"I WANT THE WORLD TO THINK I'M DEAD."

Dorinda stared across the white tablecloth at Emma. Her mother's eyes were dark-circled but despite the strangeness of what she'd said, the expression in those eyes was rational.

"Then I can watch you, be waiting if anyone makes a move toward you. I promise, you won't be alone for a moment. I'll guard you, Dorinda. And we can find out the truth."

Dorinda was speechless. Seeing her daughter's amazement, Emma tried to smile. "You know," she went on, "I've always tried to keep a jump ahead of everything in life. And this time—" She halted. "I've felt—" she continued, almost to herself, "I've felt all along that there might be more to do . . ."

Other Avon books by
Leigh Ellis

TESSA OF DESTINY

GREEN LADY

LEIGH ELLIS

AVON
PUBLISHERS OF BARD, CAMELOT AND DISCUS BOOKS

GREEN LADY is an original publication of Avon Books.
This work has never before appeared in book form.

AVON BOOKS
A division of
The Hearst Corporation
959 Eighth Avenue
New York, New York 10019

Copyright © 1981 by Anne Rudeen and Louisa Rudeen
Published by arrangement with the author
Library of Congress Catalog Card Number: 80-69892
ISBN: 0-380-77701-0

All rights reserved, which includes the right to
reproduce this book or portions thereof in any form
whatsoever except as provided by the U.S. Copyright Law.
For information address Avon Books.

First Avon Printing, May, 1981

AVON TRADEMARK REG. U.S. PAT. OFF. AND IN
OTHER COUNTRIES, MARCA REGISTRADA, HECHO EN
U.S.A.

Printed in the U.S.A.

For Kenneth

Prologue

Blood Alley, Newport, 1967.

Eleven o'clock rang from Trinity Church and cats scampered across dark courtyards, over weathered fences, under locked windows. Black water lapped against the glistening hulls of naval vessels in the bay. Sailors thronged up and down the waterfront, past lights glowing dimly from panes wet with sea spray. Loud music blasted out of the clubs on the Alley. Indoors was dampness and the smell of old wood, cigars, and perfume, and the clink of pool balls, glasses, coins.

The neon outline of a naked woman blinked on and off in front of the Carousel Club at one end of the short street. At the other, the paddy wagon of the Shore Patrol waited for drunks, its red light swinging around through the fog.

Ten blocks away at the Naples Cafe seven diners lingered. A black Lincoln drew up outside. Machine-gun bullets shattered the restaurant's window, and the owner stared at chairs covered with blood.

In the Alley, a shaft of red pierced the mist and faded—the revolving light of the Shore Patrol. Dogs barked at the sharp sound of hurrying footsteps, stiletto heels clicking over the old cobblestones. From the church tower, bells played a hymn: *Oh hear us when we cry to Thee, for those in peril . . .*

PART I

Chapter One

THE GLASS DOORS OF THE ARGOSY CLUB SLID noiselessly back at her touch. In the ruby light of the club's foyer, Dorinda Westerly glanced at her mother's face. Emma Westerly stood still, staring up at kaleidoscopic patterns of light whirling across the ceiling, a small sample of the light show to be found in the disco beyond.

After the starless London night, the darting sparkles of color were exciting to Dorinda, but sometimes night clubs made Emma nervous. As always, Dorinda had to guess what her mother was thinking. Onstage, Emma Westerly could convey all emotions, but offstage she was customarily very quiet and controlled.

"Well?" Dorinda said, her eyes on Emma. "Want to see if we can get in?"

Emma drew a quick breath.

"Why not?" she asked, turning to her daughter with a smile.

Pleased, Dorinda strode across the marble floor to the reception desk. A slender chap in a gray tuxedo lounging there lifted his eyes and gazed disinterestedly first at her and then at Emma, who had followed.

"What name, please?" he asked. His manner was bored.

"We're not members." Dorinda gave the clerk as charming a smile as she could manage. "But we're friends of Renata Enfield. She told us we should come."

"Miss Enfield, the actress?" The man's eyebrows went up. "She's a member all right, but we can't very well let you in without her, now can we?" In disdain, he pointed to the card on the desk before him that read "Private Club."

From behind them a masculine voice spoke in low, authoritative tones.

"Americans, aren't you?"

Together Dorinda and Emma turned to find an extremely handsome young man observing them. He nodded over their heads to the gray-clad clerk and with a slight bow announced, "I'm Edward Marsden, manager of the Argosy Club. Would you allow me to show you around?"

Gratified by the ease with which they had penetrated London's top disco, Dorinda grinned. Whenever she and her mother went places, she expected that there would be a stir. The attention they usually attracted was flattering. The manager now politely opened the inner door for them. A burst of hot Latin music greeted their ears as they walked into a second foyer, a small room with black walls and a cloakroom on one side.

"Would you like to check your scarf?" The young man raised his voice to be heard over the sounds from the disco apparently beyond a further set of closed doors.

Emma nodded, and he helped her remove her turquoise shawl. Catching sight of the three of them in a large gilt-edged mirror on the opposite wall, Dorinda gazed at their reflections. Edward Marsden seemed as suave and immaculate as a model in a magazine, a black tuxedo flawlessly fitting his elegant frame. On either side of his dark form her mother and she seemed placed to contrast with each other. At nineteen, Dorinda was now as tall as Emma, but their height and their dark eyes were all they shared. Dorinda had blonde hair she let fall long and straight; it glowed golden against the black velvet jacket that she wore with a red silk shirt and dark pants. She preferred tailored clothes; her figure was fuller than her mother's, and straight lines were becoming to her. Emma's style was completely different. She possessed an elegant, ballet-dancer type of body, emphasized tonight by a clinging, shimmery blue dress. Emma's head sat regally on her long neck, and her dark hair was drawn severely back from her sculptured-looking face. Caught by the mirror, Emma's figure seemed to float rather than stand.

Edward Marsden checked the shawl and returned, bending his head when Emma told him their names.

"Sisters," he said, as Dorinda gave him her hand.

Emma opened her mouth to correct this impression, but before she could, someone popped up from a flight of steps beside them and summoned the manager.

"Excuse me, I'll be right back." With a flash of his gold earring, Edward Marsden disappeared.

"Well, we got in, Mother," Dorinda said, moving closer to speak over the music. "Renata said every night they turn people away by the hundreds."

Emma smiled without answering; in a moment the manager was with them again. As he approached, a couple of men opened the double doors and ultra-violet light from the disco spilled into the black-walled room, turning Edward's teeth and shirt front an unearthly white. He handed them each a tulip-shaped glass of champagne and gestured to the doors.

"Let me present the Argosy Club to the Westerlys," he said, stepping aside to allow them to precede him through.

In the enormous room beyond, there were more black walls, these copiously embedded with pieces of mirror and swirls of silver glitter to reflect the lights playing from the constantly changing grid on the ceiling overhead. It was like stepping into a whirlpool of stars. A handful of patrons were writhing in the turning illumination accompanied by the beat of a current hit.

"Oh, it's gorgeous," Dorinda exclaimed, staring at the sparkling scene.

"It doesn't begin to come alive until after eleven," Edward said, guiding them toward a long bar at one end. "Let's find somewhere to sit. Did I overhear you say you were friends of Renata Enfield's?"

Emma nodded. "I've been in productions with her several times," she said.

"Then you are also an actress—yes, of course! Your stage name's Emma *Fairfax*, isn't it? You do only character parts; you're one of Broadway's—"

Chatting with Emma, Edward found three fur-covered bar stools and established himself between the two women, inclining his head toward Emma to continue the conversation. Well, there's one more lost to Mother, Dorinda thought. Actually, she was happy; Dorinda was delighted when anyone could coax her mother out of the reserved demeanor that had grown even more pronounced since the death of Arthur Westerly, Emma's husband and Dorinda's stepfather. This trip's purpose was to help Emma get over Arthur's death. Because of sterling connections in the theater, Emma had permission to act in a London play, if she chose to. Dorinda thought an entire change of scene would be excellent for her mother, and she had enthusiastically taken a semester off from college to accompany her.

Now, as Emma politely answered Edward Marsden's many questions, a curly-headed young man refilled the champagne glasses. Dorinda studied the bartender's outfit: tight satin shorts, silk net undershirt, and an opened rose tattooed on his right bicep. The Argosy Club definitely appeared to be gay. Wonderingly, Dorinda glanced back at Edward Marsden. Was he?

Her thoughts were interrupted by a loud peal of bells.

"We're starting things off with a magic show tonight," Edward said. "Let me get you good seats."

Suddenly the club seemed full of people—chiffon-and-satin-wrapped women, and men in every attire from almost-naked to totally encased in leather. Edward drew them through the fascinating throng to the chairs that the waiters were setting out upon the dance floor. Of transparent lucite, the chairs were shaped like naked men and women crouched on all fours, and Dorinda grinned when she saw Emma sit down on her man rather gingerly.

"Oh, excuse me again," Edward said, receiving a summons.

As he left them, another peal of bells rang out.

"The Argosy Club is proud to present Mr. William Hartman, master of illusion," a voice announced on the loudspeaker. The lights overhead flashed amber, blue, and green; then the room was plunged into total darkness. With a loud crash, a wild piece of electronic music started, seeming to come from beneath the floor. A strobe light clicked on for a moment, making all movements look slow and unconnected. Dorinda opened and closed her hand in front of her, enjoying the strange results.

Without warning, the curtain swung up to reveal a tall man in a top hat and tails standing in the center of a spotlit steel stage. With a calm, intent expression, he made a maroon handkerchief dance a few inches from his left hand as a blue-green one twirled near his right. The audience gasped as the scarves suddenly leapt up, hung in midair for a moment, and then plunged down into the large bottle at his feet.

The magician bowed to the applause; when it died away he began the patter that went with his act.

"Where have we seen him before—Hartman?"

Emma spoke in Dorinda's ear as more scarves floated farther and farther away from the magician's body, then darted swiftly into the green bottle.

"I don't know, Mother," Dorinda replied. "He *does* look sort of familiar." She scrutinized the man as the scarves and the bottle disappeared and, with the stage now bathed in a violent red light, the magician sawed his gauze- and spangle-covered assistant in half. "Maybe in some cabaret in New York," Dorinda said finally.

As Hartman levitated his assistant and then turned her into a canary, the conviction began to grow in Dorinda's mind that they indeed knew him. Not only onstage; they had been *acquainted* with him—but where?

Beside her, Emma said no more. She sat very erect on her lucite chair, staring intently at the magician.

Hartman proceeded to hypnotize a volunteer from the audience. After drinking five shot-glasses full of water that he was told was whiskey, the young man wearing flame-colored satin jeans with gold chains wrapped around his waist and forehead danced drunkenly about the stage until Hartman snapped his fingers.

"You shall have no memory of what just happened," Hartman intoned, and as the words left his lips, Emma rose, giving a soft cry.

"Mother?" Startled, Dorinda reached up to touch Emma's arm.

"Memory," Emma murmured, sinking back down onto her seat. "Don't you remember, Dorinda? It's Bill, Bill of the memory act at—"

Abruptly, Emma stopped speaking.

In the light from the stage Dorinda stared at her mother. It was extremely unlike Emma to create even a minor disturbance in a public place. Seeing Dorinda's expression, Emma leaned over and whispered into her ear. "For a moment—I thought the man looked like someone I knew, but I was wrong. What do you think of his act?"

When Dorinda said nothing to this, Emma returned to her absorbed state, her eyes fixed on the man before them. Dorinda watched him, too, but now the meaning of any of the happenings onstage was lost. The moment Emma said "memory act," Dorinda had remembered where and when they'd known William Hartman. Except his name wasn't Hartman. She didn't know what it had been, then. It was during the dark time, the part of their lives that Emma ordinarily never mentioned. Dorinda wasn't even sure how old she'd been—five, six. What she could remember came back with the quality of a childhood dream, fragmented and vividly colored. It was long ago . . . they'd lived in Newport, Rhode Island, and her mother had been a dancer in a club not too different from the Argosy Club in some ways, but vastly different in others . . . still, the colored lights, the loud music—was that why Emma sometimes felt uncomfortable in discos?

Dorinda's mind paused at the thought. Then, like a flower opening to the light, layers of the past seemed to fold back like petals, and she saw Bill—Uncle Bill, she'd called him—sitting blindfolded in a chair in the spotlight, and from the dark beyond, voices called names of things, "a watch, a hairpin, a man's tie . . ." After a tremendous number of things had been named, Uncle Bill called them all back in order. How strange! Emma had told her to pretend that the Newport part of their lives had not happened. They never talked about it. Dorinda had forgotten. . . . Yet, "a hairbrush, a dollar bill, a church key—" The words hung in the air as if just spoken by the man before her now awing the chic Argosy Club crowd, bowing to their applause, waving his top hat as the curtain fell.

When the lights above the dance floor came back on, Dorinda cast a sideways glance at Emma. Her mother smiled at her. She gave no outward sign of discomposure, but simply stood up.

"Dorinda, I'll only be a minute," she said. "I'll meet you over at the bar."

"Hey," Dorinda said, but before she could catch Emma, her mother had slipped through the persons crowding toward the edge of the small stage. A great many people suddenly seemed to be in the Argosy Club. It was full, almost mobbed. Dorinda pushed her way along in the direction Emma had taken. At the back of the stage was a door marked Exit, and Dorinda opened it. Beyond it extended a short hall with several doors. One door was open, and as Dorinda approached it she heard her mother's voice.

"Bill, do you remember me? I'm—"

"Of course! Em—"

Her mother spoke quickly, interrupting him.

"It's nice to see you're doing so well."

Reaching the doorway, Dorinda looked in. Emma was a step inside, the magician standing before his dressing table. As she stared at her mother's back, the young woman assistant brushed past her and entered the dressing room, giving the magician a questioning look.

"Natalie," he said. "This is—"

"Emma Westerly." Her mother gave her hand to the girl.

"This is my wife. And is this—?" The magician gestured toward Dorinda in the doorway and Emma turned and saw her. "Could this be your—"

Emma frowned. "You followed me?" she said to Dorinda. Then she turned back. "Yes, it's Dorinda," she said.

"My God. She's grown into a beautiful young lady." The affable expression on the magician's face seemed forced, Dorinda thought; he appeared to be just saying polite words. She stepped inside and he introduced her to his wife Natalie.

"Love," he added, "I've just thought of something. The canary had better be put into the van before he gets loose in this madhouse. Could you do that?"

Natalie nodded, murmuring some polite words to Emma and Dorinda as she left. The moment she was gone, Dorinda caught the magician and her mother exchanging a look.

"It's fantastic to find you here," Hartman said. "I was just—you know, I haven't seen you since—" He spoke in a soft voice, glancing toward the opened door as he did so.

Emma looked at Dorinda.

"Why don't you go back, honey," she said. "Find that handsome manager?" She smiled brightly.

"No," Dorinda said, making the word firm. "I want to know what's going on. I remember you, Uncle Bill."

The magician did not smile at this; his face kept a serious expression.

"Let her stay," he said to Emma. "She was there; she remembers—"

"No, she doesn't." Emma spoke sharply. She seemed shaken by his words and Dorinda looked curiously at her mother. "I mean," Emma continued, swallowing, "it doesn't matter, do you think? It's been so many years."

"Years," the magician said. The word sounded flat.

"But surely—" Emma stopped.

Bill gave a short laugh. As he and Emma stared at each other, for a moment it seemed to Dorinda that the three of them were not in the small London dressing room at all, but somewhere else, in a crowded, small space where outside the window a huge neon sign flashed off-on, off-on. A sign—she remembered, with sudden excitement, a green sign that was the outline of a naked girl two stories high, blinking . . . how strange! Suddenly the memory was very clear, the green light from outside going on and off and the three of them there.

"Recently, things have happened." The magician's voice was scarcely audible as he spoke the words. His face in the bright light of the dressing room seemed pale. "Maybe a new investigation."

"Oh, Bill, my God." Emma spoke softly.

After a moment, the magician seemed to try to shake his mood.

"I could certainly be wrong," he said, his voice louder. "You're looking marvelous after all these years, Emerald."

"Emma." As her mother cut off the name he called her, something in the tone of her voice made Dorinda's skin prickle.

For a short while after she spoke, there was silence. Then Emma smiled.

"It's been so long, Bill. I used to worry, but we're fine now."

"You think so?" The magician took a step toward Emma and put his hand on her arm. "It's all there, you know." He spoke so quietly that no one but them could have heard his words. "In your mind. In hers. In mine. God knows, I've spent years trying to forget. I really don't know what I know. I just know it's dangerous."

"Bill." Emma glanced at Dorinda with a gesture of warning.

"Oh, there are ways, Em—hypnotic recall. They could get it out of her. Out of any of us. Look." He glanced toward the open door again. Beyond it, the sounds of the disco were loud. "We shouldn't go into this here. Could you meet me somewhere tomorrow?"

This was all so strange, she couldn't say which part of it was the strangest, Dorinda thought. She watched Emma hesitate.

"I'm auditioning in the morning," her mother said finally. "I'm sure I'll be finished by one o'clock. We could meet at a pub."

Bill nodded.

"How about near our hotel?" Emma said. "At the end of South Moulton Street—do you know where that is? There's a place called the Catherine Wheel."

"I know it," Bill said. "I'll meet you there at one."

As he said the words his wife reentered the room, and

the anxious expression at once vanished from Bill's face. He smiled.

"Maybe not," he said, lifting his hand from Emma's arm. "Maybe it's silly to worry."

"Worry about what?" his wife asked.

"About growing old." He smiled at all of them as Emma and Dorinda said good night.

"Who are they?" Dorinda heard Bill's wife ask as the door closed behind her and Emma. She couldn't hear what Bill answered.

"Mother, what was all that about?" Dorinda spoke loudly over the music blasting from the disco as Emma opened the hall door. Her mother didn't stop or answer, but stepped out onto the dance floor where the club members now formed a single undulating mass. Pushing blindly forward, Emma forced a path through the tightly packed crowd, not stopping even when a satin- or leather-covered arm flailed out and accidentally struck her. Dorinda followed in her wake.

When they came out on the other side Emma paused as if disoriented. Dorinda looked in the direction of the bar, searching for Edward Marsden, but he was not there. Over the bartenders' heads some patrons had climbed up onto platforms jutting out from the wall, and performed solos above the drinkers. The entire club seemed to seethe in the ever-moving lights.

"Would you care to dance?"

A redheaded young man was before her, asking; Dorinda glanced over at Emma.

"Mother, do you want to go home?"

Emma's face was blank. Around them, the lights began spinning in a great circle, making Dorinda feel dizzy. The boy beside her was urging her onto the jammed dance floor. The lights flashed red, and Dorinda thought the place looked like a satanic coven meeting; blue, and they were all under water in a huge swimming pool. Then the room turned a brilliant, rich shade of green, and again a strong memory came to her—the naked girl on the front of the club where her mother had worked so long ago.

"No," she said to the redhead. "My mother and I have to leave."

In the lurid light, Emma's face was abstracted, as if her mind were completely absent from the present scene. Dorinda took her arm.

"The door's there," she said.

It seemed clear that this night was over for both of them. The redheaded boy turned away. Without a word, her mother let Dorinda guide her out.

In the street, Dorinda found them a taxi. During the trip to Claridge's Hotel, Emma sat silent. Curious as she was, Dorinda did not renew her questions. Habit was too strong. There were certain memories they didn't mention.

Chapter Two

A GOOD NIGHT'S REST RESTORED DORINDA completely, and the next morning her mother seemed recovered as well. In the living room of their suite, Emma placed their orders for breakfast with Room Service, and as she spoke on the phone, Dorinda studied her. Emma looked beautiful, wrapped in a pale blue dressing gown, her long dark hair loose over her shoulders. Dorinda regarded her with affection. The point of their visit to England was to relax and have fun, she thought. Arthur Westerly had left Emma a considerable fortune and it was Dorinda's opinion that her mother should enjoy life a little more. She did not know why she felt Emma had never yet been really happy. Of course, their earlier years were ones of desperate struggle, before Emma was established on the stage. Then Emma married Arthur, and there were no more financial worries. Arthur had been devoted to them both, but he was years older than Emma and more an ardent fan than a dashing lover. In Dorinda's view, Emma was overdue for a romantic encounter.

Last night's odd interlude was not discussed. During breakfast they exchanged only ordinary remarks, and after finishing her second cup of coffee Emma began to prepare for the morning's audition in her usual manner. Dorinda joined her, and together they meditated in silence for a while. Then they moved to the floor to begin "The Cat," a yoga exercise that consisted of a series of stretches—movements that a cat might make when awaking and sensing danger. First, one pretended to be the sleeping cat. Then, opening the eyes, body frozen, one allowed only the eyeballs to move, examining the room. In sequence, one's head turned in exploration; then the shoulders moved. At last, the entire body quivered as the cat reached total awareness, every nerve stretched, ready to fight or flee.

It was a taxing exercise, and Dorinda was breathing hard when they finished.

"That was good," Emma said, rising from the floor. "I feel ready. Let's put on some things and go."

"Is today the Dracula play?"

"Right. I've always wanted to play a batty German psychiatrist. 'Ve haff vays to plumb ze unconscious, you know—'." Emma dropped her voice into a lower register as she assumed a heavy German accent, and suddenly her face seemed that of a stern German scientist. Dorinda laughed. They were always closest when Emma did a bit of play-acting, like two friends in a private world of make-believe.

"Who is this character?" she asked.

"A Doctor Helpmann of the play's sanatarium. Beat you dressed."

The auditions for *Bride of Dracula* were being held in a sort of warehouse somewhere in Soho. A taxi took them to the address, and they were shown into a waiting room filled with wicker furniture and potted palms. Several tables there were covered with "sides," sections of the play script that contained the lines of one or another of the characters. Emma hunted through the piles until she found some sheets marked "Dr. Helpmann." Then she sat down in a quiet corner. Knowing she should now leave Emma alone, Dorinda took a place on the other side of the room after picking up a side for Wilhelmina, Dracula's intended *Bride*.

The script fragment was absorbing, and only when she finished reading it did she realize that someone sat beside her. Turning her head, she found a pair of sea-green eyes staring at her. For some reason she was flustered. She looked away, and in a moment noticed from the corner of her eyes that the owner of the green pair had now cast them down to concentrate on a side. The attraction she'd felt the moment their eyes met was confirmed by a close survey of his thick, fair hair, the long sandy lashes covering his eyes as he looked down, and the face that was just rugged enough to save it from being beautiful. Her gaze travelled to the well-coordinated, tailored clothes covering his athletic frame, then went back to his face. Never in her life had she felt so powerful an urge just to pounce on a strange man and start kissing him.

"Are you auditioning for Wilhelmina?" he asked, looking up again suddenly. His English accent was unbelievably perfect.

"Excuse me?" Dorinda was startled. Then she remembered the script in her hand. She glanced across at Emma, still obliviously preparing for her tryout, and decided it would be boring to tell the whole truth.

"Yes, I am," she replied. "I'm Dorinda Westerly."

"Paul Innowell, at your service." He laughed softly. "If you're trying out for the bride, I shall have to change my aim from Harker to Count Dracula himself." He threw the side of the character Harker onto the table beside him.

"Why?" Dorinda asked, trying to sound innocent.

"The better to suck your blood, my darling."

She made the sign of the cross, laughing. He was as funny as he was gorgeous, she decided. She added a little prayer, Please, God.

"I say, you're American—do you know if that's Emma Fairfax over there?" Paul Innowell lowered his voice, nodding toward her mother. "I think I recognize her from some plays I've seen in New York, but I'm not quite sure.

GREEN LADY 25

She always plays character roles, and they say she'll allow no publicity when she's out of makeup."

"I've heard that, too," Dorinda said, grinning. "And yes, I think that's who she is."

"She's a marvelous actress," Paul said, staring across the room. "And you," he added, turning his gaze back to Dorinda. "What have you been in?"

"Oh, this and that, you know," she said evasively. "Tell me, when were you in New York? That's my home."

"I spent some time studying at the—" Paul stopped as Emma rose and headed toward them.

"It's my turn, honey, wish me good luck," she murmured to Dorinda, bending to kiss her on the cheek.

"Knock 'em out, Mother."

Paul looked at her in amazement.

" 'I think that's who it is'," he said, mimicking her voice as Emma left the room. "Emma Fairfax's *daughter*? That doesn't seem possible. *Are* you an actress too?"

"Sorry, I'm afraid not." Dorinda shook her head, laughing.

"And I suppose your name isn't really Dorinda Westerly, either."

"Oh, yes it is. That is, Westerly was my stepfather's name and he adopted me. Before then—" She paused; the rest didn't seem interesting.

"Well, Miss Westerly, now that your *mother* is out of the room, I have a question for you." Paul smiled mysteriously.

"What is it?"

"May I kiss you?"

It took Dorinda only an instant to get over her surprise. She leaned forward and let him do as he had asked. After some exhilarating moments, she drew away, smiling at him. Reluctantly, Paul picked up his side again.

"I'm afraid I must get back to preparing myself if I'm ever to get this part. But please tell me where you are staying." His eyes gleamed mischievously.

"At Claridge's Hotel."

"Ah." Paul raised one eyebrow slightly. "I'll ring you there shortly, then, shall I?" For a minute longer they looked into each other's eyes; then Paul went back to studying his side.

A little while later Emma came out. Her face shone after an audition that she termed "okay." Dorinda introduced her to Paul, who had just time to shake hands before he was called himself.

"Who was *that*?" Emma asked as he disappeared. "Paul Innowell? He's darling."

"He certainly is," Dorinda said.

While Emma paused to speak a few words to an old friend, Dorinda could hear Paul in the next room shouting a line from the play. "You can do what you like to me— I'd give my life to save hers!"

After asking the taxi driver to take them to the Catherine Wheel, Emma fell silent. Dorinda debated whether to question her mother. Apparently the coming meeting with Uncle Bill would include her, and she decided to keep quiet and listen. Already Emma's spirits seemed subdued, the ebullience of the morning dispelled.

When she realized that Dorinda was studying her, Emma reached over to pat her daughter's hand, attempting a smile, but she still said nothing.

The magician, a tan raincoat slung over his shoulder, stood waiting inside the front door of the Catherine Wheel. He smiled briefly at them and then surveyed the lunch-hour crowd drinking and talking at the long bar.

"There's an upstairs room here, I think. It's probably less crowded," Emma said.

Nodding, the magician let her lead the way up some side steps to the second floor, where only a few tables were occupied. The three of them slid into the seats of a booth at the rear, well out of the hearing of anyone else in the place. A waitress arrived to take their orders and all three of them asked for ale, Emma ordering first and Dorinda and Bill repeating her order as if neither of them could think of anything else. When the waitress left, Bill turned to Emma.

"You look marvelous," he said, repeating what he had told her the night before. He spoke in a hurried, distracted manner. "I hate to stir this up. But—" He broke off. When he spoke again his words were even more rapid. "Kathy's here in England, did you know?"

Emma shook her head. "I never kept in touch with anyone at all," she said. "I've been out of everything. I never danced again or worked in a night club, anywhere that I would run into anybody."

"Oh." Bill was silent for a moment. "You were smart, getting out so fast. I had to talk to the grand jury. I lied my head off; those guys—Kathy came to see me and she was remembering how dumb they were. But no use going into it. Did you know Marilyn was dead?"

"Marilyn?" Emma repeated the name as if she only vaguely knew whom he was talking about.

"They *said* she hung herself in a jail cell in Providence. Cray's disappeared, and do you remember the girl who was just starting at the club? The redhead? No one knew her real name. It was a car accident for her. I got word; they said she just drove off the road one night last winter and— oh, and the cleaning woman, Matty. Strangled in her bed. Christ!"

Bill muttered all this at high speed, one hand to his forehead. He stopped abruptly as the waitress returned with the glasses of ale on a tray. She set them down and Bill paid her. After the waitress left, none of them touched the glasses. Both Emma and Dorinda were staring at the magician. What was he talking about? Dorinda wondered.

Emma seemed to know. When she spoke, it was in a whisper.

"I didn't know. I won't say I haven't worried since; the reason for my whole—" She stopped. "Surely the case is closed *now*."

"I think somebody doesn't think it's closed. Not just because of the deaths since. That could be coincidence— maybe—but things have been happening to me that I can't —believe me, since Newport I haven't been close to a place like Blood Alley. I never had a brush with the Mafia before that time and you can believe I haven't, since! God knows, we weren't on the inside! It was just bad luck, but you know what we heard could lead to the person behind—the death. I think he knows we could put the finger on him. And for some reason that's become important again. Em, it's strange that we found each other right now. I was thinking about you, you know, wondering what was happening to you."

"But nothing's been happening!"

"Do you live over here, now?"

"No, we're just here—"

He cut Emma off. "Look, I know someone was after me in New York. The telephone would ring and the person would hang up, over and over. I'm sure I was being followed. Here in London, I wasn't sure whether—but I have bookings in New York again next week. I don't know whether to go home or—maybe, change my name again. Disappear. If I were you—"

Bill stopped talking and his eyes shifted to three men who had just climbed the stairs and were now heading toward the booth next to theirs. The waitress walked behind them; the old floor protested under their feet. Bill watched them sit down. Before taking the men's orders, the waitress glanced over at their booth, at the three untouched glasses there; then she occupied herself with the new customers.

"I'm jumpy." Bill again lowered his voice so that it was scarcely audible.

"I think you're all wrong." Suddenly, Emma's voice was calm, and she spoke in normal tones.

"Oh, you're probably right. I always was a worrier." Bill tried to smile. "Look, I have to run. I've told you everything that I—it was good to see you." Speaking hastily, he rose. "Be careful, ladies. Keep safe."

In a moment his back in the tan raincoat had disappeared down the stairs.

"Mother, what was all that? You have to tell me!" Dorinda grasped Emma's arm.

"Just some old times, honey, that weren't so good for us."

Emma regarded Dorinda with a smile that actually seemed unforced. In fact, she seemed very relieved. "I don't think Bill had a thing to say, really. So why go into it? He just wanted to talk, for some reason, but actually—"

"Mother, you *have* to tell me."

However, Emma obviously was less alarmed than she

had been the evening before; the odd meeting had apparently reassured her. She took a swallow of her ale.

"Now that I think about it, Bill always had a great flair for drama," she said. "He should have become an actor. Last night I was afraid he was really onto something, but he's just babbling. Seeing me must have brought on an attack of nerves, that's all."

"But Mother, what is he nervous *about*?"

"Sweetheart." Emma spoke earnestly, her dark eyes fixed on Dorinda's face. "Believe me when I tell you you're better off if we don't discuss it. Most things you fear never happen at all, you know. And there's no use in worrying. I'll tell you what I think. Let's go have a great lunch at Simpson's and then look for some new things to wear to Renata's party tonight. Okay?"

Here she made a sure step toward changing the mood. Dorinda loved lunching at Simpson's-in-the-Strand; it was her favorite London restaurant. And the prospect of shopping afterward was cheering. Probably, she thought, it was better to let this matter rest for the present, and get it all out of her mother later. Accordingly she jumped up and followed Emma out to look for a taxi. And once seated in the crowded, baronial dining room at Simpson's with waiters hovering over them, anything sinister seemed far away. Dorinda took the occasion to order her favorite dish, shepherd's pie. She was further diverted when Emma brought up the subject of the handsome young man at the audition that morning. They discussed him, sipping the Burgundy Emma had ordered, and the vague, disquieting images formed in Dorinda's mind when Bill had mentioned names —Kathy, Marilyn, Cray—vanished completely.

A few hours later, possessing a new red chiffon gown for the evening's party, Dorinda walked into Claridge's to find she'd had a message from Paul Innowell, a small note asking if she were free that night.

"Oh, I'm sorry," Emma said as they rode up in the elevator. "Do you want to go out with him? I think if we ask Renata, you could bring him to the party if you like."

"I'll call him; he gave me his number."

However, in their suite Dorinda could reach only Paul's telephone-answering device; she left the message that she was going to a party with her mother and asked if he would like to join them. While she dressed she hoped he'd return her call, but finally they were both ready and the telephone had not rung.

"It's too bad. Do you want to wait a while longer? We can be a bit late," Emma said.

Dorinda shook her head, deciding regretfully that the wisest course was to go on to Renata's. Her mother was wearing a striking black-and-gold dress purchased that afternoon at Xandra Rhoades, and she had an anticipatory sparkle in her eyes already—Emma loved theatrical gatherings. Dorinda didn't want to do anything that could possibly disturb Emma's restored spirits.

"No, let's go on. I'm sure he'll call again," she replied.

At several of the London parties they'd attended they'd been confronted by apartments turned into mini-discotheques, with silver balls spinning from the ceiling and attempts at disco lighting effects, but this was not Renata Enfield's style. Renata preferred pure opulence, Dorinda learned as soon as they stepped inside her apartment at the top of an exclusive Mayfair building. There were many rumors that Renata had benefited from hot romances with wealthy lords of the land; at any rate, she could not have achieved her standard of living on the salary of an actress in Britain no matter how good she was or how long she had acted—one look around convinced Dorinda of that.

Flame-haired Renata, standing in a mirrored foyer to greet her guests, wore a gown of golden sequins, slit to the hips on each side. After enthusiastically kissing Emma and Dorinda, she passed them on into a living room that was breathtaking. Stark white walls served as background for gorgeous Chinese vases set into niches everywhere, carefully lighted for optimum effect. The result was breathtaking. The room, carpeted with a cream-colored Aubusson rug, was crowded with sofas and ottomans covered in soft blue, rose, and green velvet, picking up the colors of the Chinese vases. Little inlaid French porcelain tables scattered about held art objects and small vases of white and yellow roses. Louis the Fifteenth side chairs in rosewood with needlepoint upholstery completed the furnishings. At the end of the room, double doors revealed a balcony and beyond, the lights of London.

From those already established on the comfortable sofas a buzz of conversation was to be heard, as uniformed maids passed by offering platters of hors d'oeuvres. Everyone seemed to be drinking champagne. The party looked extremely inviting.

"Isn't this room lovely?" Emma said, giving Renata's butler her coat.

Dorinda nodded, taking in not only the room but the varying outfits of the crowd assembled there. The women all seemed elegant, whether wearing pants, long dresses, or short skirts with feather-trimmed gauzy tops, and the men were uniformly in black dinner jackets. A tall man beside a dragon-decorated urn caught her eye; he was staring in their direction as if he wanted to meet them. Emma was at once claimed by two men, who rushed up to exclaim over her dress; their excessive interest in Dorinda's appearance as well confirmed her suspicion that they were gay. Smiling at their lavish compliments, she glanced back at the man beside the urn; he was too old for her but he looked a perfect age for Emma, she thought, when she heard a familiar voice behind her. Familiar since that morning, at least! Happily, she turned to find Paul Innowell standing there grinning.

"So you're here," he said. "This was where I wanted to take you. I should have guessed you'd know Renata too."

"I was going to bring you."

"I rang back as soon as I got home. Sorry I couldn't earlier, but I was called back for Harker. This time I had to play one scene over and over while the director argued with the producer. Finally, they decided on a completely different interpretation of the character and I thought it would go on all night. I couldn't get off the stage."

"Oh, I understand," Dorinda said, overwhelmed by the sight of him in a tuxedo. Paul Innowell, she decided, was more handsome than the manager of the Argosy Club. He was, in fact, the most handsome man she had ever seen.

"Oh, Paul, hello," said the man from the urn. He had moved toward them as Dorinda and Paul talked, his gaze not leaving Emma.

Paul at once introduced him to them. His name was Trevor York. Hearing who Emma was, Trevor York seemed impressed.

"I saw you in a play in New York," he said. *"The Changers."*

As Emma responded politely, Dorinda examined Trevor more closely. He was all scars and dimples. The dimples showed when he smiled, while the scars on forehead and jaw gave him the appearance of having led an adventurous life.

Paul put his hand under her arm and she let him lead her to a love seat with down cushions.

"Now this is comfort," Paul said, sinking beside her and waving to a waiter passing a tray of champagne.

Watching Trevor York incline his curly brown head to hear Emma's words, Dorinda asked Paul, "Who is he?"

"Would you guess he's a policeman? And before that he was a ballet dancer in the chorus of the Royal Ballet."

"I don't believe that combination."

"His mother was a dancer and his father was somebody important at Scotland Yard, so first he followed in his mother's footsteps and then in his father's. He got a bit big for the ballet. We should ask him to tell us about his Brixton beat. He's on duty there now, about as dangerous a spot as you could find in London."

Paul made no move to get up to join Trevor, however, and in fact moved closer to Dorinda on the satin cushions, asking for details of her own life.

"Where I was born?" Dorinda repeated Paul's question, and the noontime scene in the Catherine Wheel suddenly came back into her mind. She would not go back that far. "I'm a New Yorker," she said. "My stepfather died not long ago and Mother decided we needed a change so she got this idea to come to London."

"Acting in England pays far less than on Broadway," Paul said, leaning toward her. He was so near she could almost count the golden flecks in his green eyes. After a moment of enjoying his closeness, she realized that his statement had been more a question. He was looking at her curiously.

"Oh, I don't think Mother cares. I mean—she inherited a lot of money."

"I see. What did your stepfather do?"

"Manufactured fabric. He was a great theater-lover, and fell in love with Mother when he saw her onstage. He'd send her roses and jewelry and finally managed to meet her and get her to marry him. He died of a heart attack just recently."

"How did you escape the stage?"

"One in the family is enough. I'm thinking of becoming a writer."

"Oh." Paul let his eyes travel over her face and figure. "That's literature's gain."

Dorinda began to feel very warm and she had to struggle with the desire to slide over even closer on the down cushion and kiss him. She thought the same idea might be in his mind, since he seemed to be looking at her lips. Unfortunately at that moment the butler announced dinner.

When they went in, Paul hastily traded the place cards around so that he was sitting next to Dorinda in the elegant jewel-box of a dining room. Dorinda gave him all her attention, noticing peripherally that Trevor York, who was seated directly across from her mother, talked to nobody else throughout the long meal. Emma seemed animated as course after course was served—oysters, lobster bisque, roast beef, salad, meringue cake, savory, and finally Stilton cheese. Passing up the cheese, Dorinda began to scheme. If Trevor asked to take Emma back to the hotel, she thought, perhaps Paul could take *her*. The idea was a pleasant one.

However, when dinner was finally over Emma seemed not to think of this arrangement at all. Turning to Dorinda as cordials were served in the living room, she made a remark indicating that she expected them to leave together. Renata was sending them in her Rolls. At this point both Paul and Trevor eagerly offered the services of their cars, but Emma seemed not to want to change the arrangement. Dorinda gave her mother a sharp glance. Something had thrown Emma back into herself; she was suddenly quieter.

Immediately, Paul asked Dorinda to go out with him the next day.

"I have another audition in the morning," he said. "But may we spend the rest of the day together? Tea at Harrod's, say; then, somewhere for cocktails, and somewhere else for dinner; and afterward to a play, or dancing. Is there a play you want to see?"

"We've been to a lot of plays," Dorinda said. "But it sounds great—whatever you want to do."

Their coats were brought for them, and reluctantly Dorinda said a well-bred good-bye to Paul at the door. Going down in the elevator, Emma stood staring ahead of herself, lost in thought. At night, things seemed worse than in the day, Dorinda thought. Emma perhaps wasn't so recovered from the Catherine Wheel meeting as she had seemed. Damn, Dorinda reflected; now wouldn't be a good time to demand the details, either. It seemed as if she was never going to find out what was going on.

"Did you like him?" she asked as they crossed the lobby.

"Like whom?"

"Mother, Trevor York, of course!"

"Oh, yes, he's charming. Forgive me, honey; it's been a hard day. I'm a little tired."

Although this evening had proved far gayer than last evening, again the night had a quiet ending. Inside Renata's lavishly appointed Rolls, the two of them sat silent as they traveled the streets between Mayfair and Claridge's.

Chapter Three

BRIGHT, SUNNY WEATHER MADE DORINDA DEcide to wear a tweed jacket with tan pants the next afternoon. If Paul meant his invitation to dinner and to spend the evening together as well, she decided to come back and change into a two-piece lavender satin dinner suit. She rinsed her hair with lemon juice after washing it, dried it and let it hang long.

"I hope you have a good time," Emma said, surveying her.

"You have one, too." That morning, a bouquet of lilac heather and orange roses had arrived for Emma, with a note from Trevor York asking her to dinner. Dorinda was delighted to think that she wasn't leaving her mother to sit alone that night. "What are you going to wear?" she asked.

"Oh, I hadn't thought." Emma looked vague. "What would you say? The white chiffon?"

"Perfect. You look so young in white."

"I'm not sure youth is what Trevor York is—"

Emma was interrupted by the ring of the telephone. Although there were still ten minutes until three o'clock, Paul was calling from the lobby.

"I'll be right down," Dorinda said, wondering if she sounded too eager.

Paul's car turned out to be a shiny black Jaguar parked at the hotel's curb. Dorinda admired it and then, during the trip to Harrod's, secretly admired Paul's handsome profile as he concentrated on making his way through London traffic.

"How was the audition?" she asked.

"Terrible," he replied cheerfully. "That's a role I'll never get. I couldn't keep my mind on it, wonder why?" He grinned but did not look over at her.

"Oh," she said, and fell silent.

"I have hope, however, for the *Dracula* situation. You inspired me, yesterday. If only you'd been there *this* morning."

"What role was it today?"

"Mine are always the same. Handsome rotters. I wish I could brag I was as versatile as your mother."

"Sometimes I can't believe it, when I see her on the stage," Dorinda said. "She's really quiet at home, you know. She's always just Mother."

Paul looked over at her. "Between you and me, I believe Trevor York is heavily smitten."

Dorinda reported the morning's flowers and invitation as Paul pulled the Jaguar into the parking area below the ornate, block-long store.

As if to match the grandeur of the great emporium itself, Harrod's version of afternoon tea turned out to be magnificent. In a huge room with a decorated dome ceiling they were led to one of numerous pink-covered tables. As a pot of tea was fetched, Paul escorted Dorinda to a central buffet covered with hundreds of cakes, pies, tarts, scones, sandwiches, candies, and pastries. The array was astonishing.

"I can't believe it," Dorinda said. She forced herself to exercise will power and not heap her plate, but each thing looked better than the last as they passed by.

Back at the table, she poured the tea, and as they attacked the goodies Paul asked her some further questions about her past.

"Who was your real father?"

"A high school football captain. Ricky Nichols. And that's all I know. I'm illegitimate—I never saw him in my life."

"My God. I was born on the wrong side of the blanket myself." Paul looked extremely surprised at the coincidence.

"You were?" Dorinda grinned, surprised herself. Elegantly turned out in a dark blue blazer and gray flannel pants, Paul looked much more the son of a lord than a fatherless waif.

"And not only did *I* never see my father, I don't even know his name," Paul said. With a mischievous expression he leaned closer to enjoy the sensation he was creating.

"You don't know his name?"

" 'Fraid not. My mother never told me; she died when I was seven and left me to be brought up by my grandmother. I imagine a scandal was connected with my appearance. Anyway, my late grandfather was a viscount and the family hushed it up. I finally escaped."

"Escaped?"

"My grandmother's unbelievable. When I told her I wanted to become an actor, she went mad—madder than usual. She's a rampant mystic. She thinks people can lose their souls when they act."

Paul delivered the last sentence dramatically and Dorinda said, "What?" The strawberry tart still on her plate forgotten, she stared at him.

Chuckling, Paul continued. "Her idea was that I stay in Hertfordshire and help manage the estate. She cut me off when I left and I've had to live on a little trust fund from my mother since."

"But why does she think that about acting?"

"Who knows? Grandmother is the queen of the local dotty gentry. There's an odd circle around her, and some house guests you wouldn't want to know. They're always communicating with each other by telepathy, or with the dead by osmosis or something. Never a dull moment around Darkbourne."

The moment that Paul uttered the word, a chill feeling shot through Dorinda, like the inward thrust of an icy knife. She would go there—somehow she was going to see his grandmother and Darkbourne. The sudden premonition left her shaken.

"What's the matter?" Paul said.

"Oh—it sounds spooky."

"It is spooky." Paul grinned at her. "A queendom for Lady Victoria, full of daft subjects. At least a football captain is something normal."

Normal, Dorinda thought. Her momentary hunch about the place called Darkbourne faded, and she cut off a bite of the strawberry tart. "I think it was actually a cliché," she said. "The football hero and the poor girl. Mother had a terrible childhood. My grandmother was an alcoholic and her husband deserted them. Then this hotshot football captain started dating Mother and got her elected Football Queen. That was a big honor in her high school. And then he wanted a payoff—he doesn't sound too nice, does he? But awfully normal. Anyway no one would help Mother; she got thrown out by my grandmother and after I was born—" Here Dorinda discreetly skipped a few years. "—she came to New York to act."

"With historic results," Paul said. "You know, she looks so young out of makeup."

"She was only seventeen when I was born, and I'm nineteen. She's just thirty-six."

"Nineteen. I can hardly remember what that was like. I'm twenty-three."

"Oh, *well*, then," Dorinda said.

"Do you think that's too old for you?"

"We're not the same age, but we are both—" She paused and glanced at him with a smile.

"Bastards," he said. "Right. Good luck, I say. We must stick together."

• • •

Pulling on the lavender dinner suit, Dorinda wondered why she had reacted so strongly to the name "Darkbourne." Perhaps the two encounters with Uncle Bill had left her more jumpy than she'd realized, or put her subconscious into a sensitive state, made her more aware of both past and future. Could you be aware of the future? The past, her early past, came back in such strange flashes of memory. Could you sense the future in the same way?

"Dorinda, do you need help with a zipper or something?"

She grinned when Paul called to her through the half-closed door of the bedroom.

"Come in, I'm almost ready."

She was fastening a gold chain bracelet when she felt her hair lifted up from the nape of her neck and a kiss pressed there. Paul crossed his arms around her.

"Mmmm, satin."

She leaned back against him, looking at the top of his bent head in the mirror.

"Sure you want to go to dinner?" he asked, nuzzling her collarbone.

"Depends where," she said, turning her head to kiss his ear.

"Precious."

"You mean me or dinner?"

"Dinner, actually." Turning her toward him, he kissed her lips lightly and then continued. "It's a club. I think you'll like it."

"A club called Precious? What next?"

"Lots, I hope," he said.

As soon as the *maitre d'* led them through the doors into the club's dining area, Dorinda felt as if she had stepped off a boat into Polynesia. Bamboo and palm trees sheltered an authentically tropical scene, wrought-iron tables and deck chairs placed against a background of Pacific blue and jungle green. Gorgeously tanned waitresses wearing bikinis crunched over the tiny white shells of the floor in stiletto-heeled sandals. Dorinda and Paul were seated beside a porthole aquarium through which they could catch a distorted glimpse of the club's disco on the floor below.

From a waiter who wore Bermuda shorts, Paul ordered a string of Polynesian delicacies. Dorinda dubiously pictured the plateful of raw fish and eels that might be coming, but when the courses began to arrive she revised her opinion. Paul fed her delicious morsels with his chopsticks and told her about parts he had played. Once, he had been a "rich young hoodlum" in a BBC television production she could remember watching in New York. Though she didn't specifically recall his role, it made her feel she had known him longer, since he more or less had been with her in her living room.

"Shall we dance in the octopus' garden?" he asked when the meal was over.

Taking his arm, she threaded with him through palms and jungle foliage to flagstone steps that led down to the disco. If the dining room had resembled the patio of a Polynesian hotel, the dance floor was buried in the heart of a tropical rain forest. Water flowed everywhere, sliding down the walls in silvery falls, circulating inside clear plastic tables filled with goldfish, shooting up in spumes from fountains with naked water nymphs dancing in their spray. Multicolored lights hidden in hollow bamboo shoots cast rainbows over the palm trees that shadowed large carved wood statues. Dancers rhythmically twisted to the drumbeats of the music in what seemed like some wild native ritual in a dark grove.

Paul located the grass hut containing the bar and returned with two coconut shells full of coconut milk and champagne. They found side-by-side chaises and stretched out with their drinks to watch the glistening fountain girls and the intricate patterns of light inscribed on the entire scene by red, violet, and gold lasers rotating over the dance floor.

"I love it," Dorinda told Paul. "It's not like being in England at all."

"Except that it's watery," Paul said. He leaned over and nibbled her cheek as a pulsing reggae tune was followed by a set of soft love songs, the room growing gradually darker until it was lit only by the phosphorescent glow of the fountains and waterfalls. Dorinda felt too contented to move, until the light show burst over them again and the slow music gave way to a disco piece with an irresistible beat.

Paul rose with her and they moved to the dance floor; Dorinda, her hair swinging around her shoulders, felt a dreamlike mood descend over her. As her body responded to the music, she imagined she was losing contact with civilization, returning to a primitive state, where dancing was the only form of communication with everyone around her, the girls in the fountains, the persons on the dance floor; most of all, with Paul.

Finally, breathless and laughing, they left the floor and lay down under some jungle ferns. The pounding music softened again and the circling lights turned blue.

"Dorinda?" Paul's voice saying her name brought back her drifting attention. "Do you want to go to my flat?" His green eyes in the blue light were almost aqua. All night she had been aware of the desire he was exciting in her. She didn't want to resist it, couldn't resist it any longer. She stood up, ready to accompany him.

The street outside the club was empty and still, the only sound the faint echo of drums and laughter from within. The crisp, bracing air restored Dorinda's energy and she enjoyed their swift journey in the little sports car. Paul parked near a modern apartment building with black marble trim, *not*, Dorinda thought, her idea of the home of a poor struggling actor. His flat upstairs turned out to be elegant. The living room boasted a high cream-colored ceiling that seemed like a floating reflection of the soft ecru carpet beneath it, and the brown walls were hung with play posters. Paul threw his blazer onto one of two sofas covered with ivory satin.

"How about a brandy Alexander?" he asked, before she could think of a suitable comment to make about his excellent taste.

He concocted the drinks in a blender at the rosewood bar in one corner.

"Are these posters from your productions?" she asked, gazing around.

"Afraid not. Look inside the Bard. He contains my life work to date." Paul indicated a bust of Shakespeare standing on a corner bookshelf. Dorinda examined it and found that the head opened at the hairline. Inside were three playbills. She leafed through them, looking at the cast write-ups for "Paul Innowell."

"Paul," she said reproachfully as he came over with her drink. "Each one says something completely different about your past. You're shameless."

Paul opened a gold candy box sitting next to the bust and hunted through the collection of odds and ends there.

"Here," he said, drawing something out. "Ever play pieces-of-eight?"

"What?"

"This is a genuine piece-of-eight." He showed her the small golden coin, but when she tried to take it, he snatched it away.

"Oh, no, you don't. This coin is my master. I have to do what it tells me."

Wondering if he were a little like his grandmother after all, Dorinda laughed when he knelt at her feet and flipped the coin.

"Heads I undo a button; tails, the strap of your shoe," he said, peering at the coin where it had fallen. "Heads it is."

"Hey." She struggled, but not very hard, as he undid the top button of the lavender jacket. When he flipped the coin again, she tried to catch it, but he was too quick, and before she could defend her foot he had undone her shoe.

"Don't I get a turn?" she protested.

"Only when you're naked."

He claimed the next "heads" gave him the right to remove her skirt, and she let him, dropping back onto the sofa. In a few minutes he had taken off every piece of her clothing, and he gave her the coin and crowded onto the sofa, lying full-length beside her. Her undressing of him was hampered by the fact that he was kissing her with rising passion. Finally, she managed to pull off his clothes, and then they were locked together, their naked bodies pressed against each other. In a moment, Paul lifted her up in his arms, and she felt herself carried into the next room, where the bed was lower than the floor, in a square pit lined with shag carpeting. She felt her arm brush the soft sides as Paul laid her on a mound of pillows. He stretched out beside her and murmured her name, and it was a pure sensuous delight to feel the down quilt beneath her and the movement of his muscles against her body as his arms circled her and cradled her. When he licked her nipples it sent a delicious tingle down her back, and she probed with her tongue around his ear.

"Is it all right, Dorinda? Can you—?"

"*Yes*," she whispered back, and he was inside her, moaning softly in his efforts as he pushed. She reveled in the pleasure that she felt in pressing against him; she arched her back and clung to him and her feeling of urgency built until she pulled her lips away from his and cried out. She felt him shudder deeply; she tried to say his name but she could only moan as he drove into her, climaxing wildly. They both trembled.

At last she felt their bodies relax and separate. Paul was still gasping; he bent over and started to kiss her, beginning at her throat and working downward, evoking delicious sensations that again quickly became so intense that she held onto his shoulders with both hands and felt pleasure spiraling through her body until even her perception of herself was swept away and she felt boundless and pulsing, helpless to stop the tide of feeling that swept over her and left her only after an ecstatic moment that went on unendurably, past all boundaries, shattering in its impact.

After a while she realized that she was wrapped in Paul's comforter and he was kissing her hair. She had to go home; what would her mother think? How much time had gone by? "Paul," she said, trying to make her body move from its soft wrapping. "I should go."

"Not yet." He moved his lips to her mouth and the comforter parted to let her feel him ready to make love, and she was incapable of resistance, wild and importunate in her response.

In her mind, she remembered Paul's green eyes. The teasing promise they had held when he looked at her was now more than fulfilled, there in the dark.

Chapter Four

AS THE NEXT DAYS PASSED, DORINDA FOUND herself more and more involved with Paul Innowell. At first she worried that he might think she had given herself to him too easily, but then she began to sense that he was as taken with her as she was with him. He was never out of her thoughts. The time away from him passed like a slow dream, and when they were together again she could tell that Paul was as pleased as she.

Emma teased her about her preoccupation and she responded by pointing out that her mother was seeing Trevor York with as much frequency. This observation did not discompose Emma. She *looked* so proper, Dorinda thought enviously. No matter what Emma might do she impressed the world as being innocent and virtuous. It was clear from the way people treated her. There was certainly no sign from Emma as to what inroads Trevor York might be making on her rectitude.

Two weeks later, coming home at dawn from a rapturous night in Paul's apartment, Dorinda paused in the hall of Claridge's before she put the key into the lock of the suite's door. Was it madness to wonder if Trevor York might be there? He'd taken her mother out to celebrate a rumor that the role in *Bride of Dracula* was hers. Thinking this, Dorinda smiled to herself and turned the key. Her own evening must have put her into a crazily romantic mood to make her think such thoughts about prim Emma.

When she opened the door the living room was empty. As she started toward her bedroom she noticed that the door to Emma's room stood open. Halfway across the living room, she heard Emma's voice call to her from inside the bedroom. Emma sounded funny.

"Mother?" Dorinda said, crossing to the doorway of Emma's room.

Emma was sitting facing the windows of the bedroom, and the rays of the sun that had just cleared the building across from Claridge's struck a face as set as a marble statue's. Emma was wearing a nightgown and a negligee; something in her tense posture convinced Dorinda that Emma had been sitting there for hours.

Emma looked at her, and gestured toward the table beside the bed. A couple of newspapers lay there, an opened tabloid on top.

Puzzled, Dorinda approached the table. The black headline on the inside page of the tabloid read "Magician Dies Onstage." Beneath the headline was a picture of Uncle Bill.

"Oh, my God," Dorinda cried.

Emma said nothing.

Dorinda forced herself to scan the story. "William Hartman, master illusionist, a recent performer here, died during a performance at the Chelsea Theater in New York last night," she read. "Playing a benefit performance, Hartman was attempting the climax of his act, in which he is tied to a post and becomes a target for his dagger-throwing assistant. Ordinarily, a few moments later the assistant, dressed in a hooded executioner's robe, turns around and reveals himself to be the magician in person, while the tied-up figure is found to be a dummy. Apparently, last evening, a trap door failed to open as scheduled and the audience watched as the knives struck Mr. Hartman himself.

"Hartman's wife, his onstage assistant, collapsed after Hartman failed to appear to take her place during the visual distractions meant to engage the audience's attention as the substitution was made."

"Mother, that's ghastly. And—Mother, he was afraid!"

"Yes," Emma said. "And I said he was crazy." She spoke flatly, lowering her gaze to stare at her hands, clasped tightly together in her lap.

Dorinda, legs weak, sat down on Emma's bed.

"Mother, maybe it really was an accident," she said.

Emma made an effort to stop twisting her hands; she pressed the palms together.

"Maybe," she said. "But we can't count on it. I've been sitting here thinking about it all night. We have to talk, Dorinda. It's just—so difficult to begin."

Dorinda leaned forward. Bill's death was apparently going to force Emma to tell her what she had for so long denied in their past, she thought. Again, shadowy figures gathered in Dorinda's mind. Neon lights, and a little street that looked very old. She fixed her eyes on Emma and watched as her mother swallowed.

"Can you remember when you were five?" Emma's voice was so low that Dorinda had to strain to hear her even in the absolute silence of the room.

"Five." Dorinda looked down at the carpet, frowning, willing memory to come to her. "After we left Grandmother's in Kingston, Rhode Island?"

"Yes."

"Just vaguely," Dorinda said. "The first thing I can remember really well is New York, and going to first grade. But before—well, you know, you told me about Kingston and Grandmother, so it's like I can remember it, and then—weren't we in Newport? We lived in a room—and in the place you worked, there were dogs."

"*Yes,*" Emma said. "The dogs. That's what I wanted to

know. The man who ran the club kept lots of dogs in the kitchen. Can you remember that?"

Dorinda wrinkled her forehead with the effort. "They used to lick me," she said. "And I knew all their names. I can't remember them now."

"Can you remember anything else?"

The shadows in Dorinda's mind became clearer images.

"Costumes," she said, closing her eyes. "You had a green one with fringe—and long green gloves. And one girl had white hair, even though she was young. I remember her bending down and talking to me—Marilyn! That was her name. And Uncle Bill, in a spotlight, saying names of things . . . oh, and it was the first time I'd ever watched someone make pizza. Didn't they make pizza in the place with the dogs, the kitchen? The cook would throw the dough into the air. And—" Dorinda opened her eyes and looked at Emma. "That's it. All I can remember." The effort at concentration had left her feeling drained.

In the sunlight from the window, Emma's face was wan.

"I wanted to divide us from it utterly," she said. She sounded very tired. "I thought if I never, never spoke of it, you would never remember. But—there was a very famous murder. It was—but I should start at the beginning. I worked in a club on the waterfront in Newport. Newport was a navy base then, full of sailors. The man who owned the club—not the manager, but the man who got the profits—was a millionaire socialite in Newport. We knew that much, those of us who worked there; nobody knew who he was. The Carousel was the only club he owned. The rest of the waterfront, and the other places on Blood Alley—that's what our little street was called—anyway, the rest were controlled by a Mafia leader named Giotto. I guess the vice rakeoff was very profitable. Apparently there was a struggle for power between the millionaire and Giotto. The night Giotto was murdered, you and I and Uncle Bill were in the kitchen of the club."

Emma paused a moment and Dorinda drew a breath, wondering what was coming next.

"You were petting the dogs, and some men came in." Emma's voice dropped to a whisper. "They named some names—never mind. At first, Bill and I had no idea what they were talking about. We kept quiet. But the men saw us, and asked what we'd heard and we said, nothing. But we had heard a code name. We had no idea whose—but anyway, they ended by threatening us. They said we had to keep quiet—then the manager came in, and there was some confusion and we got away. The next day, after the murder, Bill found me and said, 'My God, do you realize that's what those men were talking about? The murder of Giotto?' Both of us were appalled, and scared. The town was a madhouse; the police said they had caught the killers. There were arrests. But—"

Emma stopped. The words had poured out once she started. She pushed one hand through her dark hair and stared unseeingly at the opposite wall.

"Then two men knocked on the door of our room," she continued, still speaking very softly. "It was just after I saw Bill. I had hurried home with you and I remember, you were hungry and I fixed you a peanut butter sandwich in the kitchen and took it upstairs and you were eating it when they knocked. I could hear their voices and I told you not to make a sound. I hoped they'd think we weren't home, but the landlady came up. I'd gotten a call on the telephone and she'd come to get me; she knew I was there. The men told her I wasn't answering, and she unlocked the door with her key—I mean, she was alarmed, but I can still remember the way I felt when I heard the sound of that key in the lock." Emma paused, swallowing. "I rushed out into the hall and pulled the door closed behind me so they wouldn't see you. I said I had been asleep. Afterward I couldn't recall a single thing about the men except that they were rough-looking. I wanted to get them away from you. I walked downstairs and thank God, the landlady stayed up on the second floor. The men followed me down and in the living room they grabbed me. One held his hand over my mouth and the other hit me. They said they were taking me with them, that I'd tell everything I knew before they were through.

"Then—it was just luck—one of the boarders who was a policeman turned up. The men caught sight of him climbing the front steps outside and they pulled me into the hall and toward the back door. I bit the one with his hand on my mouth and kicked and—anyway, as the policeman came in the front door, they let me go. They threw me onto the floor and ran out the back. I was dazed—the policeman helped me up. He hadn't seen the men and I said I'd fallen down the stairs. And I ran back up—"

As Dorinda stared at her, Emma broke off again, shaking her head slightly as if to free herself of the memory. Then her eyes went to her daughter's face.

"Dorinda, do you remember being in the club's kitchen, that night?"

"Not at all." Dorinda shook her head.

Emma sighed. "It was so horrifying, and I was so sorry. So sorry I had gotten us mixed up with anything so seedy and terrible. The club—suddenly I saw it for what it was, realized what I had drifted into. It was a disgusting life, but it paid our bills, and in a way, it was exciting. I was young—I don't know how to explain or justify it, I guess I was just desperate, there was you to take care of, and I didn't know what else to do. I used the name 'Emerald' then. I was a stripper—they used to call us go-go dancers —with a clientele on the side. The day of that murder, it was like I woke up out of a dream and saw my life for what it really was. It shocked me; I knew I could do better, and all I could think of was getting us out while we were still alive. I grabbed you and we ran. We were on a bus just a couple of hours later. I didn't know if I knew something important about the murder or I didn't, but I didn't care. I wanted us safe. I thought if I told anyone what I remembered I'd surely be killed, that you would be left all alone, or—anyway, there was a grand jury, an investigation, and finally the case was closed. Only it never was really. Again and again new theories would be brought up, new suspects dug out; it dragged on and on, but nothing happened to us. And the trail to us has got to be stone cold now."

Emma shivered as she spoke. Dorinda, amazed by what she was hearing, kept silent.

"The Mafia," Emma said finally. "You'd hear, on the waterfront, that they never gave up, that once you had dealings with them, they knew where you were, had a file on you forever. And they don't forgive. Giotto's death is as real to them today as it was then. If a rich, powerful person was behind it, if it was a takeover—I don't know, I guess he might not want anyone alive who could finger him. I used to fear—but I got over it. Only, Bill seemed to think that for some reason it had become important again. And now, he's—" She stopped and had to swallow again before she could add, "I love you so much, Dorinda, and I've put you into this danger!"

"But Mother, I don't remember anything."

"It's in your mind, and there may be a way to—but don't worry. I'm sorry I—"

"I love you, Mother!" Dorinda interrupted her. "I don't blame you for anything. My God, look what you've done for me! I mean, I'm glad to know the truth. But do you think someone really *killed* Uncle Bill?"

An expression Dorinda could not read passed over Emma's face. It seemed compounded of fear and despair, and an attempt to conceal them.

"It's almost like he had a premonition, isn't it?" Emma said after a minute. "But—it's still a good policy for us not to talk about it. What we need—" She paused, and seemed to gather herself. "Let's order some breakfast, and I'll explain what I've been thinking about."

Dorinda nodded, repressing a yawn. She'd gotten only a couple of hours of sleep and she would rather have gone straight to bed, but she realized that her mother's fear had to take priority. Emma picked the telephone up, and Dorinda ordered bacon and eggs. Giving the order made the world seem more normal again.

They walked into the living room to wait for Room Service, and Emma sat down and asked Dorinda if she had enjoyed her evening with Paul.

That evening seemed far away now. With the idea of distracting her mother, Dorinda offered some details, describing the restaurant where they had eaten dinner. When she finished, a silence fell until the breakfast arrived.

When the table was arranged and they had pulled up their chairs, Emma made an effort to eat, but Dorinda could tell that her mother was just going through the motions. In a minute Emma put down her fork and said, "Dorinda, I have to be free to investigate this. I have to find out whether anyone might possibly be after us. And I've thought of what I want to do."

"Do?" Dorinda repeated the word in puzzlement.

"I want the world to think I'm dead."

"What?" Dorinda stared across the white tablecloth at Emma. Her mother's eyes were dark-circled, but despite the strangeness of what she'd said, the expression in those eyes was rational.

"Then I can watch you, be waiting if anyone makes a move toward you. I promise, you won't be alone for a moment. I'll guard you, Dorinda. And we can find out the truth. If nothing happens, no one appears, then when I feel you're safe, that our lives are safe, I'll reappear and we can say the report of my death was a mistake."

Dorinda was speechless. Seeing her daughter's amazement, Emma tried to smile. "You know," she went on, "I've always tried to keep a jump ahead of everything, in life. And this time—" She halted. "I've felt—" she continued, almost to herself—"I've felt all along that there might be more to do."

"Mother, look. I've got to get some sleep. I'm bushed and this frankly just isn't making any sense to me."

"Of course," Emma said quickly. "Go right to bed and get some sleep."

"And will you try to rest, too?"

"I'll try." Emma rose, her features a little more composed now. Dorinda went into her bedroom, dragged off her clothes, and crawled between the sheets. On the other side of her door, she could hear her mother moving around restlessly. What was Emma doing, what was she going to do? Dorinda wondered. For the moment, she was too tired to worry about it and she fell asleep.

She awoke in the afternoon and put a dress on before she went back into the living room. There she found Emma waiting for her. In the grayish light from the windows, Emma smiled and her face looked white.

"Did you sleep, too?" Dorinda asked.

Her mother shook her head. "I couldn't. Paul called you; he asked if you'd call him around six."

Emma was sitting on the sofa and Dorinda took a chair opposite her.

"Are you hungry? We can go out for tea," Emma continued. "But first—there was another call. Renata. She's arranging a house party at her villa in Ibiza, and Dorinda, I think that will be exactly the chance I need."

Emma spoke in a neutral tone, evidently trying not to appear too excited. For a moment she wore a faraway expression, as if she were choreographing a dance, imagining steps to fit imaginary music. Dorinda stared at her in silence, and she went on, "We'll both go to Ibiza but only you will come back—here, to England. I mean, that's what we'll let everyone think. I'll be alive, but even you won't know who I am."

Dorinda's bewilderment turned to laughter. "Oh, come on," she said. "You mean, be in disguise or something? You think I wouldn't know *you*?"

"Well, if you guess, you must play along. Everything will depend on that."

"Mother, this is the nuttiest thing I've ever heard. You mean, stake me out?"

"Oh, no; well, yes, in a way." Emma smiled ruefully. "But don't you see, this is far better than just to wait helplessly, or maybe change our names and run away and spend the rest of our lives looking over our shoulders. And it's practical, really—wait, just listen. I'm going to sell what we have in the U.S.—what Arthur left us, everything, all the stocks. I'm going to transfer the money into a Swiss bank account; you and I will both know the number. Then you can withdraw whatever you like to live on, and so can I. There won't be an inheritance problem, when I'm thought dead—I would probably reappear before that's an issue, anyway, but—"

"Mother!" Dorinda studied the woman before her. Emma's hair was carefully drawn back, her face rouged to minimize the ravages of her sleepless night; she looked rather like a model out of *Vogue* magazine, in a chic wraparound heather-colored skirt and lavender cashmere sweater. And yet she was talking collectedly about Swiss bank accounts and phony deaths and secret surveillances.

"We'll take it one step at a time," Emma said, standing

up. "Just trust me. Now, how about going out to the Ritz? They have a good tea."

"Mother, you're crazy."

Dorinda arose, grinning and shaking her head. Tea at the Ritz was the only part of Emma's words that had sunk in. And yet the world did seem different. Following Emma out, Dorinda thought suddenly that the ornate hall beyond their door, the polished, mirrored elevator, the gleaming black-and-white marble floor in the lobby below, the carved wooden arches that led to the street seemed vaguely like a stage set, like the false flats of a Western movie town. Roofs harboring shadowy figures atop empty buildings, doors leading nowhere, existing only so the enemy could burst through.

Emma's high heels clicked sharply on the sidewalk as they walked together. At the corner kiosk a man selling newspapers yelled something about the evening edition, Emma's footsteps quickened, and one fact was suddenly back in Dorinda's mind. Two weeks ago they'd drunk a beer with Uncle Bill. He'd been frightened. They apparently knew the same information he knew, and now he was dead.

One jump ahead of everything, Emma had said.

Chapter Five

THE PIPER CHEROKEE TOUCHED ITS WHEELS ON the sun-baked pavement, bounced up to fly for another moment, then settled onto the ground. It rolled a short way toward the base of a bleached rock mountain, turned, and taxied toward the aqua Mediterranean where several hangars stood not far from the water's edge. Paul shut off the motor, and the hot stillness of the island airport invaded the cockpit.

"Ibiza," Paul announced.

"It was a wonderful flight," Emma said. "Thank you so much."

Dorinda said nothing. All the way from London, crossing the Channel and then Spain, she'd stared silently out of the window. In the last few days, Emma had proved intransigent. She'd put the finishing touches to her mad plan, and, knowing how much Dorinda liked Paul, she had incorporated him into her scheme, suggesting to Renata that she invite Paul to Ibiza. Learning that Paul had a pilot's license, she'd paid for chartering the plane. "You won't feel so alone if Paul flies you back to England," she'd said, and then calmly added that Paul would take Dorinda straight to Darkbourne.

"Darkbourne!" Dorinda had cried, remembering her premonition. But her anger at all these arrangements, her mounting feeling of depression, seemed not to count with her mother.

Now Emma opened the plane door and climbed out. When she was gone, Paul put his arms around Dorinda, pulled her close to him, and kissed her insistently, holding his lips over hers until she unwillingly responded.

"I know how you feel," he said when he finally raised his head. "But we have to help your mother now. It's really a brave thing that she's doing, and I know she wouldn't, if she didn't feel she had no choice." He smoothed Dorinda's hair with his hand. "You know I don't want anything to happen to either of you."

She frowned at him. Damn actors—they all stuck together. Somehow Emma had gotten Paul on her side and now he was treating her like a little girl.

"Far out," she said rudely.

Ignoring her words, he kissed her brow and her eyelids. "So," he whispered, softly, "let's have a delicious vacation and enjoy ourselves immensely."

"Paul—"

Dorinda's reproach was interrupted by Renata's throaty contralto. "Romeo and Juliet," she called, "we're waiting."

Climbing down, they found Renata and Emma sitting in a white jeep pulled up next to the plane. Looking at the glamorous actress, one hand on the gear shift knob, her loose red hair tangled with the white ribbons trimming her lace blouse, Dorinda was reassured that she had worn the right outfit herself, for this casual island house party. And that, she thought sourly, was about as reassured as she was going to get during this weekend.

She managed to speak politely to her hostess. A Spanish boy piled their luggage into the back of the jeep, and in a few moments they were traveling rapidly through tropical foliage, the sparkling water of the Mediterranean showing through the trees on one side. The narrow road wound through the jungle for a mile and emerged at a small fishing inlet with a marina.

"My villa is on a private beach you can only reach by boat," Renata explained, hurrying them toward a motor yacht. Their luggage was loaded aboard, and the Spanish boy skippered the boat across the rippling cove. Dorinda enjoyed the cool breeze on the speeding boat after the hot island, as she sat on the bridge with Emma and Paul. Paul took her hand and gave it a squeeze. Looking at her mother, Dorinda wondered if Emma were wishing Trevor York were there, too. Trevor and Emma had begun to seem as attracted to each other as she and Paul were. Dorinda followed her mother's gaze out toward the gently swelling bay. Emma was staring across the surface of the turquoise water as if measuring the distance between various points on the land they were approaching. Then she glanced back toward Ibiza. It was not Trevor at all that she was thinking about. Dorinda could guess what it was. She began to feel queasy.

In a moment they had arrived at a dock, and Renata led her guests up some worn stone steps set in a hillside. Above was a whitewashed Spanish-style dwelling, handsomely tiled in red, its balconies adorned with crockery planters filled with red and white geraniums. From the piazza above they were greeted by some waving house guests, all dressed in shorts or shiny tight bathing suits.

"Welcome to *Entre Dos Luces*," Renata cried dramatically when they reached the open front door.

"What does that mean?" Paul asked. "It translates 'Between Two Lights'."

"Literally, yes, darling," Renata replied. "But to the Spanish it means many things. One of them is 'twilight,' and another is 'half-drunk'."

Paul grinned. "I'll go for the last meaning," he said.

Renata smiled at him and then swept up the wide mat-covered stairway, beckoning them to follow her. A short hall upstairs led out to a rear patio built into the hillside and shaded by twisting vines. They sat down on large suede

GREEN LADY

pillows and immediately were handed tall iced glasses of sangria by a dark-faced woman in a peasant skirt and apron.

Sipping the fruit-loaded drink and listening to the Spanish words exchanged among Renata's help—a bustle of preparations was apparently going on in the next room—Dorinda relaxed a little. Emma seemed charmed by her surroundings and perfectly at ease. The other guests proved to be lively and interesting, or at least appeared so after several glasses of sangria.

They were called in to a luncheon served by the brown, weathered hands of the cook herself, who was named Juana. Good-naturedly, she supplied the Spanish names of the dishes for the guests—*salpicon de mariscos*, which was shrimp and lobster salad, *gazpacho*, and several others. The meal ended with peaches and strawberries.

"Now for siesta," Renata said. The room where they had eaten was in the cool interior of the villa; outside, she said, the sun was scorching. At midday in the Balearic Islands, everything closed down, she told them, and everyone slept.

Casually, Renata led Dorinda and Paul to a single bedroom. Paul's smile as he drew the curtains to block the sun showed he was as glad of the arrangement as Dorinda was.

"I guess we're not a secret," Dorinda said, throwing herself onto the white coverlet of the bed and enjoying its crisp texture.

Paul lay down beside her and began kissing her throat. "Do you think they notice the way I look at you most of the time?" He unbuttoned her shirt.

"Paul, do you think we should?"

"Why not?"

"But I'm just so worried about what's going to happen."

"That won't help your mother." When Dorinda tried to sit up, Paul pulled her back, rolling over her body to pin down her arms. "What you need is something to take your mind off all this worry."

Her subsequent struggles for freedom ended in a passionate embrace. They began to take off each other's clothes, racing to be the first to finish, but the heat won, causing them to slow their pace and become more leisurely. As if by cue, the old-fashioned wooden fan hanging from the ceiling clicked on, and its whir drowned out their mumbled words and soft moans, while the slight wind it created cooled their moist bodies. Finally, they slept, until there was a soft knock at the door. Dorinda raised her head from Paul's chest and stared in surprise as the house boy slipped into the room, laid a tray with two tall glasses upon the table, and glided out.

There was certainly not much privacy here! Curious, she rolled off the bed and went over to the table, helping herself to one of the glasses, which was filled with pale rose liquid.

"What are you drinking?" Paul asked from the bed.

"I don't know, but I love it." She climbed back onto the bed beside him, the glass in her hand, and he lunged for it. Laughing, she tried to keep it upright; finally he won, and sipped it.

"Tastes like lemonade and wine, doesn't it?"

From the other side of the door, Renata rapped and called, "Drink your *limonada* and come on. We must make '*la rambla*'."

"What?" Dorinda turned to Paul.

"All I know is, recess is over. Need any help with your buttons?"

She let him smooth her body with the scented powder that she found in their bathroom, and then she put on a cotton shirt and a pair of white pants. When they were ready they went downstairs, where Renata, wearing a white dress slit up the side to her hips and down the front to her cleavage, was waiting. Emma, in a more conservative outfit, joined them and Renata led the way to the boat. Soon they were all in San Antonio, the town next to the airport, and the *rambla* turned out to be a street full of little shops and cafes near the park, where the entire population came at sunset to enjoy a drink and a stroll in the cooler air.

They sat at a little wrought-iron table in one of the outdoor cafes, and were presented with glasses of golden, mellow Spanish sherry and crockery dishes of *tapas*, a mixture of spicy hors d'oeuvres from kidney to eels. Dorinda looked anxiously over at Emma whenever the conversation lagged, but Emma was calm, eating her eels and drinking her cocktail, while fending off an Italian film director Renata had invited to meet her. Lovers wandered past them, arm-in-arm in the growing dusk. It began to seem more and more unreal that anything but pleasure could be experienced here.

Paul and she got up to join the strollers, and as they paced around the park her blonde hair attracted considerable attention. Paul grew slightly annoyed. When they returned to the other guests, she found a Spanish message for her. Someone had sent over an exotic drink "for the golden-haired one," as Renata translated the message.

The guests left San Antonio in a jolly mood, and while Juana feasted them with *paella* and chicken, a successful young French painter toasted Dorinda with every sip of his wine, offering to paint her portrait free. It was rather exciting to see how jealous this made Paul. Dorinda thought the painter might get a plateful of *paella* in his face.

But how could she be so lighthearted? How could there be time for sex and food and all sorts of other concerns, when all along she was filled with foreboding? Life, she thought, was a paradox.

After dinner, Emma casually suggested that the two of them take a walk on the beach. Paul didn't ask to join them, and Dorinda did not glance back at him as she left the lighted patio with Emma. The night had grown chilly, and the sand felt cold and clammy under her feet when she kicked off her sandals to cross the beach. She shivered and then, abruptly, she began to cry.

"Don't, you'll make me start," Emma said, putting an arm around her shoulders.

"All right, I won't, but what's going on?"

"I'll tell you now." In the quiet of the night Dorinda could hear the lapping of the water as tiny waves broke on the shore of Renata's beach. A crescent moon hung in the sky, so bright that near it only a few stars could be seen. In the black water of the cove, the moon was broken into hundreds of sparkling glimmers. The flashing red light on the buoy at the cove's edge seemed very remote, blinking two-seconds-on, one-second-off.

"Tomorrow, I'm going to take out a little Sailfish," Emma said quietly. She still held her arm across Dorinda's shoulders. "I've checked Renata's boathouse and she has a couple of them. I'll explain I sailed in Newport and all that. I can launch the boat alone, so no one will notice that I'm taking a plastic bag with some clothes and my pocketbook. I'll sail over there." She gestured out to sea. "I'll keep going until I'm around by San Antonio, then capsize the boat. You know I've never been an athlete—I'm a disgrace on a tennis court. But I can swim forever."

That was true, Dorinda thought; Emma had spent her childhood at some sandpit lake, and the sports she was really good at were swimming and sailing. But it wasn't reassuring to know that. Dorinda's throat closed; she said nothing.

"I'll swim to land," Emma continued, "put on the clothes in the plastic bag, and walk to the nearest road, or to wherever I can find a taxi. I hope I can hit the outskirts of San Antonio. I'll go to the airport and take a commercial flight out of here under another name."

"Mother, that's stupid. Anyone could find out you did that."

"I don't think so. You tell the police, if they inquire, that I could not swim very well. Say I liked to sail, but I couldn't swim. I'm taking along a wig, and with the help of some makeup, people won't dream I'm the American tourist who leaves San Antonio tomorrow afternoon."

"But your passport?"

"Dorinda, Trevor helped me. He got me a different passport stamped with an Ibiza entry. I'll be someone new—a part I'm sure I can play." Emma's arm grew tighter around her. "Listen, think, the whole thing is just a challenge . . ."

"But, Mother, you will go back to England?"

"Honey, don't look for me. Let me watch you."

Suddenly a sharp noise came from the trees higher on the hill and both she and Emma swung around, startled. They listened for a few minutes but only silence followed, interrupted now and then by the call of a night bird. The nervous moments made Dorinda think that perhaps they were right not to sit and simply be hunted by forces they didn't even know. Maybe Emma *was* right to turn and fight.

"Mother, I want to help," she said. "Why can't we both pretend to drown?"

"No," Emma said, taking her hands. "I can't expose you to the danger we might find does exist. I can't let you live a life of fear. Either way—Dorinda, look. You know that I trust Paul. You'll be safe at his grandmother's estate. It's exactly the place we need—out of the way enough that someone after you will be quite obvious."

"But let me—"

"No. It was my stupidity years ago that got us into this. Now it's up to me to get us out. I wouldn't do it, if I didn't think it would work."

In the moonlight, Dorinda looked at Emma's resolute expression. Then a cloud drifted over the moon, turning the sky dark as if to signal the end of their conversation.

"Please?" Emma's word was only a whisper.

"Okay," she said finally.

Emma leaned close and kissed her cheek.

The next morning as the guests ate Seville orange marmalade on brioche and drank espresso, bells began to toll from the ridge above the villa. Stepping to the edge of the balcony, Dorinda watched the road below fill up with nuns wearing long robes that twirled and rippled in the morning breeze. They seemed like daylight ghosts, black instead of white, as they floated in silence through the tree-filtered beams of the sun.

"Sisters of the local convent," Renata said, joining her and noticing her gaze. "It's enough to make you feel like repenting the sins of the night before, isn't it?" She laughed.

"What's on for today, if not church?" Emma asked.

"I think we should go and loll on the beach."

The morning air was crisp, the sun bright, and Renata's words met with universal approval. Dorinda followed Paul to their room to change. He pulled a small blue swim suit out of his suitcase and grinned at her.

"This'll drive you mad. Couldn't we just go snorkeling in bed?"

"Leave me alone, Paul," she said, turning away. "I don't feel like fooling around." She threw her clothes off and into a heap on the floor and pulled on a one-shouldered black bathing suit.

"Look, your mother is going to be just fine."

She said nothing in response. When she tried to fasten her gold ankle chain, her hands trembled; Paul came quickly over, knelt, and fastened the catch for her.

Renata paraded down the steps in a bright green bikini, her sandals slapping the stones, and they all followed. Emma had put on a white tank suit with gold rings ornamenting it, and she carried a gold beach bag, Dorinda noticed. Her mother carefully covered herself with suntan lotion, stretched out on her towel, and pulled a paperback novel from her bag. Paul enticed Dorinda into a sand castle-building contest, while Renata and the film director played Frisbee. Only the sporadic laughter of the latter disrupted the lazy calm.

When the Frisbee game wore the players out, they subsided onto beach chairs, and Emma rose.

"Are there boats in your boathouse?" she said to Renata.

"Two Sailfish. Don't tell me you sail?"

"I love to. Mind if I take one?"

"Of course not—that's what they're for." Renata pulled a large sun hat out of her beach bag to shield her redhead's complexion.

"Mother, want me to help you rig one?" Dorinda asked, joining them.

"No, I can manage. Stay here with Paul. You don't want his castle to get bigger than yours." Emma smiled at her, sounding so normal that Dorinda felt awed.

"Be sure to come back in an hour," Renata said, transferring to a large beach towel and rolling onto her stomach. "Juana will be bound to have something delicious for luncheon."

Emma leaned close to Dorinda.

"Go back to Paul," she said softly; then she turned and walked away. Dorinda could not move. She stared at the retreating figure.

"Come on, let's swim," Paul said, coming up behind her. He took her hand and dragged her toward the water. She let him pull her, watching Emma open the door of the boathouse. Her mother carried first the light hull and then the mast with the sail out beyond the boathouse, away from the view of the guests on the beach. With Paul, Dorinda swam into the cove. They turned when they had Emma in sight, and watched her. Emma fitted the mast in place, raised the sail, and pushed off, hopping dextrously on board. Luckily for her plan, an offshore breeze that morning made it easy to head briskly for the bay. With the wind coming from behind the sail, the boat made rapid progress from Renata's little cove.

"Mother! Good-bye!" Dorinda shouted after Emma, waving wildly.

Emma waved back. "This is great," they heard her call. "See you later." Then the sailboat made its way directly toward the bay beyond, where a bend of land at the edge of the cove hid the crossing to San Antonio. Dorinda strained her eyes to watch.

Finally the white sail disappeared, and her tears overflowed. Paul wiped her face with wet fingers.

"She'll be fine," he said. "She'll be just fine."

It took Dorinda a while to compose herself enough to swim back. Finally, with Paul's encouragement, she managed it. When they reached the beach and walked out of the water, her legs were trembling under her, but her resolve was strong. Emma had gone ahead as planned, and now they were committed. For better or worse, she had no choice but to play her own part.

When Emma did not reappear in time for Juana's luncheon, Renata was upset, but Dorinda smiled calmly and pointed out that since Emma had sailed out with the wind behind her, she would need to tack back and forth on returning, a process that would take her much longer.

"Also, I think the wind has lightened considerably," Paul added.

This nautical information left Renata wide-eyed; she kept the sailboats solely for her friends' amusement. Her concern made her dispatch the house boy in her motor launch to look for the tardy guest, but having done this, she switched her attention to Juana's *pisto manchego*, over which she regaled them with an account of the latest sex scandal brewing in Parliament. The details of this left the French artist and the Italian film director whooping with laughter.

Occasionally during the meal Dorinda excused herself to go to the edge of the balcony and scan the cove and what she could see of the bay. By dessert, she let herself seem a little more nervous.

When Lope brought the yacht back to the dock and reported no sign of Emma nearby, Paul was ready with the suggestion that Emma might have put in to a cove or a beach. Showing alarm, Dorinda insisted on accompanying Lope on another trip to search all nearby points. Paul went along. When they returned in an hour, a strange boat was tied up at Renata's dock and the actress came hurrying down the stone steps, speaking in agitation.

"You didn't find her, darlings? I'm terribly sorry—it's probably a mistake. But there's a policeman here, come over from San Antonio. An hour ago a fisherman found my Sailfish—it has my name on it, so they—they brought it back." Gasping for breath in the smothering heat, Renata paused at the foot of the stairs and shaded her eyes with her long-nailed hand as she looked at them, standing together on the gently rocking dock. "I mean, don't be upset. She's probably all right. But the boat was floating upside down out in the bay, and there was no sign—"

Chapter Six

WHEN THE RENTED AUSTIN SWERVED SHARPly around a corner, Dorinda awoke with a jolt. She had slept through most of the flight across land and water. When Paul arrived at the airfield outside Ware in Hertfordshire, she'd opened her eyes only long enough for the transfer from airplane to car. She had been physically and emotionally exhausted, and now troubling images crowded into her mind again. The excited Spanish authorities; the distressed house guests; Renata twisting her beautiful hair in distraction as she tried not to believe the worst; finally, their abrupt departure. Emma had told Paul she wanted her disappearance and probable death to be reported by the international press, and she wanted Dorinda to vanish at the same time. Accordingly, Paul informed Renata that Dorinda was in hysterics and had to be institutionalized immediately. Then, before Renata could fully take in the situation, Paul had commandeered the motor launch, rushed to the airport, and put the Piper Cherokee into the air. God knows what Renata was thinking, Dorinda reflected, with two more of her house guests evaporating on her. Paul had filed no flight plan. A sleepy official at Ware gave their passports only a cursory glance, and now they were traveling a deserted country road on a moonless night. There were no other cars at all.

"Finally awake?" Paul took his hand from the steering wheel to touch her cheek, and Dorinda kissed his fingers. What would she have done without him? Emma had been entirely right to think she'd need support.

He glanced over and smiled at her in the dim light from the dashboard. When he looked back at the road, she found herself wondering what the next few weeks were going to be like.

"Paul," she said. "How come you are willing to go back to your grandmother? I thought you'd left forever."

"We've just gone through Stevenage—it's not much further now," Paul said, ignoring her question.

"Paul?"

"Well, I'd been thinking I needed a bit of a rest from the stage, even before you came along to provide such a lovely alternative." Again he glanced at her with a smile.

"But what happened to the part in *Bride of Dracula*?"

"Oh, I didn't get it."

"I don't believe that."

"Shall we just drop the subject?"

"No." What, Dorinda wondered, had Emma made Paul do? Was he giving up a part to take her somewhere safe?

"All right." Paul sighed. "I wasn't going to tell you, but perhaps I should, so you can see how seriously I'm taking this. They offered me the part and I refused it. And here we are at Darkbourne."

"Oh, Paul!"

Before she could say another word the car had rounded a bend and stopped in front of two heavy iron gates. In the darkness beyond them, a long avenue of stately trees formed a black passageway to the manor house at the end. Dorinda's concern for Paul's acting career was swept away in sheer wonder, and she sat silent as he got out to undo the latches of the gates. The huge mansion ahead had white stone walls illuminated by what seemed to be flickering fires.

"Are those *torches*?" she asked, when Paul got back into the car.

"Grandmother's expecting us." Paul sighed. "I've tried to prepare you. I mean, you'll be perfectly safe here from everyone—*except* Grandmother." He gave a short laugh. "When I described her to your mother I think she thought I was kidding. But no such luck."

"Paul, I can't believe this—it's a castle—"

He chuckled, and stopped the car near a wooden bridge that crossed a stream running past the front of the house.

"You have a *moat*?"

It was too dark to see much, as she peered upward at the stone mansion looming across the bridge. Paul jumped out and helped her from the car, then unloaded their luggage. Dorinda held onto the iron handrail as they crossed the moat, and, on the other side, Paul pulled the iron chain beside heavy double doors.

In a few minutes, the doors creaked open, and a face peered out, illuminated by a candle. Dorinda wanted to laugh hysterically. A *candle*? All they needed was crashing thunder and lightning and they'd be in the middle of a horror movie. However, instead of a stiffly starched mobcap, the woman who answered the door was wearing a hair net; though she did have on a white apron, it covered a short skirt, not a long black one.

"Mr. Paul," she said, smiling slightly and standing back for them to enter.

"This is Mrs. Pomerance, Dorinda," he said. "Pommy! Is the lack of electricity for my benefit?"

In the wavering of the candle flame, Dorinda could not tell whether there was a twinkle in the woman's eye or not as she answered, her face perfectly grave, "Mr. Paul, we've done without it for a month. Lady Victoria had a dream—"

"Don't say another word." Paul raised one hand, shaking his head. "How can you take it, Pommy?"

In answer Mrs. Pomerance only gave a slight bow, then turned and went silently ahead of them through a cavernous entrance hall and into another dark room on the right. The unsteady glow of her candle brought elegant furniture and rich fittings into view, then buried them in the dark again. Dorinda held Paul's hand. She felt that if she yelled out suddenly, the whole place might just melt away.

Soon they were standing in front of a red leather-padded door, embossed with gold that the candlelight picked out. Mrs. Pomerance signaled them to wait, and went in to announce them, plunging the small passageway where they stood into darkness.

"Hey," Dorinda said softly.

In answer, Paul lifted her hand, kissed the palm, and then chuckled. "Remember me, if Grandmother has me thrown into the oubliette with the rats," he said. He was actually enjoying this, Dorinda thought.

The door in front of them opened again.

"So you've decided to be sensible," a deep voice said.

Paul led Dorinda into the room, which was lit by several candelabra and a roaring fire in a large carved mahogany fireplace. Set off by a massive red leather wing chair, the woman who had spoken sat very erect, swathed in peacock-colored silk. Silver hair surrounded her fine-boned face, hair only a shade or two bluer than the fur of the large white Persian cat in her lap.

"Grandmother," he said, "this is—"

"You have come back to stay?" The woman cut him off. Her gaze did not leave Paul's face. "You will leave the theater?"

"Well." Paul hesitated. "Anyway, for now."

A moment more, Paul's grandmother stared at him. Then she seemed to make up her mind.

"You may embrace me," she said firmly.

Paul did as he was ordered, kissing her on the cheek. Afterward, waving him aside, his grandmother turned her attention to Dorinda, surveying her from top to bottom. Dorinda expected her to sniff, but instead a faint smile came to her face.

"You're the reason this ruffian has returned to me?"

Dorinda glanced at Paul, who answered for her.

"Yes, Grandmother, Dorinda Westerly. She's the whole reason."

"You are not an actress?"

"No, I'm not."

The woman, whom Dorinda gathered she should call Lady Victoria, looked pleased. "Then welcome to Darkbourne," she said. "I've warned Paul Jeffrey many times about his profession. He is in grave danger."

The cat on Lady Victoria's lap at this point delicately stretched out its forepaws and yawned widely, displaying a mouthful of pointed teeth, as if showing contempt for Lady Victoria's words. Opening his eyes, the cat stared up at Dorinda, who looked back in fascination. The cat had one eye of clear blue and another of pale, shining green.

"What kind of cat is that?" she asked. "Lady Victoria," she added.

"Trinculo is very rare." Lady Victoria's heavily jeweled hand stroked the cat's back. "An odd-eyed white Persian. Sometimes they are called 'jewel-eyed' because the colors resemble sapphire and emerald."

"*I* call him old scratch-paws," Paul said. "He'll give it to you if he feels like it."

As he spoke, Trinculo turned his eyes on Paul, yawned again, and then settled more comfortably against the peacock silk.

Lady Victoria's eyes, themselves light blue, Dorinda saw, also traveled to Paul's face and she lifted one hand.

"I've ordered a supper for you. Pomerance—"

The housekeeper, or whatever she was, had been standing respectfully to one side. Now she indicated they should accompany her. Following Paul's example, Dorinda said thank you and good night to Lady Victoria, who nodded in response.

By the light of Mrs. Pomerance's candle, Dorinda caught sight of tapestries high on the walls as they climbed a double staircase to the columned splendor of an upper reception hall and a long gallery filled with dark oil paintings. Past that they arrived at a small drawing room with a bright fire, where a table had been laid with at least a dozen covered casseroles.

"Good heavens," Dorinda said.

She managed to down a meat pie and to drink some broth, and after a glass of wine she was a little revived.

"Grandmother was too bloody much tonight, as usual," Paul said as they finished. "We'll have to put up with her ideas, but they are good for a laugh. She's not a bad old crock when you get to know her."

"I think you love her!" Dorinda said. "So would Mother. Talk about acting—*she's* acting, just sitting there. But she's nice to take me in."

"I think *I'll* have a dream tonight that we'd better get the electricity turned on bloody quick. It's a real wonder she can keep a staff in this place."

"Speaking of dreaming—were you thinking of bed?"

"I'm always thinking of bed." Grinning, Paul got up. "Let me find out from Pommy where we've been put."

When Paul came back he was chuckling. "My lady's installed us in separate bedrooms. Oh, well, if we get tired of mine, we can move to yours."

Borrowing a candelabrum from the desk in the room, Paul led her up yet another staircase, to what had obviously been his bedroom when he lived at Darkbourne. Around the walls were banners and souvenirs of Harrow and Cambridge.

"I didn't know you'd studied in such places," Dorinda said, looking around.

"I wasn't clever enough to escape them," Paul said. "And anyway, they were heaven after Darkbourne."

A big trunk, like a theatrical trunk, stood at the foot of the large brass bed, and Dorinda examined it.

"Doesn't that look like the trunk of some actor touring the provinces?" Paul said, noticing her interest. "I found it in a dark recess of the attic; I used to pretend it had belonged to my mystery father, Laurence Olivier."

"Laurence Olivier!" Dorinda laughed.

"Well, or someone just as good. Look inside."

When she threw back the lid she saw a heap of velvet and satin, which upon examination turned out to be costumes trimmed with braid and fake jewelry.

"What's this?"

"I got an old seamstress to make them for me. I'd lock that door and play Shakespeare to the mirror."

"Maybe your father *was* Laurence Olivier." Dorinda pulled a wine velvet cape out of the trunk and flung it around her. Even in its wrinkled state it gave her a certain air, she thought, as she turned in front of the full-length mirror.

"Ah ha. Now say 'if music is the food of love . . .' "

" 'If music *be* the food of love . . .' " she corrected him.

"Oh, you perfectionist!" He picked her up, cape and all, and dropped her into the middle of his bed. His unmerciful tickling stopped only when she promised to do anything he wanted. She had a pretty good idea what that would be, and tired as she was, it was consoling to let him make love to her.

"Hurry up and dress and let's get something to eat," Paul said, waking her the next day. "I'm famished, and the breakfasts here are the best thing about the place."

She threw a pillow at him for disturbing her, but once awake, she found she was hungry, too, and hopped out of bed to put on the same clothes she had been wearing the night before. Looking at them made her wonder where Emma was, but before she could pursue the thought, Paul was leading her downstairs, and the magnificence of Darkbourne in the daytime engaged her full attention. She had been in splendid mansions out on Long Island, but nothing she had seen could be compared to Darkbourne, except perhaps a castle on the Hudson she once had visited. However, Darkbourne seemed to have more tasteful furnishings, and far better art.

"Yes, the Innowells were all collectors," Paul said when she commented. At the end of the hall he escorted her into a handsome breakfast room with french windows overlooking a formal garden. A servant was just clearing away some plates, as if several others might have preceded them at breakfast. On the long sideboard were enough dishes for a king, baskets of rolls, plates of elaborately cut grapefruit anointed with something green, bowls of steaming oatmeal and porridge, platters of kippers, eggs, sausages, and stewed tomatoes. There were even lamb chops. As sunlight streamed into the room from the garden, they progressed down the buffet and then carried their plates to the long Queen Anne table.

Dorinda tasted her grapefruit. "Creme de menthe," she exclaimed, determining what the green coloring was. "That certainly improves grapefruit."

As they finished their plates, Lady Victoria suddenly appeared. She was wearing a billowing salmon-pink robe, tied with a silver cord, and looked a little less formidable by daylight, although she carried herself just as erectly, this time sitting at the head of the table.

"The aspect of your stars today, Paul, is very favorable." She turned her head toward Dorinda. "Miss Westerly, give me your birthdate—exact place and time—and Julia will cast your horoscope. Although you may have had this done, Julia shall repeat it. She is far better at it than most—Julia Ramsay, *quite* successful in astrological circles."

"And around here, no one moves in any other circles," Paul muttered, but Lady Victoria ignored him.

"I'm a Taurus," Dorinda said politely. "That's all I know."

Lady Victoria looked alarmed at such remissness, and Paul chuckled.

"Well, Grandmother, your nutty Julia Ramsay said I was destined for riches, but *that* didn't come true."

Dorinda smothered a laugh, not looking at Paul. When she glanced again at Lady Victoria, she found that Paul's grandmother was giving her a searching scrutiny. After a few minutes it grew disquieting. Mrs. Pomerance came into the breakfast room, poured a cup of coffee, and brought it to Lady Victoria, but Lady Victoria waved the housekeeper away and rose.

"Come with me," she said to Dorinda.

"Grandmother—" Paul spoke in a warning tone.

"Hush, Paul." Lady Victoria gestured for Dorinda to accompany her.

"Oh, God." Paul stood up. "Let's get it over with, then."

Dorinda wondered if she might be going on a tour of the house, but Lady Victoria led her without comment through many rooms, into another wing, walking rapidly. Dorinda gave Paul a puzzled glance and he made a funny face at her.

In this wing a narrower set of stairs led to the third story, where there was a low-ceilinged hall full of closed doors. At the end of the hall Lady Victoria took a silver key on a chain from around her neck, and fitted it into the lock of the door there.

Opening the door, she stood back, motioning for Dorinda to enter. Hesitantly, Dorinda looked through the doorway. Inside was a small room whose heavy red curtains were drawn over the windows, making it dim in spite of the sunshine outside. The walls were painted dark red. The only furniture was a large oval table with a dozen high-backed chairs around it. At the center of the table stood a silver bell.

Somehow, the place struck a chill into Dorinda's bones. She moved over the threshold and was immediately struck by a change in the atmosphere. It was musty and oppressive in the room; more than simply the smell of a place that had been shut up—there was a dank odor that made her feel dizzy. Still, she seemed to be drawn forward. There was something intangible here, like a consciousness apart from her, Paul, or his grandmother. She shuddered, staring at the bell.

"I see," Lady Victoria said.

"Let's cut this out, Grandmother." Paul stepped in and took Dorinda by the arm. "You really shouldn't do it to people."

He pulled Dorinda out into the hall. With great composure, Lady Victoria closed and locked the door, then looked at Dorinda and smiled.

"What is that place?" Dorinda asked.

"My seance chamber," Lady Victoria answered. "There is something about you, my dear. I sensed it immediately—not last night, but at once, today. You will make a valuable addition to our group."

"Oh, no, she won't," Paul said. He was still holding Dorinda's arm and he shook it slightly. "None of that stuff. I'm surprised at you, Miss Westerly. *I* registered zero on Grandmother's spook scale, when she stuck me in there. Steady breathing, steady pulse, never smelled the other world at all—just an empty room where more mumbo-jumbo's gone on than in the houses of Parliament."

Following behind them with measured paces, Lady Victoria said nothing to this.

Paul apologized for the after-breakfast excursion when they unpacked their suitcases.

"Grandmother never rests until she takes everyone in there," he said. "Boys home with me on the holidays from Harrow, Cambridge classmates—anybody."

"Don't you really feel anything when you go in?"

"Only amusement. One of my friends, Roland Parker, pretended to hear voices and Grandmother got all steamed up and thought he was having a mystical seizure until she realized he was laughing so hard he was in danger of choking to death. She never spoke a word to him for the rest of his visit."

"Well, I felt something," Dorinda said. Paul shot her a glance and then dived into her suitcase, coming up with a peach lace bra.

"I've never seen this on you."

"You haven't known me forever, you know."

"True, and you've not yet seen me in red chiffon knickers."

"Or a purple silk cape. Paul, what are you doing?"

Over her protests, he scrambled together the things in her bag, swept them up in one armload, and deposited them in one of his drawers.

"There, now you're unpacked. We must go shopping—you didn't take much to Ibiza that you can wear here. No jodphurs for riding to hounds."

"Does your grandmother have horses?"

"Indeed, and all named for cards in the tarot pack, a Darkbourne touch."

"Lord." Dorinda glanced out of the open windows at the meadows and woods that bordered the sloping acres of side lawn; the place should have beautiful riding trails. "What's a tarot pack?"

"Fortune-telling cards," Paul said, pulling her toward his bed. She let him push her down onto it, and rolled over to make room for him beside her. "Grandmother could predict my grades at school—of course, so could I—but she used the tarot, and claimed the card called Fool always came up."

"Is Fool one of the horses?" Dorinda put her head against Paul's shoulder.

"No, but there's one called Priestess, and then Chariot, Hermit, and Strength—"

"I'll have him."

"Her. She's a bay mare. Speedy—sure you can handle her?"

"Central Park lessons, camp in Maine. Which will you take?"

"Wheel of Fortune's my favorite. Old Roulette, I call him."

Dorinda let her entire body slide against Paul's. "Where shall we ride?" she asked.

"When we leave the stables, we can skirt Mill Pond and then take off across some meadows," he said, staring up at the ceiling, his head on the same pillow as hers. "We'll slow down when we get to the woods, and take a footpath I know through the pines. It's covered with needles and smells wonderful. Smell it?"

"Yes, it's good. What comes next?"

"The path turns in a sharp bend and ends suddenly at the bottom of a large hill all over wildflowers. You can put some in your hair—I'll pick you some gorse."

"Shall we weave some into the manes of our horses?"

"Yes," Paul said, his arm under her tightening. "Then we'll ride around to the other side of the hill, where there's a waterfall I want to show you, but the noise alarms Strength. She snorts and starts to run."

"What?" When Dorinda tried to sit up, Paul's arm held her closer against him, pinning her down on the bed.

"You pull on the reins, trying to halt her breakneck pace, but she's spooked; she doesn't listen."

"Fine horse!" Dorinda said.

"Meanwhile Roulette and I are right behind you, galloping madly in our attempt to catch up."

"Oh," Dorinda said, relaxing again. "And then you do get abreast." She turned her head to kiss Paul's cheek. "You reach out for Strength's bridle, but we're headed for a stone wall and you have to fall back or we'll all be killed. Strength takes a beautiful leap, with me holding on for dear life, and a second later you clear the wall, too, and race to get beside us again."

"Then I can reach out for Strength's bridle and quiet her, talking her down to a walk. When she stops she's panting and you tumble from the saddle into the lush grass of a glade that no one has ever set foot in before. I jump off Roulette. Your hair has blown wildly across your face; your clothes are torn. I reach down and pull them away." As Paul spoke, he ran his fingers through Dorinda's hair until it spread across the pillows in twisting locks. Then his hand caressed her cheek and traveled down to unbutton her blouse. Moving so that he could pull off her clothes, Dorinda took up the story.

"Now I've recovered from the shock of the ride and I'm with my rescuer and I'm very, very grateful." She ran her hand down Paul's chest and began to unbutton his shirt. "I can't think of anything else. The ground is soft under us, and we roll into each other's arms. When I open my eyes an instant, I see the tops of the pine trees over us, dark green against the blue sky."

Here Paul halted the tale with a kiss, and neither spoke again; in Dorinda's mind, the deer standing startled at the edge of the virgin glade witnessed their first scene of human love.

In a few minutes, Paul opened his eyes and stared into hers from two inches away.

"Still want to go for a ride?"

"Umm. Tomorrow." Dorinda burrowed against Paul's warm body, closing her eyes. Clasped together, they both slept.

Later, waking slowly and in a state half-conscious and half-asleep, Dorinda dreamed. She was on Strength and Paul on Roulette. They were cantering, and a black horse galloping madly behind them was trying to catch them. He had no rider. Her heart pounding with fear, she urged Strength forward, desperate to escape. . . .

In the next second Dorinda's eyes snapped open. As her heart slowed down, she wiped her sweaty palms on the sheet and blinked at the ceiling, trying to orient herself. It had been a dream! But she must have seen a tarot pack somewhere. Because in the dream, she had known that the name of the black horse was Death.

Chapter Seven

IN THE NEXT WEEKS TIME SEEMED TO HAVE two paces. The days in the country flew by, the hours from morning to night completely filled. Paul thought of many ways to divert Dorinda. They rode horses, hiked, and bicycled all over Hertfordshire, stopping at village pubs and lunching at country inns, or they tore about doing more extensive sightseeing in Paul's Jaguar, now brought up from London, or flew a Piper Cub rented at the airport in Ware. Twice, Paul piloted them up to Scotland for a weekend there. He seemed to spend practically no time managing the estate, as he was supposed to do. Aside from having the electricity turned back on, he primarily spent every moment keeping Dorinda busy. But the hours rushing past did not stop her from realizing that a long period was passing without any word of Emma. The days were quickly over, but Darkbourne with its mistress, its servants, and house guests formed an unchanging setting, emphasizing Dorinda's suspended life.

Emma's disappearance and probable death had been reported by the press and then dropped. So far as Dorinda knew, no one in her mother's circle was aware of where Emma's daughter was, or cared. Personally she felt very safe with Paul always beside her. But what was actually happening? Was Emma peering at her through pinholes in newspapers, sitting on park benches and watching her pass? Was she following her? Her mother had always told her the truth. If she said she was watching over her, she was, Dorinda told herself. Still, she felt no emanations in the air, no sense of her mother's presence.

When Lady Victoria announced she would give a large party on Midsummer's Eve, Dorinda was delighted. Surely her mother would manage to be among the guests, and clever detective work on her own part might very possibly ferret her mother out.

Her hopes were high as she dressed on the evening of the gathering. Wondering what disguise Emma would assume, Dorinda picked up Trinculo, who was stretched across her makeup area on top of Paul's highboy, and moved the cat over to the bed, where he continued to watch her preparations for the party. Trinculo had become attached to her, following her around Darkbourne and occasionally jumping heavily into her lap, sometimes when she wasn't expecting it. Unblinkingly, Lady Victoria's cat now peered at her as she pulled a long green frock over her head, a dress bought for the event with money from the Swiss account. Settling the soft muslin into place, she debated whether to wear her hair up and perhaps add a rose.

"What do you think?" she asked Trinculo.

"About what?" Paul said from his dressing room.

"Shall I wear a rose in my hair on this pagan holiday?"

Paul appeared at the door, wearing a smoke-colored dinner jacket. He examined his buttonhole.

"Yes, if I can put a matching rose in my lapel," he said. "Though I think garlic flowers would be better. To ward off witches, you know."

"I really can't wait to see this crowd. Will they all be weirdos?"

"Guaranteed—the cream of psychic society. However, I don't believe the invitations went out by telepathy. I caught sight of some white cards engraved in gold."

Paul smiled as he spoke. His attitude toward his grandmother's doings seemed unfailingly good-humored, and Dorinda marveled at his lighthearted way of dealing with what might drive someone else crazy. Certainly everything at Darkbourne was done in unique style. When she offered to help with the party, Dorinda had been given a crystal prism on a chain by Lady Victoria, who told her to hold it over the cuts of meat in the village butcher shop. "If the meat is fresh, the pendulum will swing up and down," Lady Victoria solemnly told her. "Now, if it goes sideways, don't buy. Make the butcher show you another cut." Dorinda had relied on her eyes instead, during the shopping trip; while she was at the butcher's, Paul had taken the pendulum into the stationer's shop next door and later claimed that when he held the prism over a display of paperback books, it had unfailingly picked out the sexiest one.

Dorinda grinned now at the memory, and took Paul's hand.

"Let's get some white roses from that bush by the dining room window," she said. "Bring the scissors."

They took the back stairs leading past the kitchen wing, where the sound of frantic preparations could be heard on their passage down. When Dorinda stepped outside she paused, struck by the beautiful balance of light and shade in the garden. The sun was still high, but had declined enough to send slanting rays across the scene, illuminating every leaf and blade of grass in a warm evening glow.

"It seems much earlier than eight o'clock," she said. "A perfect English evening. There's such peace—"

As she spoke, Dorinda searched among the roses on the bush for two just-opened ones.

"Careful—don't prick yourself." Paul took the first rose Dorinda cut and pinned it into her knot of hair. She found another for him and put it into his buttonhole and he pulled her close and kissed her in spite of her protests that

GREEN LADY

he would crush his rose. When he finally lifted his head, he looked down into her eyes.

"Could you live in England?" he asked.

"I'd have to think about that." She smiled up at him and he gave her another, quicker kiss before she pulled away and turned toward the house.

Guests were arriving when they reached the entrance hall. No one was greeting the incoming partygoers but this seemed not to matter. They all apparently knew one another and were rushing into each other's arms with exclamations of pleasure. Paul beside her, Dorinda paused at the grand staircase and took in the scene. The variety in dress was breathtaking. The women's costumes ranged from flowing robes tied with daisy chains and ropes of flowers—one middle-aged lady wore a corn-yellow silk gown with hay woven into her coiffure to form a halo effect—to designer jeans topped by rainbow-hued Lurex jackets. Some men wore conservative dinner wear, but many were in robes. One gentleman's garb was a coat of many colors like the Biblical Joseph's. Several men carried flowers; one very thin, tall man wore a pure white suit and carried both an ivory cane and a white lily.

As a few people said hello to Paul, Dorinda turned her attention from the colorful guests to the extra servants hired for the evening. Lace-aproned maids rushed about with hors d'oeuvres and butlers carried around trays filled with glasses of champagne. Could any of the maids be Emma? Dorinda scrutinized them all, but not one was the right height. That was one physical factor Emma could not alter.

Disappointed, Dorinda sighed and looked back at the guests. "Where's Lady Victoria?" she asked Paul.

"Grandmother makes a great entrance down the staircase at precisely nine," Paul said. "They're all accustomed to that. Shall we dance a bit?"

The two largest drawing rooms had been joined together, and an orchestra installed on a raised platform opposite the french doors to the terrace. As they walked into this ballroom, the musicians struck up "Greensleeves."

"Maybe they see you in your green dress," Paul said.

"It hasn't any sleeves," she started to answer, but suddenly her eyes were arrested by the sight of a strikingly beautiful woman standing across the room beside an open door. The woman wore a bizarre costume, a black silk body stocking covered with jet sequins; it showed off the perfect proportions of her figure. High black boots reached to her knees, straight dark hair fell to her shoulders. Heavily painted with kohl, her dark eyes seemed to slant upward.

Dorinda felt a burst of joy. It must be her mother!

"Paul, look." She seized Paul's arm. "Or rather, wait; don't look right now. In a minute." Emma's warnings came back to her: *Don't appear to recognize me.*

"What?" Paul seemed confused.

"We'll walk out the door." Dorinda's excitement made it difficult to speak. "When we pass the woman in black, pay close attention."

Unable to wait, Dorinda began to move as she spoke. With Paul following, she headed for the door where the woman stood. As she brushed past, the man to whom the woman was speaking said, "Got it completely wrong about sex magic—"

The woman turned her head. "Hello, Paul," she said.

Dorinda did not stop; she continued rapidly to the stone railing of the balcony, keeping her back to the woman.

"She *spoke* to you?" she whispered to Paul. Cautiously glancing sideways toward the door, she saw the woman throw back her head and laugh.

"Dorinda, honey." Paul said her name softly as he put his arm around her waist. "I'm sorry. But that's Julia Ramsay—the woman who's supposed to cast your horoscope, remember?"

"Julia Ramsay? Are you sure?"

"She's been in Egypt and just got back, Grandmother said. I'm afraid I've known her all my life. You remember, I showed you the turreted house in the village where she lives."

"Oh, Paul." Tears of disappointment came into Dorinda's eyes.

"Paul, darling, where *have* you been?" From across the terrace, a woman in a brown monk's robe bore down upon them, trailed by a young girl in a bridal gown, veil and all.

"Oh-oh." Paul took Dorinda's arm and hastily pulled her toward the house, going in at another entrance, not the one where Julia Ramsay stood. He hurried Dorinda through the crowded drawing rooms and out again, into the hall, where he opened doors until he found a small room that was empty. Dorinda's tears were spilling over by this time.

"Don't cry." He put his arms around her.

"But I thought—" Dorinda pushed her face against his shoulder. This was stupid, she told herself. She was surprised at her emotion. She must be more nervous than she realized.

Paul patted her back. "I know how you feel," he said. "Anyway, I think I do." The serious tone in his voice made her raise her head and look at him. "When I was growing up, I used to look at all the men who came here. I wondered if one of them might have been my father. I'd always hope there'd be some way I could recognize him—but of course, there wasn't. I mean, I probably couldn't have. But still, I was always looking."

As he gave her a sympathetic squeeze, Dorinda pictured Paul as a little boy wandering amid the party guests, and she felt sad for him. Certainly she wasn't the only abandoned child on earth—and she wasn't really abandoned, anyway. She felt ashamed of her lack of fortitude.

"I wish I'd known you as a little boy," she said, letting her lips trace the curve of his chin.

He smiled and kissed her. "We would have been great playmates," he said.

When they returned to the party a short while later, the orchestra was playing a waltz, and they joined the dozen other couples dancing. Outside, the light was fading from the sky, and most of the guests had come indoors. Champagne was flowing at a rapid rate and the chatter of the onlookers around the dance floor mingled with the music from the orchestra, vying in volume.

"If we keep dancing we won't have to talk to anybody," Paul said, making her skirt swirl as he executed a fast turn.

"Is it almost nine?"

Paul consulted his watch. "Two minutes till."

"I'd like to see your grandmother."

In answer, Paul danced her through the high arched doorway and into the great hall. There the large standing clock by the door played the Westminster chimes as its minute hand touched twelve, and then it struck nine times. Precisely as the last stroke died away, Lady Victoria appeared at the head of the stairs and began her progress down them, watched by a hushed group in the great hall. From the drawing room came the strains of "The Girl from Ipanema," but Lady Victoria ignored the frivolous beat of the tune and proceeded as if to an inwardly-heard grand march, making her descent in stately magnificence. She wore a gown of delicate gray lace over gray satin, the bodice decorated with a ruby-set gold filigree pin whose design matched the pattern of the lace. On her fingers, ruby rings glittered, and her white hair was pinned into a high chignon held by a ruby chiffon scarf wound dramatically about it and decorated with five sparkling ruby pins, giving the effect of a ruby crown.

"How terrific," Dorinda murmured to Paul.

"The stage definitely lost an actress," Paul said, watching his grandmother's performance. "She dares to criticize acting to *me*."

"Well, her role is real," Dorinda said. "What is it such women are called? Dowagers? *Grande dames*?"

"Queens," Paul said with a chuckle.

Lady Victoria reached the bottom of the stairs and began to greet the line of guests forming in the hall. Dorinda and Paul were turning to go back to the dance floor when Lady Victoria caught sight of them.

She gestured and then, pacing between persons eager to speak to her, made her way over to them.

"A lovely gown, my dear," she said to Dorinda. "You, Paul—"

Before she could say more she was interrupted by a man in a red goatee. "Dear Lady Victoria—" he began.

"Laddie Olcott, what nonsense *was* that?" Lady Victoria spoke imperiously. "Your article in last month's *Magick Digest*? You must explain more to me about holistic mental images—but not now." Cutting him off, she turned back to Dorinda. "My dear, I wish you to meet a few persons. Would you accompany me?"

Dorinda could not refuse, although beside her she heard Paul sigh. Actually, she felt curious about these guests, and she willingly followed Lady Victoria, who seemed already to know the locations of the persons she sought.

"Baroness Gard first," Lady Victoria said, and led the way to the library, where a pale old lady was sitting in a window seat eating chocolates out of a fancy pink box. The Baroness peered vacantly up at Dorinda and Paul, and said nothing when introduced.

"Coro Richardson next," Lady Victoria said, returning to the hall and then leading them into the dining room, where in a corner under a large Vermeer they found a middle-aged, enormously fat woman dressed in a sky-blue caftan talking to several effete-looking young men. Coro Richardson dimpled all over when she smiled to acknowledge the introduction, but not allowing more to be said than "How do you do," Lady Victoria returned to the front hall.

"Lord Cobhill," she said, approaching a man just taking a glass of champagne from a tray. Fair, almost Nordic in appearance, he had cold blue eyes, Dorinda thought. Formally, Lord Cobhill bowed.

"And Julia—just back from Egypt." Lady Victoria walked swiftly toward the drawing room, and Dorinda hurried after her. The woman in black was dancing with the man in the white suit, now minus his cane and lily. Stopping in mid-step as Lady Victoria appeared, the astrologer immediately came over to join them. Again, Dorinda was fascinated by the sight of her. It really *could* have been Emma. She was sure her mother was capable of the high, cultivated English accent with which Julia Ramsay spoke.

"I shall set to work on your chart," she said to Dorinda, her eyes traveling from the rose in Dorinda's hair down to her face. "Ah, Egypt," she added, turning her head to speak to Lady Victoria. "Full of astral light; almost dangerous. And then there's typhoid."

The orchestra struck up another waltz and Julia Ramsay's partner in white reclaimed her.

"Grandmother, may I have a dance?" Paul asked.

"Later. The sun enters Cancer at 10:02 p.m.; the summer solstice. We shall have time to gather and communicate with friends not present before all souls depart at midnight."

Dorinda wondered what Lady Victoria meant by this speech. So far as she knew, the plans called for a grand buffet dinner to be served at twelve, instead of the guests departing. Paul, however, was not puzzled.

"Grandmother—" he began in a warning tone.

"You may sit in the circle to protect her if you wish," Lady Victoria said to him. Then she turned to Dorinda. "We hold a seance tonight. I would like you to attend."

"You'll scare her to death," Paul protested.

"Hush, Paul. Let Dorinda decide for herself." Lady Victoria spoke firmly.

They both turned to Dorinda. She drew a breath, wondering how she *did* feel. More curious than frightened, she decided.

"I don't mind," she said, returning Lady Victoria's rather imperious stare with a direct look of her own. Lady Victoria smiled.

"I'm coming too, then, and the ghosts had better be amusing," Paul said. At this, Lady Victoria bristled and then, with a nod to them, turned away to be immediately claimed by some waiting guests.

"Are you sure about this?" Paul murmured as they performed a slow foxtrot to "Some Enchanted Evening."

"That room made me feel strange. I guess I would like to go back," Dorinda replied. At any rate, it would keep her mind off her frustration at not seeing anyone whom she thought might be her mother. She was examining everyone they passed or danced near, but unless Emma had surpassed herself with her disguise, Dorinda did not think she was present. She had so far caught no one, man or woman, watching her with more than an admiring or curious expression.

In a few moments they were summoned, and with Julia Ramsay and the others to whom Lady Victoria had introduced her they mounted to the seance chamber. Lady Victoria went down the narrow hall first, taking the key from

GREEN LADY

around her neck. They stood in silence as she unlocked the door. When she flung it open, Trinculo, with a loud clatter, burst out of the room and ran right over the feet of the guests, racing away.

Dorinda jumped violently and Lady Victoria said "Trinculo!" in an admonishing voice. Quickly Paul put a protective arm around Dorinda's shoulders.

"We're not forced to take part in this charade, you know, love," Paul whispered.

For a moment, Dorinda was tempted to say "No thanks" and go back to the lively scene below. But really, what could happen? And it might be interesting. She took Paul's hand and together they followed the others into the room.

The seance chamber seemed subtly different, she thought, the walls and curtains now a darker red, almost black-red, lit by tapers in wall sconces. New, spicy aromas had been added to the dank odor, not quite masking it completely. Dorinda was sure the number of chairs at the heavy wooden table was not the same.

Lady Victoria arranged the seating, placing Dorinda next to Lord Cobhill and Paul across from her. Sitting down, Paul gave Dorinda a grin and a wink, making the proceedings seem less eerie. Imitating the others, Dorinda placed her hands palms-down on the table. Julia Ramsay took the chair on her other side, as the circle was completed by three guests Dorinda hadn't met, two men and a woman in eccentric clothes and jewelry. Without introducing these last, Lady Victoria made a slight bow to the four corners of the room and then sat at the head of the table, murmuring, "Now is the hour of the solstice, the hour of soul-gathering of the departed who are bound to Earth; let us begin."

A long silence followed her words. Lady Victoria's rubies seemed to glitter even more intensely in the candlelight, Dorinda thought, staring at Paul's grandmother. Then she closed her eyes, feeling the soothing coolness of the table where her palms were pressed. On her closed eyelids she seemed to see red veins outlined, glowing. She opened her eyes to find that one of the velvet curtains had parted, allowing a shaft of bright moonlight to fall on the bell in the center of the table. Alarmed, Dorinda looked over at Paul, and was relieved to see him smiling. She knew he would say this was just a trick, like many he had seen onstage.

However, his expression changed when the silver bell rose up several inches over the table and began to ring violently. At the same instant the curtain closed again over the window, abruptly blocking out the moon, and the nine red candles in wall sconces guttered in a gust of wind. As if by cue the flames died, plunging the seance into darkness. Dorinda cried out and felt Lord Cobhill's icy hand clamp firmly over her own in warning. She managed to sit still, and closed her mouth.

"We have seen the sign of entry. You are welcome," Lady Victoria said when the clanging of the bell ceased. "Tell us who is present," she added.

A shrill laugh rang through the room, making Dorinda shiver. The sound seemed to be coming from someone near her. She leaned forward and peered across the table with eyes newly adjusted to the dark. Finding Paul's outline there was comforting; he turned his head to his right and when her eyes followed, she saw Baroness Gard slumped over in her chair, her mouth open and her features oddly twisted as she laughed once more.

"Who is present?" Lady Victoria said again.

"Margaret," the Baroness replied, her eyes closed and her voice sounding as if it did not belong to her.

"My sister!" Julia Ramsay exclaimed. In the darkness Dorinda could make out the astrologer's face. She had turned it upward as if addressing someone in the air. "How are you, Margaret?" she cried.

"Cold," the Baroness said, then moaned. "It's so cold here, Julie, cold and dark. And the water is so heavy, all around me—I will never be free of it, will I, Julie? I will never be warm!"

The woman's voice died away in a sigh and Julia Ramsay bent her head.

"Please find peace, Margaret," she whispered. "Please."

"I am present," the Baroness said suddenly, and Dorinda gasped in shock and disbelief; the voice that now came from the old woman's mouth was distinctly that of a man!

"The spirit guide has entered the Medium," Lady Victoria said softly. "Michael, what words do you have for the members of our circle?"

The man's voice spoke again, deep-toned and full of personality, Dorinda thought. As he began by addressing Julia Ramsay, saying something about "Margaret," Dorinda caught herself wondering what he had been like when alive. She shuddered; she was beginning to believe in Lady Victoria's spirits! The sound of the voice was mesmerizing as it went around the circle, addressing each person in turn, telling the fate of dead loved ones or foretelling events to come. To Paul, Michael predicted "luck in your immediate future." Then the voice passed on. Overwhelmed by the power of this presence, Dorinda thought the chamber seemed to alter again. As her turn came closer, the candle flames appeared to flicker faintly once more, the walls to change to dead black in color. The dank, musty atmosphere grew so close and heavy that she could feel it touch her skin like many gently-pressing fingers.

"There is a stranger in the circle," the voice said. At his words, fear coursed through Dorinda. Pushing at the table in a sudden frantic attempt to get away, she caught sight of her hands and arms enveloped in a glowing mist. The panic she felt then immobilized her.

"Dorinda Westerly," the voice went on. "I see only scattered fragments of your past, that are joining now to make your future. I can smell the sea, and through the shadows of time—"

The voice paused. In the silence Dorinda felt her bearings slip away until her mind was adrift, spinning in currents of confusion and fright. She was never really sure she heard Michael's voice say the word *emerald*.

Chapter Eight

WHEN DORINDA OPENED HER EYES, PAUL was placing her on the bed in his room. Over his shoulder she glimpsed the familiar theatrical posters on his wall, now washed with moonlight.

"What—" she began, but he stopped her question with a kiss, then took his arm from under her shoulders and turned on the bedside lamp.

"You fainted, silly girl," he said, his grin not quite able to mask the concern in his eyes. "Grandmother's spook show had you going even more than a first-class horror film."

"Nonsense," Lady Victoria snapped from the doorway. "She's just remarkably sensitive."

"Exactly," Paul said, "but not to spirits—she's sensitive to theatrical tricks like ventriloquism!"

Lady Victoria joined Paul at the bedside. Her rubies glittering, she peered down at Dorinda.

"How do you feel now, my dear?" she asked.

Dorinda looked from one to the other. Paul was probably right, she thought; she was gullible. Still, she could not quite forget the way the chamber had seemed to change before her eyes, or the eerie feeling of another presence she'd had the first time she entered the room, the feeling that had returned when "Michael" announced himself. However, she didn't feel like thinking about that right now.

"Is anything left from the banquet?" she asked, and was rewarded by Paul's relieved smile.

"I'll go down and make you up a plate," he said, leaning over and kissing her cheek. Lady Victoria turned to leave with him.

"I must attend to my guests," she said at the door. "But I shall discuss this evening's events with you at a later time."

"You'll do nothing of the sort," Paul said in a stern voice. Dorinda could hear only the first few words of Lady Victoria's retort as they went out the door and on down the hall.

Dorinda closed her eyes, trying to relax and put the evening into some sort of perspective. She hadn't seen her mother, or anyone who could conceivably be her mother; that fact had put her into a vulnerable condition, probably the answer to her reactions in the seance chamber. She told herself this firmly.

"Pheasant, truffles, and spiced ham?" Paul said, back in an unbelievably short time. Dorinda laughed and sat up straight against the pillows as he joined her on the bed with a large tray. Nothing would do but that he feed her, bite by bite.

"I'm not sick," she said, trying to grab the fork. "What's going on downstairs? This house is so big I can't hear whether the band is still playing or what."

"It's still playing," Paul said, giving her a bite of ham and with his free hand stroking her hair back from her face. "Want to go back down?"

"We might as well," she said.

"Have some champagne first." He gave her a sip from the glass he had brought and for a moment she let her head rest on his chest. Paul was so comforting. In a few moments she was ready to jump off the bed and rejoin the party downstairs, which had grown noisier but not larger. The midnight buffet was in progress. Those guests who weren't eating or drinking were dancing. Everyone seemed to be having a wonderful time. Paul thought perhaps Dorinda shouldn't dance so soon after fainting, but she kept assuring him she felt perfectly well and at last got him to do a slow waltz with her.

At two in the morning most of the crowd, after saying good night to Lady Victoria, strung out across the moat, white coats, robes, and flowered dresses retreating in the outdoor torchlight. Julia Ramsay alone of those who had been at the seance sought them out, but it was only to say good-bye. She did not refer to the night's main event. Dorinda thought that perhaps it wasn't protocol to do so.

A single couple was still dancing to the band's arrangement of "Summertime" as Paul and Dorinda climbed the stairs to his room. In the bedroom Paul helped her pull off the long gown and heap it on a chair. He asked hesitantly if she felt like making love. In answer she hugged her body against his. When they lay down on the bed she thought he was trying to be especially tender. He kissed her face so lightly that she could scarcely feel his lips, just the warmth of his breath on her skin. He moved down, outlining her body with light kisses as if trying to memorize her shape with his mouth. She reached for the silky hair on his bent head, starting to tousle it, but then she had to hang on, gripping his locks fiercely. The kisses were having the effect he wanted. She moaned as a wave of pleasure spread through her. Paul murmured into her flesh, saying words she couldn't hear, and she tugged on his head to make him come back to her, to join his lips to hers. By the time he reached his own climax he had stopped being particularly gentle, as if he had to treat her as an equal partner in his rapture. Finally they both sank into a deep sleep.

The sky was just growing light with dawn when Dorinda roused a little. Paul's arms were around her and his body was curled to encircle her. Smiling, she nestled deeper into his warmth and fell asleep again, grateful to be with him.

The telephone was ringing somewhere in the house. Dorinda opened her eyes to a flood of sunshine from the window, and realized that the telephone she heard was the one on the bedside table. As she blinked, Paul stirred, groaned, and reached out to lift the receiver.

"Hello. Yes, Paul," he said. Beyond his head Dorinda could see the clock; it was already eleven. "No, look, Freddie, I told you—" Paul broke off and listened to what sounded like excited words on the other end. "Very well, Freddie. I'll drive down right away." He hung up, rolled over to face Dorinda, and gave her a hug.

"Good morning," he said. "Still sleepy?" He kissed her lips softly, and she returned the kiss.

"What did your agent want?" she asked as he stroked her back.

"Wants me to go to London, I'm afraid. He says he's got the part of a lifetime. Tom Prentiss, the playwright, apparently has personally asked that I audition." Paul spoke calmly but Dorinda could tell that he was agitated; his eyes shone.

"That's wonderful!" she cried.

"Yes. Well, but. What if I do get the part? We'd have to go back to London, and I don't know about that."

"Paul, please. If you gave up another part for me, I'd never forgive myself. I'd leave, I mean it! Promise me you'll take it. I'd be fine in London. I mean, this whole thing—no one's bothered us, and Mother should show up any moment and admit that."

"You'd leave, would you?" Paul tried to worm his hand under her armpit to tickle her, but she kept her arm clamped tightly to her side and in a moment, the tussle turned into a bout of something even more fun. It was half an hour before Paul jumped out of bed and opened his closet to find some clothes to wear. It never took him long to dress, and Dorinda sat on the side of the old-fashioned tub and talked to him while he shaved. While not saying that she couldn't accompany him, Paul did not complain when she suggested that she stay at Darkbourne. She thought perhaps he wanted to put his mind entirely on the audition facing him, during the drive to London.

"I'll be back for a late tea, love," he said. "Sure you'll be all right?"

Dorinda nodded. "Of course. Want lunch first?"

"No, I really should get started."

"Well, don't go ninety—and Paul, break a leg!"

"Thanks," he said. In a few minutes, watching from the bedroom window, she saw Paul jump into his Jaguar and turn it to enter the long drive to the road.

"Good morning, Dorinda," Lady Victoria said from the doorway, and Dorinda turned to find Paul's grandmother looking at her. Lady Victoria was wearing a silver and green silk dress, with a matching turban on her head.

"Oh, good morning," Dorinda replied, full of wonder at how stately Paul's grandmother always managed to appear. She herself was still wearing her bathrobe.

"And where is Paul off to, without even a cup of tea?"

"London," Dorinda answered; then, remembering Lady Victoria's views on acting, she added, "it's some sort of business trip."

"Hum." Lady Victoria seemed to repress a snort. Her eyes fixed upon Dorinda's face.

"Shouldn't we use this time to good advantage, then?" she said.

Something in Lady Victoria's manner struck Dorinda as odd; it was as if the woman felt a suppressed excitement of some sort.

"I beg your pardon?" Dorinda said.

Lady Victoria paced into the room, closing the door behind her. She gestured for Dorinda to sit down in one of the bedroom chairs, took the other one, and leaned forward to speak, her voice low.

"My dear, last night I became aware of something in your past," she said. "Something that is—troubling to you. If you will let me, I can try to help you."

Open-mouthed, Dorinda stared at her. "But how?" she said finally.

"Together, we can locate what it is, I believe." Lady Victoria was silent after these words, as if turning something over in her mind, and Dorinda had the impression that she was pleased to have her suspicion confirmed.

Abruptly, Lady Victoria rose. "After luncheon, I will show you," she said. "I must leave you to dress now." With her usual measured gait, stiffly erect, Lady Victoria made her way to the door and took her exit.

What did that mean? Dorinda wondered. For sure, she wasn't going back in that seance chamber! But now that she looked around the sunny room, she had to admit that last night's doings seemed dreamlike and vague, not really so fearful. And how odd it was that Lady Victoria knew there was a secret in her past—perhaps the "Spirit Guide" had said more than she herself had heard.

She pulled on a blue cotton dress and descended to the dining room. At present only a handful of house guests were staying there, and in the aftermath of the party they had a rather quiet luncheon. At length Lady Victoria rose, summoned Dorinda with a gesture, and led the way through the east drawing room, to Dorinda's relief not turning toward the wing of the house that contained the seance chamber. They continued into the library, with its impressive high stacks of leather-bound books, its massive desk, and comfortable, overstuffed leather furniture. Sunlight came through the large windows of the room and the place looked cheerful, not frightening.

Lady Victoria indicated a leather chair, and Dorinda sat down. Lady Victoria pulled another chair quite close to hers. She had closed the room's door and except for the ticking of a large clock on the desk, there was absolute silence. When she leaned forward slightly, a shaft of sunlight from a window picked out the silver threads of her turban, making them glitter. As Dorinda gazed at her, Lady Victoria opened her hand to reveal a heart-shaped gold locket. She held the locket up by its delicate gold chain, positioning it in the shaft of sunlight so that a pattern of reflections slid over the smooth gold case as the locket dangled.

"Now, look at the way the light plays on the locket," she said. "Are you comfortable? Sit back; just look at the locket."

Dorinda obeyed, thinking that Lady Victoria's voice

sounded less imperious now. It had taken on a soothing tone. The chair was very comfortable and she felt herself begin to relax.

"What is this, hypnotism or something?" she asked. "No one's ever been able to hypnotize me."

"Just concentrate on the locket," Lady Victoria said softly. She let it swing slightly, and Dorinda found that it was hard to take her eyes away.

"Now begin to count," Lady Victoria said.

Dorinda felt warm, almost sleepy, and she took a deep breath before she did as Lady Victoria asked. It seemed silly—no one could hypnotize her—but she said "One . . . two . . . three" slowly. It seemed to take her a long while to reach *ten*.

"Please say your name," Lady Victoria ordered.

"Dorinda Westerly." She heard herself reply without really knowing that she did; her conscious self seemed wholly occupied in watching the swinging golden heart.

"How old are you, Dorinda?"

"Nineteen." It seemed to Dorinda that the world was now bathed in a soft yellow light, and the only other person in it was this woman with the deep, inquiring voice.

"I want you to be eighteen," Lady Victoria said, and suddenly Dorinda was sitting at her desk in college. She could hear Jenny, her roommate, moving around in the next room, and some books were spread out on a desk before her in a disorderly array. "Now seventeen—sixteen." As the low voice continued, counting backward, Dorinda's mind went with it. A crowd of memories were released in her mind: high school, grade school, summers at camp. Lady Victoria asked her for details and she supplied them.

"Now I want you to be five," Lady Victoria said.

Dorinda frowned. She was in Newport, sitting on a wooden dock in the Port of Call, dangling her feet over the dark water that was dotted with seaweed and scum. Her socks were pink, frayed, and worn through at the heels.

When she was silent, Lady Victoria said, "What is happening, Dorinda?"

"Mother—Mother says to put on my shoes," Dorinda

answered. It seemed to her that her voice was high and childlike. "We have to go into the club."

"What club?" Lady Victoria asked, speaking gently.

Dorinda let her eyes close. Even in the darkness, she could still see the swinging gold locket in her mind. Then there was another image.

"The club—behind the green lady," she said. "Mother works there. I like the kitchen, because there are dogs—so many dogs. Laddie, and—I like Laddie best. He's licking me. And we're by the pizza ovens—Mother, and Uncle Bill, and me. They don't see us."

"Who?"

"The men. They're going to kill someone; they say Mr. Bellevue—Bellevue—he wants it done. And they're going to the place where he will be, and do it like—they say, like the Mafia would. That's the way—"

She broke off, drawing her breath sharply.

"Now they see us," she went on, speaking rapidly. "Oh, they're bad. They have Mother's arm, they're hurting her. And Uncle Bill is saying we didn't hear anything; we won't say anything. We won't say anything! We won't say anything—" Her voice rose in a shrill cry. Then her eyes opened, and she stared unseeingly at Lady Victoria.

"Dorinda, wake up." Lady Victoria spoke sharply.

Slowly, the room came into focus again. She was in the library at Darkbourne. Dorinda blinked.

"Where was I? What did I say?" she asked.

"You were where someone was going to be killed. You mentioned a Mr. Bellevue?" Lady Victoria raised her voice in question.

"So *that* was the code name." Dorinda spoke in her normal voice, but she had difficulty putting her thoughts into words, even to herself. Suddenly she felt terribly tired. "Did I say anything else?"

In the sunny room the scene before her seemed unreal itself, Lady Victoria leaning forward in deep interest, the gold locket now clasped in one hand.

"Apparently you were threatened. Who was the green lady?"

"Green lady." Repeating the words, Dorinda closed her

eyes again. She could see the naked girl outlined in green neon, blinking off-on, off-on. Suddenly, she felt heavily oppressed.

"Do you mind, Lady Victoria, if I don't go into it all?" she said. "I guess I didn't learn much that was new. It just—brought back a part of my life that my mother never wanted me to remember."

Lady Victoria reached forward and patted Dorinda's hand. Dorinda looked at her; Lady Victoria's face was bright with interest.

"Tell me about last night," Dorinda said, casting about for another topic. "Who was the man with the lily?"

Lady Victoria allowed the subject to be changed. They chatted for a while about the guests at the ball; then Mrs. Pomerance summoned her mistress to a consultation. Left alone, Dorinda had to struggle against a wave of depression. She had smiled and laughed with Lady Victoria. She was sure Paul's grandmother had no idea how down she felt, but last night and this afternoon together had left her quite dispirited. She remained in the library, trying to read, but she couldn't find anything that held her attention. The weather outside was beautiful, but she did not feel up to going out. She simply sat and wondered when Paul would come back. The afternoon dragged.

Paul returned in a jubilant mood. Dorinda heard his voice in the hall; then he strode into the library, closed its doors behind him, and picked her up in his arms, interrupting her questions about the audition by kissing her breasts, her throat, and finally her mouth. She kissed him back, and he allowed her body to slide down against his until her feet touched the floor.

"What happened?" she cried when he lifted his head.

"Darling, what do you think? Prentiss all but said he had written the play with me *in mind* for the part! He'd seen my work in *Measure for Measure* last year and liked it, and he kept nodding and smiling all during my audition. He gave me the role straight off as soon as I'd done!"

"That's wonderful! What's the play called? What's your part?"

"It's called *The Starling*. It's about a young Englishman, me, who goes to America—you can help me with that, my love—and keeps getting mistaken over there for some spy everyone wants to kill. The scrapes he gets into and the ways he gets out of them are really quite funny. I'm sure it will be an enormous hit. But—" Paul pulled back from her a little, and looked closely at her face. "Dorinda, your safety is much more important to me than any part in a play. You must believe that."

"Oh, Paul, you have to take this part!" Dorinda seized Paul's arms. "I'm sure—" she began.

Paul's serious expression did not change.

"I really do think you'll be all right in London now," he said slowly. "But if you feel at all frightened about going back—"

"Oh, I'm not a bit frightened. I'm excited!" She hugged Paul to her.

"You could stay—" he began.

"No, listen." She released him, so she could look up into his face. "Darkbourne is beautiful, but the only thing to do around here is sit and worry about Mother. In London, I'll be better off. There's so much going on." She stopped, not adding "and London is where Mother probably is, right now." After all, her mother had certainly not seemed to show up in the country.

"Dorinda," Paul said, "you have to promise me that you won't take any chances once we're there."

She nodded solemnly, inwardly resolving not to tell Paul about the experiment with hypnotism; she would let that remain a secret between her and Lady Victoria.

"You mustn't go out without me," Paul continued. "And there are some places you shouldn't go at all. No Argosy Club. You could be recognized there."

"But how do you know that?" Dorinda asked. "Did Mother—"

"You know she told me all of it. Dorinda, I don't want anything to happen to you just because I'm thinking of myself in taking this part." Again, he looked uncertain.

"Oh, for heaven's sake, don't worry," Dorinda said. "I'll be just fine."

"Well, it may be boring for you to stay at home every night, or come to every rehearsal—still, that's the only way I can be sure you're safe. Will you do what I ask, love?"

"Of course," she said.

As they left the library, Dorinda wondered what Lady Victoria's reaction was going to be.

"Maybe I'd better tell Grandmother myself," Paul said, looking slightly apprehensive.

Dorinda was happy to leave this task to him, and went upstairs to dress for dinner. When Paul joined her, all he could do at first was say "Whew" and shake his head.

"Bad?" she asked.

"Let me just say that if I send her first-row opening night tickets, I won't be at all surprised to have them returned to me in ash form."

"Oh, dear."

"I believe I stand a good chance of a second disinheritment. She says the wrath of the spirits will be on my head if I return to my accursed profession."

Thinking of the seance and the later hypnotic session, Dorinda couldn't wait to pack her things.

"Should we go to dinner?" she asked.

"Oh, of course," Paul said, pulling a dinner jacket out of the closet. "I imagine we'll have a treatment of cold scorn tonight, though, and more fuming tomorrow—let's get up and get out fast."

"I really don't want any supernatural curses brought down on my head."

"Oh, she's not mad at you," Paul said, kissing her cheek as he passed her. "She said something I didn't quite understand—"

Before he could go on, the dinner bell rang.

"Well, at least let's not be late," Dorinda exclaimed, hurrying Paul to distract him from that line of thought.

From the head of the candlelit table, Lady Victoria made her displeasure plain, and it took all Paul's charm to keep his grandmother even passably civil. After an uncomfortable meal, Dorinda politely told Lady Victoria that she was quite tired from last night's party, and hoped she could be excused for the rest of the evening. Paul's grandmother assented with a regal nod. To Dorinda's relief, she had said no word about the revelations of their hour in the library; she seemed too distracted by the thought of Paul's coming defection.

Paul accompanied her upstairs, and while she got ready for bed he packed their clothes and put the suitcases beside the bedroom door for an early-morning getaway. Really tired, Dorinda fell quickly asleep.

In the morning they found the dining room at seven o'clock occupied only by Mrs. Pomerance, who poured them cups of coffee.

"Now, Pommie, don't let Lady Victoria turn the electricity off again," Paul said, gulping his cup's contents hastily.

Before the housekeeper could express an opinion about the likelihood of future candlelight, Lady Victoria swept into the room. She was dressed in a long black lounging robe, her white hair as immaculately combed as usual, and her blue eyes bright. Trinculo accompanied her.

"Good morning, Grandmother!" Paul cried heartily, jumping up to pull out a chair for her.

Lady Victoria ignored this and lifted one hand. Paul immediately forestalled any prediction, curse, or blessing by seizing his grandmother by the shoulders and giving her a kiss on one cheek.

"We're off, then," he said behind her back, gesturing to Dorinda to rise. "We had a super time, Grandmother, and we'll be back soon—just leave the drawbridge down and keep that beast off the attack." Trinculo had seized his trouser leg.

Releasing his grandmother and shaking off the cat, Paul grabbed Dorinda by the hand and started rapidly for the doorway. It took Lady Victoria a moment to recover her equilibrium and her stately manner.

"Paul," she called after him commandingly.

"Cheerio," he said at the door. "Give it some foot," he added under his breath to Dorinda.

Their suitcases were already loaded into the Jaguar, and the car was standing ready in front. The two of them fled through the reception hall and out into the sunshine, Dorinda grinning at Paul's performance. In a second she was over the bridge and loaded into the passenger side of the sports car and Paul had started the engine. It throbbed into life and he threw the car into gear. As they pulled away, Dorinda looked back. Lady Victoria had appeared. She stood in the open front doorway with both arms flung upward in a gesture that could have meant either defiance or despair.

Apparently spotting her dark figure in the rear vision mirror, Paul rolled down his window and gave a jaunty wave of his hand as the Jaguar turned down the driveway.

"You know, you two are a lot alike," Dorinda said. "There's drama every minute."

"Well, now we've made our escape." Paul chuckled.

Escape—Dorinda pondered the word he used. Darkbourne had seemed safe, and for the most part she'd been happy there, although wondering every minute where her mother was. Her disappointment at the ball, and the later events of the seance and the hypnotic regression had served to bring home more keenly the fact that months had gone by, and she had heard nothing. Just being in London would seem more of a link with Emma because they had been together there. Once again Dorinda remembered the flashing lights of the Argosy Club, red, green; Bill's act . . .

She glanced over at Paul. His words yesterday, "No Argosy Club," came back to her. Was Paul hiding something from her? Did he know more than she did? She felt annoyed that she should have to sit there and wonder. Emma was *her* mother, after all. Had Emma actually told Paul every tiny detail of their dilemma, even about that first meeting in the Argosy Club with Uncle Bill? Or was Paul somehow currently in contact with her mother? The unfairness of this possibility stirred angry feelings in her.

Deciding to ask a clever question, something that would trap Paul, she frowned, studying him. But before she could think of anything to ambush him with, he reached over and without taking his eyes off the road found her hand and gave it a squeeze. She gazed at the broad shoulders under his dark brown jacket, his handsome profile, and her irritable mood gave way to one of gratitude. She should thank heaven that she had Paul. He never seemed to worry about Emma. At least, he didn't bring the subject up. But he was obviously anxious for Dorinda's own safety.

She sighed to herself, tired of going over it all. There didn't seem to be an answer. But of course, there was one, and in London she would definitely be closer to finding it.

Chapter Nine

"MY DEAR, THAT IS SUPPOSED TO BE A *FUNNY* line!"

Lavinia Montgomery, the dark-haired, pixie-faced heroine of *The Starling*, glared across the footlights as her director, famous Rollo Jones, shouted this comment.

"Then laugh, sweetie," she said venomously, spitting out the words and directing a look of hatred toward the first row in the deserted Laurence Olivier Theater, where Jones lounged.

From a seat a respectful distance away in the second row, Dorinda watched as again there threatened to be a scene on the stage better than anything in the script of *The Starling*.

"You don't think it's an amusing line, then, Lavinia?" Jones lowered his voice ominously, his tone full of menace.

GREEN LADY

In answer, the actress emitted a short, piercing scream.

Paul, who had been about to find a small bomb hidden under his broccoli as he shared some chicken divan with Lavinia in her "Greenwich Village apartment," paused with his fork held in mid-air as the echo of Lavinia's cry died away.

"I mean, *really*, to say at this point 'So you've never heard of broccoli, honestly? Well, take a taste—it won't kill you.' " Lavinia's inflection was scathing. "That is just in there for a cheap laugh—there's no *motivation*!"

Tom Prentiss, the author of the line, strode onto the stage from a position in the wings, a rolled-up script in his hands. His pale blond hair was in wild disarray and he appeared to have reached the bottom of his last store of patience.

"Lavinia, it's your *timing*," he cried. "You've got to say it—"

"If you think—"

As Lavinia and the playwright squared off, Paul laid down his fork, while on the fire escape outside the set's window Donald Snee, who played a Scotland Yard inspector, swung upside down from his knees, a prop gun dangling idly from one hand.

"I'm trying. I am trying. I'm trying to maintain my sanity!" Lavinia shouted.

"Reggie, call the others," Rollo Jones ordered in a weary manner, speaking to his stage manager, whose head had just popped up from the trap door where he was awaiting the cue to detonate the broccoli. Reggie ascended from his position under the card table that held the chicken divan, crawled around the arguing pair at center stage, and loped off toward the dressing rooms. Slowly, Rollo Jones arose and climbed the steps to join his cast.

"Now we're going to *stop* this," he said firmly. "Come down, Donald. On second thought, everybody take ten, and then we'll assemble here."

Released from his post, Paul jumped up and hurried into the darkened theater to join Dorinda. "God," he said in an undertone, sinking into a seat beside her. "How many times is this going to happen, and previews starting in forty-eight hours?"

Dorinda reached up and touched the worried crease in his forehead.

"I'm sure it'll be okay," she said. "Relax."

Paul sighed, taking her hand in his. "I know it's wrong to complain all the time, but when Lavinia changed her character last week it threw everything I've been developing right out the window. She insists that the 'carefree hippie' image was wrong, but the slummie tart she's become—"

Dorinda shook her head at him and gestured toward the other end of the row, where one Lord George Higbee leaned pensively forward, his eyes on his girlfriend, the dark-haired Lavinia. Onstage, Lavinia abruptly wheeled away from Rollo and Tom and stamped off to her dressing room. Lord George Higbee rose and headed in the same direction.

"That twit of a fellow is part of the problem," Paul muttered. "Can you believe we're having scenes like this and tomorrow night is actually wet tech?"

"What's wet tech?" Dorinda asked.

"Didn't you ever hear that? It's the last run-through before previews begin. The final dress rehearsal, when everything has to work. Opening night's so close!" Paul's expression grew even more worried. He stared in front of him and bit his lip.

"Well, Paul, *you're* excellent," Dorinda said.

"That's not much comfort if the production fails. I feel for Prentiss. Oh, why did Lavinia have to have a boyfriend who is an amateur theater critic? He's probably in there with her right now feeding her more nonsense."

Dorinda wanted to say something soothing, but she was fast running out of comforting observations. *The Starling* had been in rehearsal for almost a month and from the start there had been personality conflicts, literary disagreements, and general ill will. Paul had at first cheerily maintained that this was often true of productions that opened to raves and ran for years, but now he was worn down by it all. Dorinda knew that some of Emma's plays had been battlegrounds backstage, or so her mother had told her; she had usually been in school and not around. She wondered if any hit had ever had so many problems as

The Starling; it seemed about to founder, perhaps never having a chance to be either praised or panned by the critics.

"Everybody back onstage," Reggie called.

"That was a short ten minutes," Paul muttered, rising. He filed back up to the stage with the others, and gave his attention to Rollo Jones, who was explicit and direct. They were down to the wire, and he would brook no more rebellion. Not looking toward the seats, where Lord George Higbee had rejoined Dorinda, Rollo announced firmly that after this session rehearsals of *The Starling* would be closed, meaning no onlookers at all.

For the rest of the night Lavinia controlled her temper, playing her tart role to the hilt and leaving Paul to take corrections from the director. Dorinda suspected what this would do to Paul's mood, and when rehearsal was finally over she looked anxiously at his face as they walked downstairs, past the empty lounges and bars of the National Theater complex.

"You want to walk, don't you?" she asked.

Paul nodded. Since the beginning of the week, when the company had moved to the National Theater on the South Bank, Dorinda and Paul had walked across the Hungerford Foot Bridge to Charing Cross every night on their way home. The bridge spanning the Thames afforded a beautiful view of London, its riverside buildings brightly lit. In the summer darkness the water of the Thames below glimmered in the moonlight.

Tonight Paul did not spare a glance for the scene. He strode steadily ahead, his hands thrust into his pockets. Dorinda matched her stride to his and preserved silence, hoping that the soft night air would at least partly revive Paul's spirits. Actually she did not feel overly cheerful herself. It was wearing to have spent nearly a month watching rehearsals of *The Starling*. But Paul expected her to be near him every minute. Since the part had proved more difficult than he expected and the enmities of the cast were so nerve-wracking, Dorinda hadn't wanted to add to Paul's worries by going off alone. Yet days and days had passed, and finally weeks and weeks, and there was no sign or word from Emma. As if she had truly drowned in the sea at Ibiza, she made no appearance and neither did anyone connected with her.

Again the question of what Paul knew rose in Dorinda's mind, and she glanced sidelong at the silent figure beside her. He was managing to oversee her almost every minute. She continually had to smother her annoyance at the sight of Paul rushing to answer his telephone when it rang. He had asked her not to answer it, or make any calls out. Although she listened carefully to Paul's side of all telephone conversations, they never seemed to be with anyone but his agent or some friend. A week ago she'd dialed Renata's number while Paul was in the shower. A servant had answered and told her that Renata was in the country. When he asked her name and number, Dorinda hung up in frustration. It wouldn't do for Paul to get Renata's return call.

Two days after that she'd been more daring, slipping out to the National Theater's lobby while Paul was onstage. Quickly she had searched a London telephone book for detective agencies. "Atkins Brothers, Round the Clock, All Investigations" caught her eye, but all that "Round the Clock" turned out to mean was that the Atkins Brothers' answering service asked for her name and number. In indignation she'd slammed down the receiver, then turned to find a scowling Paul crossing the lobby, Rollo Jones beside him.

"Finished so soon?" she'd asked airily.

"Dorinda, whom were you calling?"

"Grammatical to the end, aren't you? None of your business."

Paul drew a breath but whatever he was going to say was forestalled by Rollo.

"Oh, that's wonderful!" Rollo shouted. "That's exactly the expression you want when you ask Lavinia about the pink knickers. Paul, I knew you'd get it."

Concealing her amusement, Dorinda had followed as Rollo dragged Paul back to the stage. That night, finally alone in Paul's apartment, she had waited in edgy anticipation, but Paul had not again brought up her phone call. She supposed he didn't think she'd had time to get into much mischief. She'd almost been tempted to mention her transgression herself. Part of her felt guilty, part of her felt justified. She wanted a chance to shout, to tell Paul she'd call up anyone she liked. Certainly Paul didn't seem to be doing anything to find Emma. But of course, he was obeying Emma's wishes. She wanted to rebel against them both.

Sighing, Dorinda let her gaze scan the buildings lining the river. Emma was *there*, somewhere out there in London, carrying out some charade. But where? As they neared the end of the bridge, Dorinda strained her eyes, willing a shadowy figure to be waiting for them on the embankment. But nothing moved in the darkness; there was no one. Maybe she should be glad.

Increasingly, Dorinda brooded over the hypnotic session with Lady Victoria in the library of Darkbourne. The thought of a "Mr. Bellevue" frightened her. But if he had the power to threaten her, then why didn't he do it? Again, she heard Bill's words at the Argosy Club last spring: *"Let her stay . . . she was there, she remembers—I do think something's going on; lately, I've been concerned—"*

"Dorinda, I'm sorry about tomorrow." Taking one hand out of his pocket, Paul put his arm over her shoulders and pulled her close to him, leading her down from the end of the bridge. "But maybe you've heard enough bitching for a while."

"I would like a day off," Dorinda agreed, forcing herself to sound casual. Paul led her toward the street, and then waved for a taxi.

On the ride to his flat Dorinda looked out of the window as the streets of nighttime London passed. Finally she turned to Paul.

"What time is your rehearsal tomorrow?" she asked.

"We begin at noon," he said. "God knows when we'll be done. I think the entire third scene needs reblocking. That entrance of Donald's isn't working. God, I'll be lucky to see you again before opening night."

She patted his hand consolingly. "I'm sure things will go better than you think," she said. "It's really a funny play. I'll bet it will go to Broadway."

Paul groaned. "They'll need a new lead, then. I'm fast running out of boyish charm."

When they reached home, Paul was too bushed to do more than hug her good night. He quickly fell asleep. Dorinda lay awake longer, staring into the darkness, trying to analyze her feelings. She felt balked, frustrated, like someone pent up too long in a maze without an exit. Well, she was going to take action, jump over walls if she had to. She lay still and felt the commitment build in her. Only by trying could anything be gained.

Chapter Ten

THE NEXT MORNING, PAUL'S MOOD WAS SOMEwhat improved.

"You won't go out without me, promise now," he said over coffee. "There's plenty of food around here, and I'm sure there's something on the television you can watch tonight. You've been wanting to read a couple of my books, and—"

"Really, Paul, you'd think I was a child," Dorinda said. "I'll be fine. I'm just worried about you."

"Lord knows what Lavinia and Lord Higbee have cooked up to throw at me today. Thank God, he won't be in the theater to set her off. But I'm going to miss my own inspiration." Leaning over, he kissed her on the cheek.

"I'll be dying to hear what happens," she said, walking to the door to see him off.

Once Paul was gone, the hours dragged. Dorinda made herself a salad for lunch, and watched some striking firemen's wives being interviewed on TV. At four o'clock, Paul called her.

"How's it going at the theater?" she asked.

"I'm not alone here," Paul said in a muffled voice. "But are you okay?"

"Sure. You sound *grim*."

"You guessed it. Have the hemlock warm." He whispered this last sentence and then said he had to go.

"Will you get home pretty late tonight?" she asked.

"Go to bed without me."

When she hung the receiver up, she went into the bedroom and looked through the contents of her side of the closet. Nothing she saw there appealed to her. She had not needed much of a wardrobe to sit around in a rehearsal hall. An outfit she'd bought similar to the one she had worn last spring at the Argosy Club, velvet jacket and velour pants, was too warm for summer, and anyway, she didn't want to be recognized. She was going there tonight to look for Emma, or any clue that might lead her to Emma, not to be spotted herself.

Accordingly she closed the closet door and descended to the street. Paul's Knightsbridge neighborhood was full of small dress shops. She turned into one that looked conservative. Passing some racks of padded jackets and a display of sequined disco slips, she found a saleswoman and asked for "something black."

"We have a beautiful lace gown," the woman told her. "It's just in."

When the saleswoman produced the dress, Dorinda tried it on and paid for it. It was nothing she would ordinarily have chosen to wear—in fact, it reminded her of something that would appeal to her mother, dark and not attention-getting, with a demure high neckline and medium-length skirt. Its price was also high, but she put down the cash and hurried back to the flat, her spirits rising. Now with pale makeup, and her hair in a dark cloche, she would look completely unlike the girl who had drunk champagne with and admired Edward Marsden last spring.

After a cup of tea, Dorinda took a shower and spent a

long time achieving a pallid face, using pale pink on her lips and silver shadow around her eyes. The paleness aged her, she thought. To kill time until the Argosy Club would open, she spent an hour filing her nails and painting them silver, then another half hour adjusting a black scarf around her head to look like a fashionable cloche. Finally, the scarf was arranged to her satisfaction, and she pinned it with a silver stickpin. Not a tendril of blonde showed.

She had to hunt to find some panty hose to wear with her one pair of high-heeled pumps. Finally she pulled on the black lace dress, and was pleased by the image in the mirror. She looked like someone in her late twenties, she thought, and not so much mysterious as just uninteresting.

"Now, Mother, be there!" she thought to herself as she left Paul's flat.

The streets were just drying from a short summer shower when she stepped out of Paul's apartment building. She flagged a cab and asked the driver to take her to the Argosy Club. She could feel her excitement rise as they sped through the damp, hot night. Something was going to happen. She could sense it.

Now to get into the club. The same lighted foyer met her gaze as she hesitated beside the glass doors. Should she mention Renata's name again? Wondering what chance that would have of getting her into trouble, she was just pushing open the door when a crowd of five jaunty young Englishmen in school ties and white flannels swept up to her.

"Allow *me*," cried one young man, holding the door for her. She stepped inside; when she gave him a smile in thank-you, he made a bow.

"Are we to be honored by your presence at the Argosy Club this evening?" he asked, his blue eyes sparkling as he scrutinized her sophisticated garb.

"Well—if I can get in," she answered, smiling again.

"Done," he said. Gallantly, he took her arm, and the entire group walked past some waiting patrons and up to Edward Marsden at the reception desk.

"My friends and I—" The young man paused. Whoever he was, he apparently had impressive credentials, because Marsden just laughed and waved them all in. Thankful for this break, Dorinda was positive that the handsome club manager did not remember her at all. He had given her a very cursory glance.

"Now for some champagne, love. What's your name?" her escort said.

"My name—uh, Nora," she answered, using the first name that came to her mind, as they passed through the dark inner foyer and into the club. The dance floor was already crowded with patrons. A Foreigner piece was playing as the colored lights she remembered so well swung to and fro across the dancers and the glittering walls.

The young man steered her toward the bar. "I'm David Selwyn," he said. He ordered champagne for her and his friends, who crowded up to be introduced to her. They were all young; she found out they were freshmen at Oxford out for a night in London. None of their names stuck in her head. After downing a glass of champagne with them, and answering all their questions very vaguely, she accepted David's request for a dance, crossed the floor with him to the strains of "Dynamite," and excused herself, beating a retreat to the downstairs lounge. No one she'd seen on the dance floor had aroused her interest.

In the lounge she took a bar stool at the end of the long bar and carefully scrutinized the customers, straining in the darkness to see the women. Several men were staring at her, but it wasn't they who interested her.

The women at the bar were all young, and they uniformly looked like the girls who sold clothes in the trendy shops of Kensington and Knightsbridge. Although Emma was small-boned and petite, she still couldn't possibly be any of this group. Turning, Dorinda tried to make out the women crowded on the banquettes around the sides of the lounge. Some of them were a bit older. Dorinda wondered how to approach anyone; if only Mother would see her, and make the first move.

From an undershirt-clad bartender she ordered a white wine, and sipped it slowly. Several men offered to buy her another drink. She declined all offers, and nothing substantial developed in the next hour. Telling herself that she had all night, Dorinda was about to head upstairs again when she shrank back onto her bar stool and wished she could turn invisible. Trevor York and Renata Enfield had just walked into the lounge!

Fortunately, neither of them looked in her direction. Renata, resplendent in a one-shouldered jade-green Grés chiffon, rushed off to speak to someone on the other side of the room. And Trevor turned to say something to a woman just coming in the door behind him, someone who had apparently followed him down the stairs.

Dorinda could not hear what he said, in her jubilance. Blonde, aristocratic-looking, somewhat nervous in manner —the lady he spoke to, who wore a Ralph Lauren cowgirl outfit, was exactly like someone she had seen before. My God, what if she had found her mother! She had to remind herself to breathe.

For the next few minutes she watched Trevor politely answer whatever the woman said to him. *Yes*, Dorinda thought. The little nervous mannerisms, like twisting her hair, fiddling with her fringed vest, picking at her turquoise-and-silver bracelets—Emma had once played a character just like that. The height was right, and the face—well, it *could* be. Emma was a genius with makeup, and in the darkness of the room Dorinda could not judge for sure the color of the woman's eyes or the shape of her cheekbones.

Dorinda turned away, allowing herself to observe only out of the corners of her eyes. Trevor's tete-a-tete did not last long; Renata came back, and gestured toward the stairs. Both of them shook hands with the cowgirl, and then turned to depart.

"Let her stay here!" Dorinda prayed. She far preferred to broach her away from the scrutiny of either Trevor or Renata, since she didn't know what the situation was. Maybe they were both in this plot with Emma, and had been since the beginning.

Trevor and Renata disappeared, and the cowgirl took a step toward the bar. Dorinda slid down from her stool and walked over to her.

"Could I buy you a drink?" she asked boldly.

The woman appeared startled for a moment. She paused, and stared into Dorinda's face, as if she were trying to place her.

"Excuse me?" she said, in an unmistakably English accent.

Yes, Dorinda thought. The voice was possible; low, throaty—and Emma could do any accent. Dorinda cursed the lack of light. The woman's blonde locks fell forward around her face, making it difficult to see her features.

"I don't think we've met," Dorinda said with a smile. "I'm Nora Payne." So there, Mother, she thought; two can play your game. The funny side of the meeting struck her for a moment. However, she maintained a grave composure.

"Oh?" The cowgirl looked confused.

"Here." Dorinda indicated the seat she had just left at the bar; there was an empty stool next to it. "Want to sit down?"

"Well, thank you." The woman slid onto the bar stool with a flutter of her ruffled skirt. She wore a checked Western shirt of cotton under the vest, with a tan cowboy hat hanging down her back. Cowboy boots completed the look. As Dorinda watched her, the woman fumbled in a small leather bag for a pack of Virginia Slims, pulled one out and lit it with a gold cigarette lighter.

"I'll have a Scotch and Perrier, darling," she said when the bartender asked for their order.

"Make it two," Dorinda said, as the woman blew out a long stream of smoke and gazed through it at her. Her eyes were dark!

When the drinks came, Dorinda gulped hers, trying to assess the situation. Perhaps Emma thought that tonight Dorinda was adequately disguised, that they could talk together without risk, or perhaps she was simply afraid that Dorinda would make a scene if she refused the contact. At any rate, here they were, side by side. Dorinda tried to give no sign of her delight.

"So, Nora Payne, you look like a little girl who's lost her mother," the woman said, picking up her drink. She seemed faintly amused.

Dorinda couldn't speak. It *was* Emma!

"My name is Lieto Clavell—"

As the woman introduced herself, the figure of Edward Marsden suddenly appeared behind them.

GREEN LADY

"Countess," he said, as Lieto Clavell turned. "How are you?"

"Very well, Edward," she replied with composure. "Do you know my young friend here?" She gestured at Dorinda.

Marsden gave Dorinda a blank look and smiled.

"Afraid I haven't had the pleasure," he murmured.

"Nora Payne," the woman said.

There was definitely something strange in the way she spoke the name. Dorinda could not read the expression on her face. Edward Marsden gave Dorinda a direct look. Almost, she would have said it was a gaze of warning. What was going on here? Marsden held Dorinda's eyes with his for a good thirty seconds, and then said, "I was on an errand, I'm afraid. I'll be back. Enjoy yourselves." He gestured to the bartender, and Dorinda's empty glass was refilled.

"I haven't seen you here before," Lieto Clavell said, stubbing out her cigarette in one of the Argosy Club's sterling silver ashtrays.

"No." Wasn't that exactly the way Emma had tilted her head, in the role Dorinda remembered? Even more hopeful, Dorinda murmured the first thing that came into her head. "Are you really a countess?" she asked. She wanted to keep Emma talking, and tease her a little, as well. Countess, indeed!

The woman's slight smile stayed the same; she pulled at one blonde curl.

"I was once married to a Hungarian count," she said. Looking down and searching again in her bag, she lit another cigarette. "We didn't suit. But I still have the title."

That was good, Dorinda thought. Her mother was certainly proving her acting talent. The cowgirl-nervous countess character was great!

"Tell me about you," the woman continued, giving her a glance full of interest, and moving closer to her.

"Oh, I'm an actress," Dorinda responded, again saying the first thing that came into her head. Lieto Clavell smiled into her eyes.

"I'm sure you're a good one," she said. "And by the way, I adore your dress. Is it a Bus Stop label? It looks like one."

"Bus Stop? I don't know; I didn't look."

"I'm a fabric designer; I have an interest in such things." The woman's long-nailed right hand touched Dorinda's knee lightly. "This is nice lace."

When were they going to get to any point in this? Dorinda wondered. Lifting the drink in her hand, she realized that she had downed the second Scotch in her agitation. Take it easy, she told herself.

"I'm glad you like it," she answered politely.

"I'll tell you what." The woman put out her cigarette. "Why don't we just call it a night here and go back to my flat? I've got lots of Scotch there, or champagne or whatever."

"That would be great!" Dorinda arose immediately, inwardly congratulating Emma on the good thought. Now they could go somewhere and have this thing out. This meeting was bizarre, but at least she had found Emma! She *must* be, or at the very least, she was somebody who knew all about everything. Hadn't she indicated that by her remark, "You look like a little girl who's lost her mother?"

The countess led the way out. Dorinda followed, feeling so many different emotions—wonder, doubt, hope, fear— that she couldn't think coherently. The countess appeared calm and in control of everything; her fidgety manner was only superficial. On the street outside the club she flagged a cab and gave an address on Pembroke Close.

"I've a place in Belgravia," she said to Dorinda. "I'd love to show it to you." She tilted her head, seeming to study Dorinda's face closely, examining each feature.

Oh, why do we have to play this game? Dorinda wondered. What was her mother trying to prove? Still, she had promised long ago to honor Emma's disguise. Yet surely here in the back seat of the taxi Emma didn't have to preserve her cover. The cowboy hat she had now donned pushed the blonde ringlets even further forward, making it harder than ever to see the face clearly.

"Here we are."

Quickly, the countess climbed out and paid for the ride. When Dorinda joined her on the sidewalk she led the way into an elegant townhouse apparently now converted to apartments. From the small lobby they entered a tiny mirrored elevator and went up one floor. At the end of a short hall the countess opened a door. When she flipped on the lights they revealed a striking interior.

Bewildered, Dorinda followed her inside the door. When would her mother have had time to furnish a place like this? But of course, the apartment could be rented or borrowed. Its decor was amazing. Living room and dining room were done entirely in black and white, the furniture all black, the carpet white, all the tables chrome, and every wall mirrored. The effect was overwhelmingly cold and confusing, and certainly distinctive.

After the door closed behind them the countess turned off the overhead lights, leaving on a black-shaded lamp, tossed her cowboy hat upon a chrome cube of a table, and gestured toward the black sofa. "Sit down," she said. "Want a Scotch?"

Dorinda did as she was invited, sinking into the dark cushions as the countess vanished through a black door and then returned with a bottle of Dewar's and two crystal goblets. She poured each of them a drink, handed Dorinda hers, and then dropped down beside her, her skirt again fluttering. Picking at its folds, she arranged it around her and then took a swallow of her Scotch; Dorinda followed suit.

"Now you must allow me," the countess said. "I have been *dying* of curiosity all night." As she spoke, she put her hand up to Dorinda's head. "Let me see what color hair you have."

"What?" Before Dorinda could move, the countess had pulled the stickpin out of her scarf and was unwinding it.

"A blonde! With those dark eyes, you could have fooled me. Is it real?"

"Mother—honestly! What is this?" Suddenly, Dorinda reached the end of her patience.

The countess fluffed out Dorinda's blonde hair, letting the scarf fall to the floor. She laughed softly at Dorinda's words.

"Darling, I don't really think I'm old enough to be your

mother," she murmured. "But I will be, if that's what you'd like." Leaning forward, she impressed a light kiss directly on Dorinda's lips.

Dorinda was immobilized. Total astonishment washed through her. This was certainly not Emma! And as surely, not any emissary from Emma, either. The Countess Lieto Clavell was simply a lesbian.

"You can stay the night," the countess said in a low, throaty voice, one hand stroking Dorinda's bare forearm and then passing up to caress her hair. "I'll take care of you, little girl."

"Oh, my God." Suddenly Dorinda's mind and body began to work. She leaped to her feet. "I'm sorry! I didn't mean—I mean, I misunderstood you. I thought—" She choked on her words. The countess hadn't anything to do with Mother! Dorinda wanted to sob.

The countess seized her knee.

"Now, wait," she said, but Dorinda didn't wait. In one bound, she reached the front door. She clawed at the knob. If the door had been locked, she would have begun screaming, but the knob turned in her hand and in one more second she was out, the black-and-white interior behind her.

She ran down some stairs to the first floor and fled out the front door, her face burning with embarrassment. Of all the stupid situations! And she had brought it on herself.

She continued to hurry, although she was pretty sure the countess wouldn't pursue her out into the street. Pembroke Close was a short and shadowy little lane, leading past a number of townhouses to a wider street she could glimpse beyond. She rushed to reach this haven, but the avenue turned out to be deserted as well. Something suddenly made Dorinda panic. She wanted a taxi; she wanted to be on her way to the safety of Paul's flat.

A man came out of a house across the street and walked in the opposite direction, the sound of his footsteps seeming loud. Intermittent rain had left the air muggy, and swarms of insects clustered around the streetlamps. Repressing a desire to run, Dorinda walked quickly toward the heavily traveled street she sighted at the end of the avenue, cursing the high-heeled pumps on her feet that made her steps shorter than usual.

When she reached the busy street she breathed easier, but in a moment she found to her dismay that a wrought-iron fence cut her off from the traffic's flow. Cars were streaming past at a rapid rate. She looked up, searching for a street sign, and instead found one reading "Subway." Beneath the sign was a flight of steps leading down.

Well, the subway would be fine. She knew how to read London subway maps. The Underground was safe, and she was confident of being able to get back to Paul's neighborhood from anywhere. She ducked down the stairs and into a tunnel, but to her dismay, after a short distance, the tunnel led only to another flight of steps leading up.

She climbed them to find herself in a totally dark little park, a traffic circle of sorts, now completely deserted and surrounded by wrought-iron railings. Some sort of building stood in the center, like a memorial. It was unlit, and there was nothing else there but grass and some trees.

Suddenly, as she stared at one of the large old trees, Dorinda saw the figure of a man detach itself from the shadow of the low-hanging foliage. This was so stupid! What was she doing in this circle in the middle of the night? She leaned over the railing to wave at the traffic, but automobiles continued to rush past in a never-ending river, no taxicabs stopping. Obviously, they couldn't stop in the fast-moving stream.

This was no place to catch a taxi! As the realization hit her, she felt her legs tremble. Turning away from the traffic, she saw the man's figure moving toward her, and she started at a run toward another sign that read "Subway." This time maybe it would *be* the subway; she didn't want to go back where she'd been. Not taking time to see whether the man was still moving in her direction, she ducked down the stairs. Was anyone coming through the darkness? Damn, another underpass! She certainly did not want to run through a deserted tunnel, yet she apparently had no choice if she wanted to get away from the dark traffic circle. How could London turn into so terrifying a place? In cursing her high heels, she ran as swiftly as she could, not even daring to look over her shoulder. Every moment she dreaded that a hand might grab her from behind and her heart pumped heavily, but she reached the stairs at the other end and sprinted up unimpeded. Now for heaven's sakes where was she?

She had come out on yet another part of the busy highway, the dark little circle behind her. Although her feet were smarting, she walked rapidly along, looking for a subway entrance. There was no sign of one as she went past some dark houses and a long hedge. Then she remembered. The subway was always called the Underground in England; "subway" must just mean an underground tunnel.

Fortunately at the next corner she caught sight of a taxi. Its light was dark, and momentarily she was discouraged, but then a cruising taxi turned into the street and she waved vigorously. He stopped for her at once.

"I've never been so glad to see anyone," she said, climbing in.

On the way to Paul's flat she tried to catch her breath and compose herself. She had acted like an idiot tonight, of that there was no doubt. Luckily she had come out of it all right. And, she told herself, at least she *had* taken some action. She wasn't that daunted, either. She was ready to do more. "Mother, where *are* you?" she said to herself, closing her eyes and letting her head fall back against the seat. "Am I alone?"

That thought was so sad that she immediately tried to put it out of her mind. But what if Emma had confronted Mr. Bellevue—and lost? Would her daughter ever know, in such an eventuality? Would the enemy come after her?

I'd rather *face* it all, she thought. Anything would be better than this vague threat, this feeling of being hunted by the unseen.

By the time the cab pulled up at Paul's flat, her nerves were not notably better. She glanced at Paul's windows; they were dark. Good. She'd have time to go in and pull herself together. Maybe she wouldn't have to confess any of this evening to Paul, who had his own troubles.

This plan was dashed as she paid her cab driver. Another taxi pulled up and Paul emerged from it.

"Dorinda!" he said, catching sight of her. "Where have you been?"

Suddenly she realized how disheveled she must look. Her hair was wild around her face—and here she was in a perfectly strange black dress and high heels. Paul paid his driver and came over to take her arm. "Hey, what on earth?" he asked, looking at her in amazement. In the light of the streetlamp above them, she stood revealed.

"I went out," she said shortly.

"Where?" Paul's question was just as curt.

"Paul, please don't start anything. Let's go upstairs. How —how was the rehearsal?"

For a moment, Paul gazed back at her without speaking. His face was pale, she saw, and he looked strained and tired.

"It was a total disaster," he said quietly. "Lavinia was high, Rollo threw a tantrum, and Prentiss walked out—for good, he says. And then—" He broke off. "Let's get off the street, at least."

They rode up in the elevator in silence. Paul surveyed her outfit without a word, only crooking one eyebrow. As he was unlocking the door he said, "I called at eleven, so I knew you had gone out."

"You don't have to check up on me, Paul."

"Apparently, I do." Paul's tone was cold.

"Look, let's have a drink." Dorinda went through the door and headed straight for the kitchen, where she opened the refrigerator door, clattered a tray of ice cubes into the sink, and finally managed to fix herself a glass of vodka. Paul stood watching her in the kitchen doorway.

"Want a drink?" she asked.

"I want some news. Dorinda, where did you go?"

"I'm not sure that's any of your business." She strode past him, collapsed on the sofa in the living room, and pulled off the torturing pumps, rubbing her feet.

"What do you mean?" Paul came over and stood in front of her.

"Oh, okay. If you have to know, I went to the Argosy Club. And instead of seeing Mother like I hoped, I got picked up by a lesbian."

"*What?*"

"Well, I thought she might be Mother—or someone who came from Mother. I mean, she knew Trevor and Renata and she said—oh, just forget it. I'm not feeling too great about it."

"Well. Just forget it. That's super." Paul sat down on a footstool. "Dorinda, didn't your promise to me mean a thing? I mean—"

"Paul, can't you see I'm sick of this? I mean *sick*. You and Mother both make me tired." Dorinda drained her vodka. She was fighting not to cry. "Listen, you can't tell me what to do. You think I'm some baby. Mother fixes me up with you and then goes off, God knows where, like she'd left me with a nursemaid, and every minute you want me to report my whereabouts to you like I'm a schoolgirl."

"You don't know what's at stake." Paul's face was paler now than it had been downstairs.

"Well, then why am I the only one who doesn't? It's high time I did know! I want some answers." Dorinda lifted her voice as she spoke. It made her feel much better to shout.

"Oh, God, look. I've had enough screaming for one day, do you mind? The play is screwed, and you—I'm taking a shower!"

He turned and strode into the bedroom. Dorinda followed him, freshening her vodka on the way.

"You can't tell me what to do," she said, watching Paul strip off his clothes.

He made no answer and walked into the bathroom. She heard the shower go on. Pulling off the black lace dress, she threw it on the floor and for a moment considered going into the shower with Paul. She decided against it, put on a dressing gown, and started brushing her hair.

Paul came out with a towel wrapped around him and fell onto the mattress of the recessed bed. After a minute she went over and crouched down beside him.

"I'm sorry," she said. "Can I get you anything?"

"Another play."

"I'm sure that things will come out all right."

Paul stared at her with his face expressionless. She had never seen him look so depressed.

"God, Paul," she said softly. She felt tears coming into

her eyes. It seemed as if everything between the two of them was abruptly drawing to a close.

"I'll be all right," Paul said. "But Dorinda, you can't go around taking chances like that. I blame myself." His tone was harsh, as if his nerves were badly abraded. "I shouldn't have gotten into this damn play."

"Oh, for God's sake, it's your career. You have a life, and—I really mean this—you have to let me have a life, too." Suddenly, Dorinda's temper spiked high again.

"Bugger off, you clot." Paul pulled a pillow from behind his head and threw it at her. She realized that he had started laughing.

"I'm *serious*, Paul."

"So am I." He reached forward and grabbed her by the wrist, pulling her down toward him.

"Stop it. Listen, I'm all sweaty. Paul, I've got to take a shower." She struggled, but it was useless. She was hot and sticky and still angry, and much as she wanted Paul, something inside her refused to cooperate this time. When Paul was finished, he seemed rather unsatisfied himself. He was still in a bad mood from whatever horrors he had faced at the rehearsal, obviously, and the sex didn't help. Again Dorinda felt cut off from him and alone. Paul turned on his side and closed his eyes without a word.

After a while, she climbed out of the bed and walked toward the bathroom, but when she got as far as the bench in front of one window her legs gave out and she sat down. She looked at her reflection in the full-length mirror on Paul's opened closet door. Her dressing gown was awry and the lace trim had been pulled loose in front during their scuffle. Her hair hung limp and straggly. There was no makeup left on her face. She stared at herself, unable to move.

She looked young. Anyone looking at her would think she was young and dumb. Why did she have to look like she did? She was plump, too. She would not cry, however. There was a desperate pain in her throat, as if it were closed up for good unless she could cry. But she wouldn't. Why did she have to live this way? She got pushed around by everybody.

Young. She looked at her hair. Maybe if she wore it in a

knot. She gathered it up and coiled it on the back of her neck. Pulling it back did make her look older. She longed to twist it up tightly, to jam pins into it until it was like a pincushion. She didn't want anyone pawing it.

She looked over at the dresser top, but of course there were no pins. She never used bobby pins. It was Emma who used the pins. There were always lots of them scattered around in Emma's room.

The feeling in her throat eased at the thought and she swallowed and realized that tears were sliding down her cheeks, leaving streaks on her face. She was crying even though she didn't want to. She looked over at the bed. Paul lay there as if dead. She blinked the tears out of her eyes and gazed at the reflection of the high-ceilinged room in the mirror. It seemed oppressive. She closed her eyes; after a while she opened them and looked again at the dresser top for bobby pins. She still held her hair clenched in a bun. It was too dark to see if there was a stray bobby pin there that had been left by some former girlfriend of Paul's.

She thought of her bedroom in the apartment in New York. She hadn't seen it in so long. It had light lavender walls. The twin beds had flounced white cotton coverlets. She always slept in the left one. The other bed was for friends who visited her. Girlfriends. Her throat closed up again.

After a while through her tears she could only dimly make out her white gown and white face, in the mirror, and she thought that she wanted to go home. She was tired, and she wanted to go home and get some answers. She was through with everything here.

She closed her eyes and pursued the thought. She was through with everything here. It was alien and English and—

Well, she could go home, couldn't she?

PART II

Chapter Eleven

"How long have you been back in New York, Dorinda?"

She had answered the telephone in the bedroom and she looked across at the lavender wall and the ruffled white curtains framing the windows.

"A week."

"Yes? Well, I heard you were back. And is your mother—" He paused.

"Mother? Mother was lost in a sailboat accident last spring. In Europe." She spoke softly.

"Oh, I heard something. So it's true. I'm so sorry. I read it, somewhere, but I was hoping it wasn't—" He paused again.

"I'm afraid it is."

"I'm very sorry to hear it. I knew your mother well."

She frowned. She had not recognized the name this man with a cultivated East Coast accent had given her.

"So where have you been since then, my dear?" he went on.

"I've just been traveling, trying to get over it; the shock, you know," she said.

"You should have come home sooner. Many of your parents' friends would have liked to help. I am sorry we've never met—"

She lost the thread of the man's words for a moment. When she recovered her concentration, she realized he was talking about Newport and in fact apparently was telephoning her from there.

"—summer of the America's Cup," he was saying. "My wife and I are living on a yacht here. I'm with the *Trophy* syndicate. Dorinda, I was wondering if perhaps you'd like to see some races? The trials are on to pick the best American boat."

Startled, she managed only to say, "Oh."

"We have plenty of room aboard," he continued, his voice smoothly pleasant. "Do you remember Newport at all?"

"Just a little," she said. She could hear her voice sounding breathless. The suddenness of the invitation had taken her by surprise. To go up to Newport certainly wasn't what she had been expecting. Nonetheless, she told herself, however it comes, isn't this exactly what you want?

"Well, that's very nice of you," she said when he paused. "I'd love to see some sailing."

"Could you come up here immediately then?" he asked. "That's because this set of trial races is almost over. I believe we go out just tomorrow and the next day, and then we rest."

"Oh, I see," she said. She waited a moment, then said, "Everybody I've called seems to be out of town this month. I really don't have any plans. I could come."

"Splendid." He sounded genuinely pleased; his tone was warm. "It takes just over three hours to get here from the city. Would you like me to send a car and driver for you—tomorrow, shall we say?"

"I can drive up myself. I'll rent a car."

"Whatever you prefer, my dear. We'll be going out on our syndicate's boat to watch the racing; the *Morgana*—that's our yacht—stays here, moored at the Port of Call. Would you happen to remember that dock? Do you think you can find it?"

For a moment she closed her eyes, memory stirring painfully.

"I can ask the way," she said. The Port of Call was the dock at the end of Blood Alley.

"You may arrive at any time. Just go aboard. I'll leave word with the guard that you're expected. We should arrive back at least by six tomorrow evening. There's a cocktail party—our syndicate is giving it. We will certainly be grateful to have a pretty girl helping us entertain—I've seen your pictures, you know. Now when you arrive, ask the steward where your cabin is, and make yourself comfortable."

"I probably won't be there until six or so."

"That's fine. You're welcome anytime. I must go now, my dear, but I'll look forward to seeing you."

Saying good-bye, she placed the receiver back on its white cradle and wiped sweaty palms on her jeans. Sitting on the edge of the bed, she replayed the conversation in her mind. *Ashcroft*. That was the name the man had given her. Sebastian Ashcroft. What a name—it sounded like a lawyer in an English murder mystery.

She took a deep breath, willing herself not to feel panicky. She hoped she had sounded like an ordinary young girl, unsuspiciously accepting an invitation extended by an old friend of her mother's. Realizing that her hands were now formed into fists, she forced herself to relax them until each finger hung limp. Now. What was the next step? Clothes.

Thinking hard, she stood up and walked out to the hall closet, her footsteps not making a sound on the white carpet. There was no sound in the entire apartment except the whir of the air-conditioning system. They were high over the street and the noise of cars below on Park Avenue did not penetrate the closed windows. The apartment was an island of quiet, sealed from the world, three doormen downstairs protecting the tenants from unwanted visitors. And which of these guardians had told Sebastian Ashcroft, or maybe somebody else in Newport, that Dorinda Westerly had come home? How much had that information been worth?

Trying to put the thought out of her head, she opened

the doors of the closet and burrowed to the back, where drawers held summer clothes and bathing suits. Digging through them, she pulled out shorts and a collection of bikinis and one-piece suits from past years. The drawers rasped loudly as she opened and closed them.

Back in the bedroom she tried each thing on before deciding whether to pack it. One pair of shorts was too tight. It must have been left over from summers ago. She discarded it and made a pile of the things that fit. Then she added jeans and some sweaters and sweatshirts, and decided it could all fit into the lightweight parachute cloth suitcase she had just bought.

Thinking of the cocktail party, she hunted through the closet and pulled out a red and black tuxedo outfit. Probably evenings by the water would be cool, and the outfit would be right. She liked its carefree look. A little red bow tie went around the collar of the tucked-front white shirt. Carefully, she folded the jacket, red-lined vest, and black pants in layers of tissue paper. When everything was in the parachute bag, she zipped it shut.

Next she arranged for the rental of a Hertz car the next day. After she hung up the telephone, she sat staring at the lavender walls of the bedroom. Was she really ready?

Carrying the purple bag into the front hall, she left it beside the door for tomorrow, then continued on into the kitchen. The refrigerator contained only a carton of milk and a dozen eggs; she'd been eating out. Pouring herself a glass of milk, she opened a box of saltines and ate several, noticing as she did so that the copper bottoms of the pans hanging over the stove had turned dark. It was hard to chew; she wasn't hungry and the crackers were tasteless.

When the refrigerator went on, she jumped; it was like the startling sound of the ringing telephone. Well, there was a cure for this. Putting down her glass and not waiting even to close the carton of crackers, she hurried to the study and the Pioneer stereo. Beside the record player was a tape deck in a walnut cabinet. She pushed "Disco Baby" into the machine and switched the sound into the living room. In a moment she reached the long mirrors there and began to dance, studying her reflection as she moved. Letting her head turn from side to side made her long blonde hair swing out. She smiled, practicing the six-beat Latin hustle and wondering if Newport had discos.

Finally, out of breath, she stopped, pushed her hair back, and went closer to the mirror. Tentatively, she smiled again at herself. Then she walked back to the lavender bedroom, to the night table of the bed she'd been sleeping in, took a loaded revolver out of its drawer, and dropped it into her patchwork canvas pocketbook.

Crossing the Bay Bridge into Newport the next afternoon, she turned off the car's air conditioning and opened the vents to breathe in the salty air. To her right lay the finger of land that was Newport; tiers of houses lined the western side of the peninsula, their windows glittering as they reflected the sun's rays. In the harbor below, a dozen small sailboats wheeled and glided across the water like gulls.

Leaving the bridge, she followed a sign directing her to Farewell Street, a road that passed an ancient cemetery. It became a one-way street lined with curbside eighteenth-century houses, all looking recently restored. So far, memory guided her, but suddenly she was confronted with a baffling set of parallel one-way streets where old Thames Street used to run by the water. She had to stop and ask the whereabouts of the Port of Call. A boy in a gas station directed her through a wilderness of shopping malls and condominiums. Finally making a lucky guess, she found herself on the site of Blood Alley—and yet, what a difference! Somewhere, she remembered, she had read that after the navy left Newport, the town had undergone extensive renovation and become very commercial in order to survive without the naval base.

Now she looked through the car window in amazement. The old Black Pearl restaurant was still in its place, but it had been joined by the Clark Cooke house, apparently moved down from Thames Street, and dozens of small shops selling everything from scrimshaw to Scottish plaids. A young girl claimed five dollars from her for the privilege of leaving her car beside an establishment selling custom-made wrought iron.

Feeling weak in the knees, she climbed out and locked

up, telling herself she was cramped from sitting so long behind the wheel. Shouldering her lightweight purple bag, she started to cross the cobblestones—were they even the same cobblestones?—when suddenly she heard a sound that was totally familiar. From the spire of Trinity Church the bells pealed six, and then the carillon began to play a hymn.

Blood Alley—she could scarcely take it in. The Black Pearl had an outdoor annex and bar now, thronged with a chattering cocktail crowd. Tourists of every description seemed assembled: three men in Bermuda shorts walked past eating ice cream cones, a redhaired girl cruised by on a bicycle, and she was given the once-over by two bearded boys wearing the red pants of the yachting fraternity. Beyond the restaurants and shops, the harbor was jammed with boats of all sorts, while the old Revolutionary War ship *Rose* was berthed beside the Black Pearl and had apparently become a tourist attraction.

Bewildered by the changed atmosphere, she walked on, past the Black Pearl, the only landmark she recognized, and then beyond a kite shop to the dock called the Port of Call. Barricaded from the rest of the wharf now, it had a guard beside its latticework door.

"I'm Dorinda Westerly. Did Mr. Ashcroft tell you?" she said to him.

He smiled and opened the door.

"Yes, indeed, Miss Westerly, and welcome to Newport. Could I help you with that bag?"

"Oh, thanks, it's not heavy," she answered. She looked down the pier. Sloops were tied up on either side. "Which is the *Morgana*?" she asked.

"It's at the very end of the pier."

"Thanks, I'll find it," she said, and turned in the direction he pointed. The sun was directly in her eyes as she made her away across the boards of the dock. She blinked as she walked, until suddenly she was in the shade of an enormous motor yacht. As she stared at the boat, a young man in a blue blazer and white pants came over to the railing.

"Hello," he said, smiling. "Are you looking for the *Morgana*, I hope?"

She smiled back at him.

"I'm Dorinda Westerly."

"I guessed." As she looked up, across the teak deck, she could see people apparently enjoying afternoon drinks in the salon beyond. The sound of chatter rose on the slight breeze. The boy, who had a dashing mustache, jumped down onto the dock beside her.

"My name's Billy Bachelor," he said, surveying her with a look of open admiration. "I've been watching for you. Let me have your bag."

He took it, and helped her up onto the teak deck of the yacht. The moment she was aboard, a man came out of the door of the salon and hurried toward her.

"It must be Dorinda," he said. "Am I right?"

She recognized the cultivated accent of the man who had called her on the telephone, and said, "Mr. Ashcroft?"

"My dear, I'm so glad you could make it." He gave her a perfunctory kiss on the cheek, and as he straightened, she looked closely at his face. He had small features, deeply tanned and quite bland in expression, but his eyes were a striking pale gray in color, making his black pupils look like two targets. As she gazed at him, he smiled.

"You're exactly as pretty as you looked in your pictures —and that was beautiful," he said. "We can't have too many like you around. Is this your bag? Billy, perhaps you'd take it below for Dorinda?"

He took her by the arm as he spoke, guiding her toward the party in the salon. "Come and meet the others," he said.

She was still amazed by the size of the yacht she had been invited aboard; Sebastian Ashcroft must be a millionaire, she thought. Through the opened sliding glass doors of the huge rear compartment she saw half a dozen elaborately-gowned women sitting or standing, all with drinks in their hands, and as many men, dressed as her host was, in white pants and dark blue yachting blazers. Mr. Ashcroft led her up to a woman wearing a black chiffon concoction that was far more attractive than the person herself. She was short, stocky, and had a hard expression on her face.

"Dorinda, let me present my wife."

"How do you do." Waving one chiffoned arm in their direction, the woman spoke flatly and without the slightest enthusiasm. Diamonds glittered around her neck, and above them the cool gray of her eyes matched the immaculately perfect gray waves of her hair. "I want to speak to you, Sebastian," she added. "Immediately. It's urgent."

"In just a moment," he said calmly, appearing indifferent to his wife's clipped phrases. "I want to introduce Dorinda around." He turned her toward a short, sandy-haired man who smiled warmly. "This, my dear, is Howard James, the designer of our boat *Trophy*."

The people she was introduced to all seemed to have been expecting a Dorinda Westerly; none of them mentioned Emma, or her fate. Sebastian Ashcroft presented her to *Trophy*'s skipper, a very thin and distinguished-looking man called "Kentucky," and his wife Coco, who was motherly in appearance and decidedly more cordial than Mrs. Ashcroft. Then she met a number of middle-aged, wealthy-looking people who had various functions in the *Trophy* syndicate, the group who, she gathered, backed the twelve-meter yacht *Trophy*'s bid to become the American yacht defending the America's Cup in the coming races with a foreign challenger. An older couple she met was named Bachelor and she wondered if they were Billy's parents. As she shook hands with them, Billy appeared.

"I've stowed your gear," he said, grinning.

"Shouldn't I change for the party?" She smiled at him.

"You look great, but you do have a few minutes if you want to dress. Let me show you your cabin. But first, would you like a drink?"

Wishing she could say yes—she definitely could use a drink!—she declined and suggested she get ready for what was coming next. In her jeans and silk blouse, she felt under-dressed for her opulent surroundings. The circular banquettes of the salon were upholstered in velvet and satin, a large bouquet of roses stood on the marble-pedestaled glass cocktail table, a liveried barman was serving drinks at the sparkling lucite bar—it seemed like a throwback to the age of the Vanderbilts.

Her wonder increased as Billy led her out of the salon, through a paneled dining room with a cut-glass chandelier and down a softly carpeted spiral staircase to the cabin floor below. The corridor's thick covering was a glowing deep green, and the walls were papered in what looked like jade silk. They padded past several cabin doors and came to Number Two. Billy opened it, and she said, "Wow."

He grinned as she looked in. The cabin could only be described as sumptuous. There was a striking blue-and-white Madras print covering the walls and the king-sized bed, and hanging over the bed's fan-shaped headboard was what looked like an original Monet oil painting of water lilies. Through portholes on either side of the bed, shafts of light from the sinking sun outside sent sparkling reflections all over the ceiling and walls, hitting the silver-backed brushes, silver bottles, and silver-framed mirrors of the built-in vanity table. On top of the vanity a large silver sea shell held multicolored cotton balls, and a silver dolphin beside it guarded a cut-glass flask of perfume. The floor was carpeted in white. The full-sized statue of a naked Venus stood posed against the far boudoir wall, while the ceiling, composed of wall-to-wall gray-smoked mirrors, dimly reflected the grandeur below.

"All yours," Billy said. "There's a head through there." He gestured in the direction of the Venus.

Stepping inside, she thanked him. As soon as he retreated up the corridor, she closed the door and bent to examine its lock. It was the sort that had a button in the center of the knob; she pushed it in and tried the knob. It didn't move. Leaving it locked, she checked the fittings on the large portholes. Each latched on the inside and the latches were working; she tried them and left them locked, turning to the bathroom.

The head had walls that were mirrors. The tiny porthole set in one mirrored wall also possessed a working latch. She locked it and went back to the cabin. Billy had placed her bag on a stand, and she brought out the tuxedo outfit and rapidly changed clothes. The red tie was just the right debonair touch, she thought, searching in her makeup bag for a brighter shade of lipstick to match it. The rest of her makeup seemed all right, she decided after studying herself critically in the triple mirror of the vanity. Finding a black silk pouch in the suitcase, she transferred everything from the canvas pocketbook into it. A little disco bag would probably look better, but she had to carry something large enough for the gun. She fitted the cords of the bag over her left shoulder so that she could reach it easily with her right hand. Part of her wanted to consider how strange all this was, to be in such luxurious surroundings and in fear of her life, but she resolutely put such thoughts to one side, checked her appearance a last time and left the cabin.

The group upstairs was just preparing to leave. Apparently the party was to be held elsewhere, not on the *Morgana*.

"Do you look great!" Billy Bachelor said when he saw her. "I've been delegated to drive you to the party."

He was the only other young person in evidence, so the choice seemed logical. As he helped her from the boat to the dock she looked closely at him and decided he must be in his early twenties. He had a handsome face and his dark hair fell over his tanned brow in engaging tendrils.

"Do you sail aboard *Trophy*?" she asked as they walked up the dock.

"Yes. I'm a jib sheet tailer." He slid his arm under hers. "Have you seen *Trophy* yet? No? Would you like to?"

She nodded as, ahead of them, the group from *Morgana* could be seen going through the latticework door. A few minutes later she and Billy reached the small parking lot across from the Clark Cooke house and he led her, with obvious pride, to a silver Porsche. *Trophy*, it turned out, was berthed at Newport Shipyard, just down Thames Street. A guard in a booth waved them in when he saw Billy, who parked the Porsche at the rear of a shed.

The reddened disk of the sun touched the surface of the sea as Billy led her down a long pier. The harbor turned a brilliant gold, and the Bay Bridge beyond gleamed like a gilded spiderweb. The first slender hull that Billy pointed out belonged to the Australian boat *Melinda*; her single mast was a silver spire that seemed impossibly high.

"So that's a twelve-meter yacht," she said, looking up. "It seems so streamlined."

"*Trophy* is down here." Billy led her past the Australian boat to another slender hull, this one white with a wide gold stripe, a pale green deck, and the word "Trophy" across the transom in gold.

"Come on aboard." Billy stepped onto the narrow stern and she followed him. The deck was pock-marked with hatches and the cockpit in front of her full of an awesome array of equipment.

"It looks so complicated," she exclaimed.

"Takes eleven of us to run her, you know. Here's my tailer's compartment." He led her forward to a small opening, jumping down into a well that left him waist-high to the deck. He tried to explain what he did while she gazed at the strips of tape and notes in Magic Marker that apparently detailed various sail settings. A strap nailed across one wall held a large knife, two smaller ones, and a heavy silver marlinspike that looked like the tooth of a metal whale.

"Come on below," Billy said. He disappeared through a hole in the tailer's bin that led to the interior of the twelve-meter, where the struts and sides were unpainted aluminum.

"It looks like a boiler factory," she said, eying the winches and various contraptions below.

"You should hear us under sail, banging like a kitchen full of tin pans." He led her up to the compartment at the front, now full of white sail bags that made it look like a vast lumpy featherbed.

"We didn't stow all our gear tonight, because of the party," Billy said. "Which reminds me—we better get going. The bar will probably close at eight-thirty."

He helped her back onto the dock and she thanked him for the tour.

"I can't wait to see you under sail," she said politely.

"You'll be going out on that boat," Billy said, pointing to a power boat tied up alongside the twelve-meter. "And I certainly hope you'll see something better than today's performance."

"What happened?" she asked, keeping step as they went back up the dock.

"We lost. That's nothing unusual, unfortunately. The hot rumor is we're going to have a skipper change."

Seeing her look a bit bewildered, Billy proceeded to explain as he escorted her back to the Porsche and drove out. It seemed that four boats were competing for selection as the American defender.

"America's Cup racing is match racing," Billy said. "That means one boat against one boat. So each day there are two sets of match races—we trade about for opponents. And the only boat not even beating the oldest twelve, *Great Republic*, is us. The crew thinks it's Tucky. He's a great ocean racer, but match racing is something else. Tucky has a lot of money in the syndicate, but I still think he's got to be replaced. After the party tonight there's going to be a meeting. The guy with the real say is Sebastian Ashcroft. He's put a million dollars into this effort, and I think he's got Big Ed on the way here."

"Who's Big Ed?"

"The most famous match racer in the world. Every syndicate has tried to get him. So far, he's stayed out of Newport, but with the kind of money Ashcroft is throwing around, I think he can be had. I just pray it's fast. We're about to get our asses shot out of the water."

"What do you mean?" she asked.

He turned and gave her a grin. "I mean, pray for us," he said, and swung the Porsche through a stone gateway with a "Private Drive" sign. After a moment an enormous stone house that looked like a Gothic cathedral loomed up against the sky.

"This cozy cottage is where the *Trophy* crew stays," Billy said.

Hearing her sound of amazement, he chuckled. "Spooky, isn't it? It used to be someone's mansion; it's part of a school now. There are dormitories upstairs."

A field to the left of the house was jammed with cars. Billy finally managed to park his Porsche between a Rolls Royce and a tree. Sounds of the party came from the other side of the house, where the lawn faced the sea, but Billy led her first to the front door. Inside, the high ceilings and general gloom of the tapestried grand hall were awesome.

Through archways, dark drawing rooms could be glimpsed on either side. Billy led her back to the french doors at the rear, open to a broad stone terrace and the lawn that was filled with chattering guests. Not pausing, he headed toward the heaviest concentration of people, thereby finding the bar. In another moment he had secured some drinks for them, and followed her as she walked curiously down to the edge of the lawn, where a sheer cliff dropped straight to the ocean. Through a chain-link fence she peered down to watch spumes of spray dashing up as waves washed onto the jagged rocks of the shoreline.

"So *here* you are, Dorinda."

She turned from the sea to find that Sebastian Ashcroft had joined them. In a paternal way he took hold of her arm, asking where they had been.

"We went to see *Trophy*," she said, trying to smile into the pale eyes of her host and resisting the impulse to yank her arm away from him. "It's beautiful."

He regarded her for a moment and then his eyes went from her face to the horizon of the ocean.

"Tomorrow," he said. He paused and then added, "An exciting day, I hope. A pretty girl always brings luck."

The reflection of the red clouds of evening shone on his face. Beyond his profile she caught sight of his wife standing a short distance away, staring in their direction with a hostile expression. Her host was still holding her arm. As she cast about for something to say, Billy's parents joined the three of them.

"Shall we plan to dine before the meeting?" Mr. Bachelor asked Ashcroft. Ashcroft withdrew his eyes from the ocean and glanced briefly at Billy's father.

"No, we'll have sandwiches sent in." He turned to her. "Dorinda, my dear, I am very sorry, but I am tied up with a syndicate meeting tonight. Billy, I believe, would like to take you to dinner."

"Of course," she said.

His grasp on her arm loosened and fell away as, not saying a word, his wife walked over and joined their group, her black chiffon fluttering in a sudden breeze from the sea. For a moment no one spoke, as if all were variously preoccupied. Twilight was just beginning. The bright clouds in the east that had been burning in the lingering sunset light were now fading, and the ocean was growing hazy.

"Come and meet some people, Dorinda," Billy said, at last breaking the small silence. Giving them all a smile, she excused herself and followed him to a nearby group of young men who were uniformly tanned and healthy-looking and who all wore white pants and blue blazers with "Trophy" written in gold braid on their breast pockets. They also all seemed glad to meet her. The preponderance of women at the party, she noticed, appeared to be middle-aged socialites.

"Welcome to the effort," said the boy just introduced to her as the "bowman." "Or what was the effort. Billy, Tom just said he really thinks we could be eliminated tomorrow."

"Eliminated?" she asked.

Her new acquaintance nodded gloomily, his curly blond hair stirring as he did so.

"The New York Yacht Club Committee would like to pare the competition down to two boats," he said. "*Great Republic* is last time's defender. Everyone's been beating her regularly except *Trophy*. If the Committee eliminated us, they could excuse *Republic* and just let *Dauntless* and *Resolute* slug it out."

She found it hard to keep all this straight; even the names of the boats sounded alike. Holding her drink behind her as the discussion went on, she managed to spill most of the contents out on the ground, but in a moment Billy saw that her glass was empty and rushed off to get her another. When he returned with the news that the bar had just closed, his crewmates were further depressed. Guests were beginning to leave. The remaining little groups dotted around the terrace and grounds seemed to be having serious, low-voiced conversations, and there was less laughter.

"Let's blow. How about eating at the Clark Cooke house?" Billy said.

Over the protests of the others, he took her off. As they departed she looked for her host and his wife, but they were no longer on the lawn.

Chapter Twelve

THE CLARK COOKE HOUSE NEAR THE PORT OF Call boasted a many-decked arrangement of attractions. In the basement was a disco, Billy said, the street floor bar and restaurant called the Candy Store was for informal gatherings, as were several floors above, while on the left in a large, beam-ceilinged room they found an elegant French restaurant complete with hurricane-lamp-centered tables, a roaring fire, and hovering waiters.

"How romantic this is," she said as they were seated at a table for two in one corner. Billy smiled at her and then turned his attention to the hand-written menu, and she studied his face in the flickering light of their glassed candle. His brown eyes looked amber in the soft illumination; they weren't the kind of dark eyes that turned unreadable in dimness. Good-humored, athletic, accustomed to privilege—Billy was not someone to fear. Thank God, she thought, I ended up with him tonight. That wasn't the purpose of coming to Newport—after all, she was here to find out who *was* after her—but still she didn't want everything to happen too fast. Go slow, get things figured out, she told herself. Then, when you're sure . . .

Billy looked up and smiled at her again, and she decided that she would definitely be safer with him tonight than alone in the cabin aboard *Morgana*.

"Why don't you order for both of us?" she said. "It all looks good to me."

He leaned closer to her, apparently pleased by this intimacy, and with one finger he touched her red bow tie.

"I like that," he said. "All blondes ought to wear red. Have I told you you're beautiful? Where have you been, Dorinda Westerly, that I haven't met you before this?"

"Well, recently I've been in England," she said.

He started to ask a question, but the waiter arrived. Billy ordered chateaubriand for two, and a Caesar salad, and asked for the wine list. After much pondering he made a selection, and once the progression of their courses began, their conversation became desultory. Billy had the appetite of an active sailor.

"The food's terrible at the house," he told her between bites. "Always chicken."

Finally they finished with chocolate mousse and coffee. Billy paid the bill and led her across the hall to an adjoining porch, where he knew at least half the customers at the long bar. As he was greeted, she recognized people who had been at the party. One crew member she remembered came up to her at once, and his manner made her suspect that he'd been drinking and not eating since cocktails. His face was flushed a bright red. Billy was accosted by a small, determined-looking brunette with a pressing question to ask him.

"Diller can tell you that, Mary Lou," Billy said, waving her toward his crew mate. "Now, Miss Westerly, what will you have to drink?"

When she hesitated he said, "Would you rather go dance? Or maybe just get out of here?"

"I am a little tired," she said, letting her eyes remain on his face.

GREEN LADY

"Hey, let's go, then."

He put his arm around her waist, waved to his friends, and started them toward the door. All the decks of the Clark Cooke house were thronged now, she saw. Some people were in elegant clothing, some in jeans or sailing gear, and everyone seemed in good spirits as they mingled together, chatting volubly.

Outside the door, the short street was full of rambling sightseers. Most of the shops were open, and under the balmy sky the outdoor bar of the Black Pearl was packed with customers. Billy did not turn toward the Port of Call; instead, his arm still around her waist, he walked her to his Porsche.

"Want to go back to the old mansion?" he asked, glancing sideways at her.

She thought of the gray gothic pile of stones beside the sea and decided that it did seem a much better idea than *Morgana*.

"Sure," she said.

She tried not to picture what he had in mind, as he put her in the Porsche and drove onto Thames Street. The sidewalks were thronged with tourists and most of the shops they passed were brightly lighted. It seemed a gay setting. The sudden bleakness of her own mood deepened in contrast, and she sat silent as Billy drove, telling herself that she was here in Newport to bring things to a head, to face the unknown at last. You're strong, she told herself. Whatever she had to do, she was ready to do. After this inward pep talk she lifted her chin.

Billy drove the Porsche through the stone pillars and up the dark driveway, parking just past the high pointed archway of the front entrance. The mansion was lit but looked deserted now. All the cars in the field were gone and only a small Chevette stood in the driveway, pulled to one side.

Billy helped her out and then looked up at the facade of the house.

"Why don't we go around here?" he said, and taking her by the arm he led her across the grass of the dark side lawn and over the stone terrace to a door connecting with a back stairway. Softly, they walked up two flights. She noticed that Billy seemed to be stepping quietly and she followed his example. Perhaps the sailors weren't supposed to have girls in their house.

At the top of the stairs he turned right, and in a moment opened the door to a small bedroom with a dormer window in one wall. The entire way she had heard no sound; the mansion seemed deserted.

Billy closed the door behind them and in the darkness turned and put his arms around her, finding her mouth with his. They kissed for a long time, and she was breathless when he lifted his head.

"Could I stay here all night?" she whispered, trying to see the expression on his face in the darkness.

"*Sure*." Sounding enthusiastic, he began to unbutton her jacket. She hung onto his shoulders as he did so. "I'll set the alarm," he said softly. "Then I can take you back to *Morgana* before anyone gets up in the morning."

He pushed the jacket off her shoulders and when it fell to the floor, she helped him find the fastening of the bow tie. In a moment more it was off and he had unbuttoned her shirt and pushed it down; as she struggled to pull it off her wrists he unhooked her brassiere and began to fondle her breasts and then to kiss them. When he got the blouse off over her hands, she felt a little uncertain of how to proceed. Should she undress him? Before she could make a move he had stripped her pants down and, bending his head, began to kiss her stomach. She felt his hot breath on her skin and she gasped. When he straightened he put his hands under her arms, lifted her up so that the trousers dropped off her legs, and transferred her naked to the bed.

She could see him outlined against the light faintly coming through the room's opened window as he stripped off his clothes in a quick, practiced maneuver. She got only a glimpse of his muscular body. In a moment he was on the bed with her and had planted a knee on either side of her waist. Without a word he tilted up her hips and thrust himself inside her. The action was so abrupt that she cried out. She had been feeling far from sexy, but oddly his silent, direct approach excited her body if not her mind. She felt herself helping him establish a rhythm between them as he bent and sucked on her right breast. He kept his hands cupped around her buttocks and she put her own arms around his shoulders, feeling his muscles tightening under her wrists. He made a soft sound and had an orgasm that lasted and lasted. She couldn't remember being with anyone who had a longer climax.

For a while afterward he held her cradled in his arms and kissed her lips and her cheeks and temples, stroking her hair with his fingers.

"Was that good for you?" he asked finally, whispering into her ear.

Without answering, she kissed his lips and then asked, "Can you lock the door?"

"No one will come in," he said softly. "I room alone." He bent his head and began to lick her nipple.

"Wait. Do you care if I lock it?"

"What?"

Swiftly she rolled her body across him and stood up.

"Hey," he said, in a complaining way.

"Just a moment." Quickly, she stepped to his door and examined it. Of heavy, old-fashioned carved oak, it had an old-fashioned lock. She twisted the knob and opened the door inward two inches, sliding her fingers over the outside of the lock.

Billy sat up and snapped on the bedside light beside him as she pulled the black key out of the outside lock. She closed the door again, locked it from inside with the key, and turned.

"Now do you swallow it?" Billy said.

"What?"

"Now do you swallow the key?" He grinned at her.

"Oh," she said. She looked down at the key in her hand, as somewhere on the floor a door slammed and she heard the voices of several men. Footsteps came down the hall, passing Billy's room. Somewhere, water started running.

"Come here," Billy said, his eyes on her naked body.

She laid the key on top of his dresser and walked back to the bed, feeling safer. The window of his room was on the third story and too high to be entered. It would be all right if she fell asleep, she thought.

"You're beautiful," Billy said, looking at her in the light. He pulled her onto the bed and against his chest and kissed her, thrusting his tongue so deeply into her mouth that she was afraid she might gag.

A sudden pounding on Billy's door made her jump so violently that her whole body jerked.

"Hey, don't panic," he whispered. Then he yelled, "Who is it?"

"Just checking—what are you doing in there?" The male voice was laughing.

"Sleeping, you bastard."

"Turn your light off, then." Whoever said this moved off, on down the hall, and there followed the sound of more running water. Billy untangled himself from her, turned off the light beside the bed, and then slid his body against her.

"Want me to make you come?" he whispered, and burrowed his face into her throat.

"No, I'm all right," she said.

"You're all right?"

"Yes." She turned, but he didn't let her go. Instead, he slipped his hand between her legs and began to play with her. She gasped. Before she had time to think, she felt herself having a violent orgasm. She had to bite the pillow under her head to keep from crying out; she squeezed her eyes shut and a wave of blackness swept over her for a moment. It was amazing! Your body could respond even when your mind was completely occupied with something else, it seemed. She shuddered and felt her legs twitch.

He said nothing, leaving his hand between her legs, and very slowly, against the warmth of his body, she began to relax. The hair on his chest tickled her back slightly, but it was comforting to feel herself being held. She was safe there with him, she thought; safe, and the door was locked.

Sometime in the night, she awoke and was startled before she realized where she was. Billy had rolled over onto his stomach and was snoring lightly, his head turned away. His snores were the only sound in the silence. A luminous spot of light attracted her attention; it was his alarm clock, reading 3:10.

Slowly, so she wouldn't awaken Billy, she slid off the side of the bed and walked over to the dormer window. Billy's room faced the sea. Beyond the lawn below, the vast dark stretch of the ocean went out to touch the dark sky, where a few faint stars and a half moon were shining. The surface of the water was only dimly lit by moonlight. Blackness was the predominant color everywhere else.

From far below, the sound of the waves breaking on the rocks could be heard. The lawn was a deserted expanse. Nothing moved out there, at all. And yet she would not have been surprised if someone *had* been there, standing and looking up at the house. She stared out for a long time, straining every sense. After a while her eyes adjusted to the darkness better, but even then she made out no more. Nothing outside moved. The only sound was the faint washing of water onto the shore and, behind her, Billy's sleep sounds. Not even a breeze stirred; there was only a subtle smell of the sea and, from the walls, a slightly musty scent, the odor of an old house with rooms that are never entered.

Billy sighed slightly and shifted his weight, and the bed squeaked. She hadn't been aware of a lot of noise during their exertions, but it had been so odd being there in the arms of a stranger that she hadn't quite taken everything in. Now she thought again that she had been very smart. Perhaps right this minute, the door to her cabin on *Morgana* was being opened. Perhaps someone was stealing quietly in and finding only her empty bed.

She groped her way over to the dresser and found the key to Billy's room. It was comforting to touch the key, to trace its old-fashioned shape with her finger. Thank God for locked doors. Her black pocketbook stood beside the pile of her clothes on the floor. She saw its shape and picked it up, feeling the hard bulge of the gun inside it. Gently, she placed the pocketbook on top of Billy's dresser, and then picked up her clothes, shaking them out and putting them over the back of a chair. Billy's things were still where he had shed them, beside the bed, but she didn't touch them. Instead, she went to the door and tried it. It was still locked; the knob wouldn't turn.

Go back to sleep, she told herself. Get all the rest you can while you're safe.

When she folded herself against Billy's body, he murmured, turned to embrace her, and after a few minutes roused himself sufficiently to slide his penis inside of her. She was surprised, but she lay still. The bed squeaked loudly until he was finished; he seemed to go through the routine in his sleep, because his eyes were closed. Musing on the sexual capacities of twelve-meter sailors, she fell asleep with his heavy body still partly covering her.

This time the ring of the alarm awakened her. At the sound Billy started, rolled toward the clock, and slapped at it until he shut if off; then he shook his head in a groggy way. Looking around, he caught sight of her and seemed almost startled. Sunshine was pouring into the room and she blinked back at him, feeling disoriented herself.

"Hey." Billy grinned at her, apparently remembering their night. She was trying to comb her hair with her fingers, sitting up and clutching the sheet to her. "Come here," he said, reaching for her.

With the realization that it was morning had come a renewal of her anxiety, and she was far from in the mood for any more sex, but her lack of enthusiasm meant nothing to Billy. After several long kisses, he dragged her to the wall for a quick encounter standing up.

"Do you think I could wash my face?" she asked as he caught his breath.

"Sure."

Hastily, she donned the tuxedo outfit again, putting the red bow tie in one pocket of the jacket. It scarcely seemed the touch for morning. She hung her pocketbook over her shoulder and took the key off the dresser and unlocked the door. Billy, meanwhile, pulled on white shorts and a T-shirt.

The bathroom a few doors down the hall was deserted. The entire household apparently was still asleep and all the doors along the hall were closed. She used the facilities, shuddering when she saw last night's mascara now under her eyes. Quickly she washed her face and after opening her pocketbook carefully so that the gun wouldn't show, put on some fresh makeup.

In a few minutes Billy led her back down the small side staircase and out the side door into a gorgeous morning. The sun was already well up in the sky, and the front of the house was washed with sunshine. The old gray stones gleamed. The grass had been heavily covered with dew and the whole expanse to the cliff sparkled brightly. A few glasses left from the party last night were scattered about and the pink tent on one side stood empty.

Both of them took a deep breath of the air, and Billy turned and gave her a sleepy smile. His eyes were bloodshot, there was stubble on his cheeks, and a hole in his T-shirt. Ruefully, she looked at her own state. The white shirt was badly wrinkled.

"*Great* weather for the races today," Billy said, looking at his wrist watch. "We'd better hurry; they'll be stirring on *Morgana*."

They climbed into his Porsche and in a moment the huge stone house was left behind. Billy drove quickly. The streets were almost unoccupied; there were several early-morning bicyclists, a newspaper truck, and a garbage collector, but the majority of the resort's citizens were still in bed.

She was silent and Billy also said nothing, apparently thinking of the day ahead. He parked beside the Clark Cooke house and walked her down to the latticework fence. No guard was in evidence as yet.

"Good luck today," she said.

"Dorinda—thank you." He spoke fervently, gave her arm a squeeze, and left her.

Morgana, as she approached, looked deserted, rocking slightly. The lines holding the yacht to the dock made faint squeaking noises; this and the crying of a flock of gulls were the only sounds in the quiet of the early hour. Taking off her slippers, she stepped on board, feeling the heat of the deck under her feet. Barefoot, she walked as silently as possible over to the open door of the salon. It was strange to feel so frightened on such a beautiful morning; the contrast of her mood with the crisp, fresh seaside air, the warm sun, and the cloudless sky was sharp. A light breeze ruffled the surface of the harbor, making small, picture-book blue waves that caught the light, dancing toward the shore. It was hard to imagine any menace in such a setting as this.

Still, the menace was there. She looked into the salon. A number of glasses and several unemptied ashtrays stood on the large cocktail table; the room was silent and empty. She walked soundlessly across the white carpet, *Morgana* rocking slowly under her feet.

At the head of the circular staircase that led down, she paused. She could hear no sounds at all, but she swung her handbag around, opened the drawstring and put her hand inside, on the gun. Then she descended.

All the doors in the corridor downstairs were closed. As noiselessly as possible, she made her way to Number Two and tried the door. It opened, and the inside of the room looked exactly as it had when she'd left it the day before. Her white pants were still thrown down across the blue-and-white coverlet of the bed, and her suitcase stood open on its rack.

After she locked the door behind her, she checked the head. It was empty. Weak with relief, she sank onto the edge of the bed in the cabin. But what had she expected? Someone hiding there, waiting for her? She sighed, and wondered how long it would be before breakfast would be served—she needed some coffee.

At least you did get some sleep, she told herself. Turning her head, she caught sight of herself in the mirror over the vanity and almost screamed, choking back the cry just in time. *God*, she thought, a wave of horror washing through her body; then she began to laugh. For a second she had been afraid someone else was in the room with her. Spooked. She was spooked.

"My God, now you're scared of yourself," she whispered. She studied her face in the mirror. There was no doubt that she looked worried and tense.

"Stop it," she said to herself. She could by no means let her nerves get into this state. Here in Newport she had a very precise manuever to carry out, she reminded herself. First, she had to find out who was after her. Second, she had to stop that person. Any way at all.

"Settle down, kid," she said to herself.

Chapter Thirteen

WHEN SHE HAD BRUSHED HER TEETH SHE felt better all over. A long shower followed. She lathered herself twice, shampooed her hair, and let hot water rinse her off for a long time, finally drying with a luxurious blue bath sheet embroidered "Morgana."

It took twenty minutes before her hair was completely dry. As soon as she shut off the hair dryer she heard noises outside. The boat's passengers were apparently stirring; she heard both light and heavy footsteps go past in the corridor. Just as she finished applying her makeup, someone knocked on the door.

"Dorinda, are you awake? Breakfast is served, upstairs."

She recognized the cultivated voice of Sebastian Ashcroft.

"I'm coming, thank you," she answered.

She had put on white pants and a red-and-white striped T-shirt; now she checked herself in the vanity mirror. Her eyes were faintly shadowed but she looked young, healthy, vibrant, she thought. Washing her hair had definitely helped. She combed through it again, fluffing it out, and then looked around for the patchwork pocketbook she'd arrived with, and transferred the gun into it from the black evening bag.

As she climbed the stairs and walked in the direction of the dining room she heard voices. The group at breakfast included her host, his wife, the Bachelors, and several others. The skipper, Kentucky, and his wife were not present, but a large stranger arose when she appeared.

"Oh, Dorinda," Sebastian Ashcroft said. "Come and meet Ed Riding."

She went over, smiling, and the man shook her hand heartily as she wondered if this could be the "Big Ed" Billy had spoken about.

"Ed is today's skipper of *Trophy*," Billy's father said when she sat down. She thought Mr. Bachelor sounded nervous; in fact, looking around the table, she could sense undercurrents of tension. Each face was too carefully noncommittal in expression.

The man she had just met smiled when she looked his way. He had a square head like a basset hound's, with heavy wrinkles at the corners of his eyes and a bald dome faintly red on top, as if sunburned.

The conversation at breakfast centered on the day's prospects, with "Big Ed" dominating the talk. Ashcroft, she noticed, was listening carefully to what the new skipper had to say.

"What did you think of the satin sheets?"

The words were repeated twice before she realized that Mrs. Bachelor was speaking to her.

"Satin sheets?"

"On your bed. All the beds aboard *Morgana* have satin sheets—didn't you notice?" Mrs. Bachelor smiled at her.

"Oh," she said, feeling herself blush. "I'm afraid I didn't."

"The sheets came with the boat. I wonder what sort of owners—"

Mrs. Bachelor was interrupted by her husband.

"Hattie, excuse me," he said. "I'm making a head count. You and Dorinda, Tucky and Coco, the Chatsworths, the Masons, who else? Oh, yes, and that Australian fellow—

GREEN LADY

Billy promised him a look at the American races and the Aussies aren't sailing today. Now, will that be all aboard *Keeper*?"

His question totally distracted his wife, and in a happy fluster she went over the list. It seemed that lunches had to be ordered from *Morgana*'s kitchen staff and various other arrangements to do with transportation had to be decided.

"Will you go with Hattie, Dorinda?" Mr. Bachelor asked. She quickly assented and finished her third cup of black coffee as fast as possible, forcing herself to eat some scrambled eggs and a piece of toast as well.

"I'm sure you probably don't get seasick, my dear, but if you'd like some Marazine?" Mrs. Bachelor said. "It makes you sleepy but at least you don't—"

"I don't usually get seasick," she said, declining with a smile.

Mrs. Bachelor made her offer to the others, and then put the bottle of pills into her satchel and led the way down off *Morgana*; the rest of her party consisted of the other wives present. A Ford station wagon held them all, and Hattie Bachelor drove to the shipyard.

As they walked toward the boats, a fresh southerly breeze was whipping at the water without actually causing whitecaps; the sky was still completely clear of clouds. Dozens of young men were dashing back and forth between the various twelve-meters and the sail sheds and buildings of the shipyard. The long dock was jammed with people. Sailors popped in and out of the hatches on board *Trophy*. She looked for Billy but didn't see him.

Several syndicate members were on *Keeper* already and came to the boat's rail to help them board. Mrs. Bachelor led her party over the deck into the salon.

"The heads are forward," she said. "One on each side. Oh, and Dorinda, come with me and take a look at this."

As she spoke, Mrs. Bachelor took her into a companionway and opened the door of the first starboard cabin beyond the salon. The room was filled with communications equipment. A switchboard covered one wall, a large computer display board was on another, and a desk held telephones and a small teletype machine. Over the control board several clocks told the time around the world. There was also a large television screen surrounded by smaller monitors. Lights blinked, ticker tape was issuing from the machine, and various devices hummed or clicked as they watched.

"My goodness, what's all this?"

Mrs. Bachelor smiled at her question, closing the door again.

"It's specially outfitted so that Mr. Ashcroft can be in constant touch with his business interests. Did you *ever*?"

Before more could be said, Tucky and Coco joined them in the passageway. The ex-skipper and his wife both appeared strained, she thought, but their faces were determinedly cheerful, and they cried hearty hellos when they greeted her and Mrs. Bachelor. Coco was a pale-faced blonde who looked as if she always wore posh dresses and could still do the jitterbug, yet her expression today was less that of a former debutante than of a tigress whose cub is threatened. Mrs. Bachelor immediately began to chat volubly with Tucky and Coco. All of them went back to the salon, talking about the weather.

In a few minutes Sebastian Ashcroft strode down the dock and swung aboard *Keeper*.

"Is Leona coming?" Hattie Bachelor inquired.

Ashcroft shook his head. "Not today," he said. "Let's go."

Under his command, *Keeper* cast off and maneuvered to a position before *Trophy*, receiving a line from her bow. The twelve-meter, which had no engine, had to be pulled to the race course by her "tender," as Mrs. Bachelor said the boat they were on was called. Big Ed waved from the cockpit of *Trophy*, and *Keeper* towed the twelve-meter out into Newport harbor. The fresh breeze still blew.

"Looks like a good day for the races."

The words were spoken in what sounded like a Cockney accent: she turned to find a freckled young man with tousled blond hair smiling at her.

"I'm Rob Meredith," he continued, pronouncing his first name like "Robe."

"Oh," she said. "Dorinda Westerly."

"I know," he responded, grinning even more widely. "Billy asked me to look you up and keep an eye on you."

"Then you're the Australian?"

"Right. I'm the tailer on our yacht, like Billy is on *Trophy*."

She smiled but could think of nothing more to say for the moment, and they watched the towing operations in silence. *Trophy* was the first twelve-meter out, leading a procession of three others that were being towed in a similar way. Rob said the race course lay seven miles out at sea.

"Let's go up to the bow," he suggested.

They took seats by the forward railing and for a few minutes she stared down at the green water as *Keeper* ran smoothly along, slicing into the waves. Behind them, the tall silver mast of the twelve-meter they were pulling gleamed in the sun. With the salty breeze in her face she began to feel a little more relaxed. They were alone in the front of the boat and Rob chatted easily, drawing her a picture of the race course and explaining the points of sailing required.

Finally the engine slowed and *Keeper* drew near an anchored cruising boat with large letters posted on her side.

"That's the Committee boat," Rob told her. "Those letters are the pairings for today. It looks like *Trophy* will sail against *Resolute* in the second start. Do you know about what's been happening? Everyone in Newport's talking about it. Billy hopes having Big Ed at the helm will make a difference in the way *Trophy* sails."

As he spoke, *Trophy* was hoisting her mainsail. She had cast off her tie to her tender, and when the huge sail filled she suddenly looked enormous.

"Majestic, isn't she?" Rob said as *Trophy* heeled over on port tack and sailed away. *Keeper* turned and followed, drawing even after a few minutes. There were shouted exchanges about the way the mainsail was setting; Big Ed at the wheel was grinning.

"Look over there, Dorinda," Rob said, directing her attention to the other three twelve-meters, all of whom had now arrived and hoisted their sails. The boats began crisscrossing each other's paths in the water, followed by their tenders, while a small flotilla of spectator boats drew around them.

Mrs. Bachelor came forward to join them as Rob said,

"I bet they'll start on time; there must be a twelve-knot breeze."

"No, the Committee always waits until they've eaten lunch," Mrs. Bachelor declared, smiling. "How about you two? I'd be glad to bring you some lunch boxes. Anything else you'd like?"

Rob jumped up. "I'll go myself. Could I bring you something, Mrs. Bachelor?"

She shook her head. "I don't usually eat," she said, her expression rueful.

After Rob left, Mrs. Bachelor lowered her voice and said, glancing toward the stern, "You know, Dorinda, everyone is very tense today. We simply *have* to win this race."

"I hope you do." She smiled at Mrs. Bachelor.

"It's awkward, with Tucky—but of course, he wants what is best for the effort. Did you know his son is married to Big Ed's daughter? His son's the navigator on *Trophy*. Tucky and Big Ed have the same grandchild—I mean, these things are always touchy but in this case—"

Rob appeared with the lunch boxes and she broke off.

"I'll leave you to eat. Dorinda, if you have any questions, I'm sure Rob can answer them." Mrs. Bachelor seemed to be implying that Rob and she would be better off on the bow and not back at the stern with the nervous syndicate members.

After Mrs. Bachelor left, Rob opened his box and assessed the contents.

"Fried chicken and those odd bread and butter sandwiches. Someone told me they always go with fried chicken in the States. Why's that?"

"I think they serve as napkins."

"Wipe your fingers and then eat them? Yankee ingenuity." He chuckled and attacked the chicken.

You ought to eat something, she told herself. She opened her box and took out a drumstick, offering Rob his choice of the rest of the contents. He ate her apple, and stored her candy bar in his pocket. She took a few bites of the drumstick.

"There's the gun for the start!" Rob said, pointing to the

GREEN LADY

Committee boat. They could see a small puff of smoke rise from her bow, and a second later they heard the report.

"Right on time. Here we go," Rob said, dropping his lunch box and standing up. "This is the most important part of a match race—the ten minutes before the start. Look at the manuevering for position."

She stood beside him to watch as *Dauntless*, a red-hulled boat, and the white-hulled *Great Republic* sailed rapidly toward each other. When they met, they circled each other, and she could hear shouted commands and the ring and crash of metal as the crews frantically worked the winches taking in the lines.

"Look at *Dauntless* try to get a death grip!" Rob cried, caught up in the action. "If she makes it onto *Republic*'s tail—there, she's got it!"

"The red boat is winning?"

"Yes." Rob looked at his wrist watch. "Only two minutes left till the start. Now—oh, look, it's a tossup."

The scene against the background of blue water was magnificent. The two yachts crossed the starting line with their bows exactly even as another gun went off.

Rob glanced away from the starting boats, and pointed out *Trophy*. "Now there's ten minutes before they start," he said. "Look at Big Ed go!"

She caught his excitement as they watched *Trophy*, now flying her jib, come toward them; suddenly *Resolute* cut into *Trophy*'s path. The finer points of the maneuvering eluded her, but she appreciated the beauty of the spectacle as the yachts circled each other like giant moths fluttering about on a summer day.

Glancing back at the stern of *Keeper*, she saw that the entire party there stood as if hypnotized, watching the two boats in silence. A gull flew over, screeching loudly; the contending twelve-meters rattled and banged, slamming from side to side, and across the water they could hear hoarse-voiced commands. Big Ed's voice was distinct. Once, *Trophy* passed close to *Keeper* and she could see four men standing in the rear cockpit, Big Ed staring straight ahead, intently steering.

The gun for the start sounded, and *Trophy* sped across

the starting line, going fast on port tack. Behind her, *Resolute* was just changing tacks, not yet having crossed the line.

"Ed wiped her off on the Committee boat!" Rob cried. "I don't believe it. What a starter that man is!"

Resolute crossed the starting line as he spoke, and someone on the stern yelled "thirty-second lead!" *Keeper* fired her engine and fell in behind the two boats. Some of the spectator fleet had gone with the first start, the two boats long gone; the rest formed a line behind *Keeper*, who with *Resolute*'s tender led the pack.

"Ed caught *Resolute* just right, you see. Broke for the line and went for glory. That was a classic start." Enthusiastically Rob recounted what they had just watched, trying to explain it to her. Meanwhile, each time one boat tacked, the other followed suit. The first leg of the race seemed to take a long time to sail. At last Rob pointed out an orange balloon in the water, and *Keeper* slowed her engine and idled as they watched the two boats approach the mark. Rob had a stop watch in his hand. *Trophy* pulled around the mark first, with *Resolute* just behind her. "Twenty-five seconds! Ed's lost five seconds somewhere."

A large white spinnaker was now blooming from the bow of *Trophy*, and Rob added, "This is *Trophy*'s fastest point of sailing—a reach. She ought to increase her lead by the wing mark."

He smiled at her, obviously enjoying his role as racing expert; she looked back at the stern and noticed that the people there now looked more relaxed. Beers had appeared in a few hands.

"The breeze is freshening," Rob said.

In a moment, she was uncomfortably aware of that. *Keeper* was hitting the waves at a slant now, instead of straight on, and the boat began to rock from side to side. She regretted the bites of the chicken drumstick. There was a greasy taste in her mouth and suddenly she was afraid her lunch was going to come right back up again.

"I think I'd better go below," she said.

Rob looked at her closely. "Can I help you?" he asked.

She protested that she'd be all right, but when she started toward the back of the boat, Rob took her arm, accompanying her. The party on the stern was too intent on the race action to notice them, except for Mrs. Bachelor, who gave her a sympathetic look. Rob helped her inside the cabin. Nausea washed through her and she could barely make her way, even with his aid. He located the head, opened the door, and gently pushed her inside.

"You'll soon feel better," he said.

Cursing to herself, she hung over the toilet bowl and lost the chicken. She hated to vomit and tears came into her eyes; this seemed like just too much. Her bag swung forward and she pushed it back, feeling the hard bulge of the gun inside. When she could manage to stand upright again, she brushed the tears from her eyes and stared at herself in the bathroom mirror. Her face looked green.

"Please, God, help me," she whispered. Her misery seemed complete; she was ill, she wasn't sure what was wrong with the situation she was in—"God, let me find out in time," she said under her breath.

In another few minutes the attack was over, and she did feel better. Taking a deep breath, she pumped the toilet clean, and in a tepid stream of water from the faucet she washed her face and then gargled. Mouthwash was in a bottle beside the sink and she borrowed a little. When her mouth felt fresher, she applied some lipstick, noticing that the boat's rocking motion was increasing. Perhaps *Keeper* was slowing down for the wing mark.

When she came out of the compartment, Rob had gone. He was probably upstairs watching the mark rounding, she thought.

She was right. Rob had joined the group at the stern, she found. He turned and grinned at her, taking her arm again.

"Feel better?"

When she nodded, he said, "*Trophy* was forty seconds ahead just now! You missed the rounding."

As he spoke, Ashcroft looked at her.

"You are bringing us good luck, Dorinda," he said. "Come and stand by me."

She obeyed and he gave her a cold smile. The engine fumes were worse in the rear, but she was not sure they were what suddenly made her feel queasy again.

Out at sea the two boats now flopped from side to side almost in unison.

"*Resolute*'s not gaining a thing," Mrs. Bachelor said in satisfaction.

"Big Ed's got that boat grooved," Rob commented. "Right in the slot, every time."

Mrs. Bachelor shot him a glance, as if she wished he wouldn't so openly praise the new skipper in the presence of the old.

"Well, I'm going to sit down," she said, taking a seat along the railing. "Won't you join me, Dorinda? Coco?"

Glad to escape Ashcroft, she took the invitation at once, and sat on the cushion next to Mrs. Bachelor. Perhaps to forestall any further sailing remarks from Rob, Mrs. Bachelor asked him about the accommodations his crew had taken in Newport.

"We're in the Beaufort house, at the end of Bellevue Avenue, just beside Bailey's Beach," Rob said. "I believe someone named McIntosh owns it."

"Oh, yes. That's just a block from your house, isn't it, Sebastian?"

Ashcroft, to whom this question was addressed, turned from his scrutiny of *Trophy* and *Resolute* to nod and seat himself across from them.

"You know Dorinda, Sebastian's rented his house this summer to the syndicate from England," Mrs. Bachelor went on. "I do hope the boys are taking care of things there."

"You live in Newport?" She was startled into asking Ashcroft the question; the fact that he was chartering *Morgana* had seemed to indicate he wasn't a native.

"It's very good of him to give the English syndicate his house," Mrs. Bachelor said. "You know, Mrs. Auchincloss used to rent out Hammersmith Farm on Cup summers."

Ashcroft had turned his attention again to the race, and as no one else was paying any heed, Mrs. Bachelor lowered her voice and continued in a confiding tone, "I think Sebastian would make a handsome governor, don't you, Dorinda?" glancing toward her host's chiseled profile outlined against the blue of the sky.

"Governor? Is he in politics?"

"My dear, didn't you know? Sebastian is running for governor of Rhode Island, and from what I see, this state needs him. Now that Newport's become such a tourist center, people are afraid the Mafia will try to make a comeback. You know, when the navy was here, the Mafia controlled the waterfront; I guess we wouldn't have known the place. But now again there's talk of legalized gambling, like Atlantic City—"

"Dorinda, want a beer?"

She realized that Rob was speaking to her only after he had repeated the question twice. Mrs. Bachelor was chatting on at her side, but her own mind had come to a complete stop. She felt chilled to the bone. Ashcroft must be Mr. Bellevue! It was suddenly clear; here, on this bobbing boat in the middle of a twelve-meter race, she had come to the truth.

"I didn't realize he was running for governor," she said softly. "He didn't mention it."

"Didn't you see my bumper sticker?" Mrs. Bachelor said. " 'Clean Up Rhode Island.' That's Sebastian's campaign slogan. He's done so much for Newport already, you know. And all along, people have been insisting that he's a born politician. Leona told me he's been urged to think about it for years. He always said no, but when the party offered to back him for governor, Leona convinced him—"

"I think this will help settle your stomach."

Rob pressed a cold beer can into her hand and she had trouble grasping it. Her fingers felt stiff, as if they belonged to someone else. This last piece of information was all she needed. Now every piece fit. If Ashcroft were Mr. Bellevue, the long-ago owner of the Carousel Club who had made his own fortune from waterfront vice, who had ordered Giotto killed; if he now had entered politics, surely he would want to make certain that there was no way he could be linked to a Mafia murder. "Clean Up Rhode Island," indeed! Good Lord, if Ashcroft was now a force against crime, he wouldn't even be able to put out a contract on the mother and daughter who could finger him. Anyone he hired to kill them might go straight to the Mafia with the information, instead. She wondered how he had engineered Bill's death—there he sat, the picture of wealth and ease, watching his elegant yacht leading in the match race, his handsome features composed, his manner seemingly imperturbable, and all along—

At least, now she knew. The fear that had held her immobile gave way to a sudden thankfulness. She was really lucky. She'd been afraid the only way she could identify the person after her would be when he made an open move to kill her. Now, she could actually plan. It had all happened right under his nose, in his hearing, if he had been listening.

In his hearing! Suddenly it struck her that she had better resume acting, and fast. She hoped she had betrayed no noticeable interest in her host's political aspirations; quickly, she asked Rob a question about the race. Where was the next mark?

"Right there. I think *Trophy*'s increased her lead again—" Rob was happy to give her some more nautical information, and Mrs. Bachelor beside her transferred her interest back to the race.

"Would you like to go up to the bow again? There will be more fumes aft on the downwind leg," Rob said.

Gratefully, she rose. She noticed that Ashcroft watched as she and Rob excused themselves and made their way back to the deserted bow of the boat.

Once *Keeper* changed direction, following the yachts, conditions on board altered dramatically. With the wind behind them, the boat was steady, and sunshine grew hot on her face as they watched the two yachts ahead making their way down the ocean.

"Is the finish soon?"

"They go downwind, then come back upwind to finish," Rob said. "The downwind leg's the nicest, isn't it?"

She nodded, letting her eyes close. The vibration of the boat's engine was soothing, almost soporific.

"Have a hard night?" he asked, sounding amused.

"Oh? What?" She opened her eyes again.

"You were almost asleep."

"No, just—thinking. Hey, look." She gestured toward two twelve-meters coming toward them.

"That's *Dauntless* and *Great Republic* going for the finish. Looks like *Dauntless* has it. Still, it's never over till the final gun."

Great Republic swept past them close enough for the blue letters reading "Great Republic" to be visible on her transom. Rob looked at the boat reflectively.

"That old tub's beaten us Aussies enough," he said.

"Do you think Australia will ever win the Cup?"

He grinned at her. "I don't tell pretty American girls such secrets." He touched her arm. "You're going to burn; do you have some suntan lotion?"

She shook her head. Softly, he stroked her forearm and then rumpled the hair at the back of her head. "You ought to wear a hat," he said. "You could get sunstroke."

She gave him a smile, wondering if Ashcroft could see them from the stern of *Keeper*. She wanted above all to appear unconcerned, like a young girl flirting, without a thought of danger. She let her eyes meet Rob's.

"What are you doing tonight, Dorinda?" he asked softly.

"I'm not sure."

"Would you like to have dinner with me?"

She smiled and nodded, murmuring, "If I can. I don't have any idea what's planned. Last night there was a party."

He moved closer to her as the twelve-meters sailed past the last orange mark, *Trophy* leading as always. Once *Keeper* turned, the smooth ride was over. The wind seemed to have piped up, and dashed spray onto the bow as they plunged ahead.

"Want to go back, Dorinda?" Rob asked as the spray hit them.

She shook her head. "I don't mind getting wet," she said.

Ahead of them, *Trophy* and *Resolute* seemed to bend forward, dashing through the waves. The sun was now low enough to send slanting light across the water, outlining each cascade of spray. The whole afternoon had passed, she realized; watching a match race was almost like being hypnotized. Time seemed to move at a special rate.

"Like another beer? Or a cocktail? I think they're drinking on the stern," Rob said. "Celebrating already."

"I'll wait," she answered. "Don't those masts look the same height to you?"

Rob stared at *Trophy* and *Resolute*.

"By God, Dorinda, you're right," he said in a startled voice.

At the same moment, from the stern, they heard alarmed voices.

"*Trophy*'s not pointing on port tack," Rob announced, squinting at the boats. "Something must have happened."

He rushed to the stern of the boat, conferred with the group there, and returned, shaking his head. Stricken expressions were on all the faces she could see.

"Tucky thinks a running backstay may have broken on the starboard side. That way, they couldn't point to port—it would put too much strain on the mast in this breeze. What a shame!"

On the stern, she saw, the syndicate members seemed to crowd together, as if for comfort, while they watched their lead melt away. She looked back, toward the drama in front of them. The shadow of *Resolute*'s sail crept up onto the immaculate white sail of *Trophy*. In a few minutes, the shadow had darkened the entire mainsail. Then *Trophy*'s sails were bright again. *Resolute* had passed her.

"Don't they make an allowance for equipment breakdown?" she asked Rob, who was groaning beside her.

He shook his head. "No. They figure, if a boat's equipment breaks down in the trials, what's to stop it from breaking during the actual Cup races? The equipment's on trial, too."

"Then—is this the end, for *Trophy*?" She spoke softly, even though no one on the stern could have heard her. "I know Billy said they had to win this race."

Just as she spoke, *Resolute* crossed the finish line and a gun sounded from the Committee boat, followed by blasting horns from the spectator fleet. *Keeper*, however, did not sound a horn.

"So close to the finish line, too!" Rob said. He looked at the stop watch in his hand, punching it as *Trophy* crossed the line in *Resolute*'s wake. "Yes," he added, looking at her as he answered her question. "Seven seconds behind. Yes, I think this is the end for *Trophy*."

On the stern of *Keeper*, there was silence. Ashcroft and the other syndicate members stood immobile, as if frozen by disbelief. In a moment, *Keeper* pulled alongside *Trophy* and they saw Billy staring glumly over at them. Big Ed transferred to *Keeper*, going immediately below with Ashcroft. The rest of *Trophy*'s crew didn't move. *Trophy* was connected to the tow line, and after her sails were dropped, *Keeper* turned toward Newport.

"Can you beat that?" Rob said. "She led all the way until the finish. That would hurt."

They had taken seats at the rail again, and she watched the late afternoon light sparkle on the water as she stared at the sea on their way in. Being at sea had seemed safe. It had lulled her. But she had to face whatever might happen now. She was head-to-head with Mr. Bellevue. Oddly, she was not so frightened as she had supposed she would be; she had something on her side. Sebastian Ashcroft thought she was a dumb young girl, a girl who had no idea he was going to kill her.

Rob's head fell forward, interrupting her thoughts. The throb of the engine on the returning boat had put him to sleep. Only when the harbor and the green shore were growing close did his head jerk upright.

"*You* must have had a hard night," she said, smiling at him.

"Not really. But I wouldn't mind one tonight; I'm all rested up, now. How about it, Dorinda?"

"I'm not—" she began, then didn't finish, as they neared the dock in the Newport Shipyard where *Trophy* and *Keeper* were berthed. A crowd was waiting. "Look at that," she murmured. "Do you think that's a TV camera crew?"

Several men surrounded a cameraman, and there were also people with tape recorders and notebooks who seemed to be waiting for *Trophy*. A group that looked like girlfriends and wives stood on the edge of the dock, Mrs. Ashcroft at their head. Her expression was dour and her cold eyes were fixed on the approaching boats. Beside her stood a young red-haired girl who held a baby. The instant *Keeper* pulled close to the dock, the red-haired girl jumped on board as Big Ed appeared from the cabin.

"Oh, Daddy," she cried. "What happened?"

"Our backstay," Big Ed answered, appearing as ebullient as he had upon starting out. He seemed to take the bad luck in stride, and reaching for his grandson, he swung him high in the air. The child screamed in delight. However, he was the only person chortling with joy as they all moved to the stern. Looking at the solid wall of persons lined up on the dock, Dorinda wondered if they could even get off the boat. A photographer shouted to Big Ed, asking him to pose at the helm of *Trophy*, and Big Ed flashed a big grin and agreed. He was still holding his grandson and he looked around; his daughter had disappeared.

"Miss Westerly?" Big Ed said. She was closest to him, of the women on board, and he gave her a smile. "Could you do me a favor and hold Bobo for a minute?"

"Of course."

He handed her the baby, who was dressed in a blue-and-white checked pair of shorts and a white shirt that had "Trophy" on its pocket.

"While you baby-sit, let me go find Billy," Rob said, stepping over to the dock and managing to squeeze past some reporters.

Jiggling the baby to amuse him, she found him to be a squirming armful. Big Ed debarked, pushed through the dockside crowd, and in a moment had boarded *Trophy*, who was being tied up just behind *Keeper*. The baby kicked her, trying to escape, but she maintained a firm grip, wondering how old he was. He seemed very strong and vigorous; he reached around her and began to pry at the opening of her pocketbook.

"No, no, sweetheart," she said, pulling the bag away from him. He made a determined effort to get it again. Finally she had to take it off her shoulder in order to hold it away from him. His big blue eyes fastened on the tie that held it closed, and he lunged for it. Having trouble hanging on to him, she looked around for help, but no one offered assistance. Mrs. Bachelor had vanished. Bobo grabbed for the bag again and she dropped it on the cushions of the banquette, trying to distract the baby by pointing out a gull on the nearby pilings.

"Birdie, birdie," she said.

GREEN LADY

"Dorinda, can you come?" Billy called to her, appearing amid the crowd beside *Keeper*. Tucky, who had been talking earnestly into a young man's tape recorder, turned at that moment and, seeing the squirming baby, said, "I'll take the young fella now. Come here, Bobo."

As the baby was lifted from her arms, Billy jumped aboard *Keeper*, took her by the elbows, and swung her over to the dock in one movement.

"You've got to see this, Dorinda," he said, pushing her forward. "The Committee's arriving."

"Wait. I left my pocketbook—"

She twisted out of Billy's grasp and turned to go back onto *Keeper* just as Sebastian Ashcroft appeared. It was the first time he had emerged from the cabin since *Trophy* lost the race, and a crowd of reporters converged on him, pushing her backward as she attempted to step over onto *Keeper*. "Damn," she said to herself, starting to push as they were jostled on all sides.

"Look. See the Committee?" Billy was saying. "They've come over in a special boat."

Someone called to Billy and simultaneously a space was cleared for the entire crew of *Trophy* to line up on the dock in front of *Keeper*. Tucky and Big Ed stood in the middle of the line. The crew members, standing shoulder to shoulder, wore smiles that were strained as their picture was taken. During this proceeding she had to be content with a perch by a piling.

Suddenly someone said, "Shhh." The crowd quieted. Looking down, she saw that a small boat filled with dark-coated men was drawing past. This, she thought, must be the Committee. A silence fell over the scene while the boat docked at the end of the pier, by the sail sheds. Then the crowd on the dock parted like the Red Sea, and six solemn-faced men, of assorted shapes and sizes, paced in single file toward them.

Her eyes swung from the dark-coated men, who seemed a delegation of doom, to Sebastian Ashcroft. He had stepped over to the dock in the last minutes, and now stood lined up with the crew, no readable expression on his face. A master at concealing his feelings, she thought, remembering his political ambitions. To his right, Tucky looked visibly upset. On Ashcroft's other side, Big Ed simply smiled.

She abandoned any thought of getting back onto the boat for the moment, noticing that Billy was trying to catch her eye. He looked less grim than the other crew members.

The Committee assembled in front of Ashcroft. In identical outfits, white shirts, black ties, black coats, and somber expressions, they resembled undertakers, she thought; all had weathered-looking faces and yachtsman's hats on their heads. A short, portly man seemed to be the spokesman for the group. He put out his hand and grasped Ashcroft's.

"We want to thank you for all your time and effort," he said, so softly that the silent crowd strained to hear his words. "You've made a magnificent effort," he went on, dropping his voice even lower. "I want to meet your wonderful crew."

A prolonged bout of hand-shaking followed, all the Committee members shaking the hands of the crew, passing down the formal line. "Oh, Dorinda," she heard a woman say, sniffing as if crying, and she found Mrs. Bachelor beside her in tears. Billy, having his hand shaken for the sixth time, began to look affected himself, she thought when she looked back at the crew. A baby started to wail and she located Bobo, now back in his mother's arms. The redheaded girl stood next to Mrs. Ashcroft, who held her head high and looked more disdainful than grieved.

Seeing the baby made her remember the pocketbook on the boat and she wondered if now she could dart across onto *Keeper*. The crew was having an official photograph taken. She decided to wait a moment, not wanting to disrupt the picture by pushing through the crew's line. *Why* had Billy grabbed her off the boat like that? she wondered in annoyance.

Later she could never remember which happened first, whether *Keeper*'s engines started up or Ashcroft turned, but before she could set foot on *Keeper*, Ashcroft had clapped Big Ed on his shoulder and jumped aboard the tender. A second later the boat moved off with Ashcroft alone on board.

She heard herself gasp. The picture taking was now suspended, and she hastily stepped to Billy's side. "Where's *Keeper* going?" she asked.

He looked surprised at the urgent tone of her voice.

"Probably taking the boss back to *Morgana*. I don't believe he wants to hang around here. What a scene! When you think of everything we've put into the effort, all summer—"

"But my pocketbook's on board! I've got to get it." Panic made her almost shout the words.

"For it *all* to go, because of a lousy backstay! Did you see how *Trophy* was sailing? Big Ed had her right in the groove, and she was—God, I can't believe it. I mean, it's *over*."

Shaking his head from side to side, Billy looked like someone in shock. Certainly he wasn't worrying about the whereabouts of her pocketbook. All the *Trophy* crew members appeared stunned, as if the afternoon's events were just sinking in. "Through. Finished sailing," a young man near her muttered in disbelief.

The Committee had re-formed its single file line and now began the walk up the dock, the crowd as before standing respectfully back on either side. As soon as their black coats were out of sight, a babble of conversation broke out. Several persons clapped Billy on the back, murmuring their regrets.

"Billy," she said, trying vainly to get his attention. All she could think about was getting the gun. She had to have it! Without it, she was helpless. She cursed fate; why had the baby been handed to her? It seemed like terrible luck. Finally she succeeded in breaking through Billy's distraction.

"Do you think *Keeper* will come back here?" she asked.

"What? Oh, I don't know," Billy answered. "I suppose so. Rob told me you two watched the race together. He's gone to see what the Aussies are doing and said to tell you he'd get in touch—but not if I can help it." As he spoke, Billy took her arm.

"Look, could we go see if *Keeper*'s over at *Morgana*?" she said, giving him as winsome a look as she could manage. "I could get my bag and we—we could have a drink."

"A drink!" That word penetrated. Billy grinned down at her. "That's *exactly* what I want! Let's go over to the Candy Store."

At that moment a concerted move down the dock seemed to testify to the same idea in many minds. The crew and their complement of girlfriends and wives started in a body to head toward a side gate.

"Well, would you mind going to *Morgana* a minute first?" she asked. "Let's see if *Keeper*'s there."

"Oh, sure," he said. He didn't let go of her as they walked through the parking lot of a small factory, across a weedy patch of ground beside an unused dock, and around another building. Then they were in the parking lot behind the Clarke Cooke house and the Candy Store.

Trying to keep from running, she hurried through the white latticework gate of the Port of Call and down the dock toward *Morgana* with Billy at her side. To her dismay, no *Keeper* was in sight.

"Where's the boat?" she asked in surprise, looking up and down the dock and over at the neighboring piers.

Billy shook his head. "She might have gone across the bay for gas, after dropping Ashcroft," he said. "The skipper usually fills her up at night, over at Goat Island marina."

"Then she'll come back to the other dock, beside *Trophy*?"

Billy nodded.

"Billy, I think I'll go back to the other dock and wait, then. Do you mind? I need—"

She was forming the words "my pocketbook" when they seemed to dry up on her lips. A figure had emerged from *Morgana*'s salon and was coming toward them. The setting sun was behind him, but she could easily tell from the outline who it was. She swore to herself.

"Dorinda," Ashcroft said. His tones were warm as he reached *Morgana*'s railing. "My dear, you're just the person I wanted to see."

Chapter Fourteen

"WE'RE ON OUR WAY TO THE CANDY STORE," she said quickly, moving closer to Billy. She wanted to be nowhere near Sebastian Ashcroft until she had her gun again.

"The Candy Store? Fine, I'll go with you." Ashcroft swung onto the pier beside her, slid his hand across her back, and clasped her lightly around the waist, all in one movement. "The greatest cure for disappointment is a pretty girl; right, Billy? It makes everything seem better."

Billy grinned at him in a friendly way; oh, where was the cold-eyed wife? As Ashcroft exerted a slight pressure on her waist with his arm, urging her up the dock, she forced herself to look up at him and smile winningly. She must act the part of an innocent and unknowing young girl, until the moment she had Ashcroft at the end of her gun. Why did she think that? Was she *really* going to kill him? The way her flesh crept at his grasp was causing her to have black thoughts; but still, realistically, what *was* she going to do? Was there anywhere she could turn for help, in time? She'd have to see what developed. Hating the way her legs were trembling under her as she walked, she told herself that Ashcroft held almost every card in this game— he had money, power, position—but he did not know that she knew why he had summoned her to Newport. He didn't know that she was aware he wanted to kill her.

It had to be he, she thought, glancing sideways at his set-looking profile. Just the few words from Mrs. Bachelor had drawn all the loose ends together. Ashcroft must think that she was the last link, the last possibility that anyone could get to the truth, uncover the facts about the Carousel Club and Giotto, and from there, God knew what else. He was going to erase that possibility, she thought, and he was going to do it himself. The arm firmly around her waist convinced her of that. If he hired someone to kill her, wouldn't it mean one more person with something on him? With a political image as a crime- fighter, he couldn't afford that. The fact that he had invited her to his yacht in Newport must mean that he trusted only himself to do the job. Bill was gone, Emma was gone—she was sure he thought that to rid himself of Dorinda would be easy.

The fact that she understood this gave her a chance, but how good a chance? She wondered if Ashcroft had always known their whereabouts. Perhaps he had been afraid of Arthur Westerly—and Arthur Westerly was dead, now. Or had he just recently had them tracked down? The thought of Bill and his death surfaced again in her mind; she could hear Bill's words in the Catherine Wheel about the others who had died—*Marilyn, and a cleaning woman, and the redhead*—don't think about that! Don't, she said sharply to herself, even as she stumbled on the cobblestones under her feet. They were almost at the Candy Store. It loomed ahead as ideas formed in her brain and dissolved again: the FBI, the CIA, the government—long before she could go to any of them, she would be dead. Ashcroft would see to that. From the way he clasped her to his side, she gathered that there would be no time for calling authorities. She was on her own. It was surprising how calmly she faced the prospect before her; maybe she had always expected it. She was going to kill him herself. She must. I'll get the gun somehow, that's all, she thought.

Billy and Ashcroft had been exchanging words about *Trophy*'s disaster as she pursued her thoughts. She realized Billy had said something to her, but she didn't know what, and she gave him a smile instead of answering. Snap out of it, she told herself. You'd better become aware of everything going on. At the door of the Candy Store she turned to look back toward the harbor. The sun was turning the water into a flat sheet of silver; the breeze had died. A boy who'd just passed them eating an ice cream cone walked toward the Port of Call, his blue-jeaned figure outlined in the shine from off the water. As she stared, she smelled the odors of cigarette smoke and whiskey that emanated from the ground-floor bar. A babble of voices emerged; cocktail hour was in full swing.

"Let's go to the bar upstairs," Ashcroft said, guiding her toward the stairs. As they walked up, Billy transferred to her free side.

"Hey, it's me," he said in a low voice. "You did it again. You looked at me on the dock that same way."

"What way?" she asked. Someone passing had stopped to speak to Ashcroft and she didn't think he had heard Billy.

"Like I was a stranger." There was a puzzled expression on Billy's face. "You do remember me, don't you?"

What he said puzzled her in turn, until she recalled the previous night. It seemed so long ago that she had actually had to think for a moment before she realized what he meant. God, her mind was really in a turmoil! She put her hand lightly on Billy's arm in answer to his question; she couldn't think of anything to say. Anyway, they had reached the bar that was on the upper porch, and she would have been required to shout over the loud, cheerful din from the crowd that jammed it, sailors and syndicate members, girlfriends and wives, spectators and New York

Yacht Club members filling every inch, all talking. Three bartenders were dashing back and forth behind the long oak bar, filling drink orders.

"Hey, there's Big Ed." Taking her with him, Ashcroft headed toward the skipper.

Big Ed turned on his bar stool and jumped up when he saw them, offering her his place with a friendly grin. She slid onto the stool murmuring thanks, grateful that the move would force Ashcroft to let go of her. However, though his hold around her waist was necessarily broken, he put his hand on her upper arm as he asked what she'd like to drink. She repressed the desire to jerk away and asked for a gin and tonic. He gave the bartender an order and then turned to Big Ed.

"Go over your start today again for us, Ed. It was magnificent."

Big Ed chuckled. "Well, I think they were a little misled by us, weren't they, Billy?" Using his hands to represent the two boats, he explained with gestures how he had used the situation to his advantage in crossing the starting line. She tried to listen, but concentration was difficult. Her mouth felt dry. She licked her lips and even her tongue felt dry. However, she was determined not to touch her gin and tonic. When the bartender put it in front of her, she ran her fingers down the wet outside of the glass and touched her lips, wondering how soon she could excuse herself and go back to see if *Keeper* was docked beside *Trophy*. Could she get back inside the Newport Shipyard without Billy? She decided to ask him to come with her.

Finishing the discourse on his start, Big Ed drained his glass and waved to the bartender.

"Billy—" she began, but at the same moment Billy asked Big Ed, "Did you get to watch the start of the first race, sir? How did *Republic* wiggle out of the death grip?"

Big Ed's face lighted.

"Wasn't that beautiful?" he said. Again, he demonstrated with his hands, angling them back and forth to describe the maneuver. When he finished he ordered more drinks for them all, not noticing that she hadn't touched hers. Throughout Big Ed's remarks, he had to stop to speak to people who came up to commiserate with him and Ashcroft. "Too bad about *Trophy*," was on all lips.

"Billy, could you and I go down to the dock now and see if *Keeper* is back?" she murmured when Ashcroft was distracted by a sympathizer.

"What? Sure." Billy immediately agreed, but as she started to rise, Big Ed's daughter, now without Bobo, and Tucky, his wife and son suddenly emerged from out of the crowd.

"Daddy, we've been waiting and waiting!" the red-haired girl said to Big Ed. "We've actually got a table here big enough for the whole syndicate; but where is everyone?"

"Oh, we'll come right away." Big Ed's voice was somewhat slurred; he seemed to have been drinking quite steadily. Murmuring "Dorinda," Ashcroft took her by the arm.

"We'll join you all in a few minutes," she said, trying to sound firm. "Billy and I have to go back to Newport Shipyard."

"What? Why's that?" Ashcroft looked sharply at her, his hand not releasing her arm.

"I left my pocketbook on board *Keeper*," she said. "It shouldn't take long—"

"*I'll* go with Dorinda, Billy," Ashcroft said.

For a second she was panicked. How stupid she had been! The last thing she wanted was to go anywhere alone with Ashcroft! She opened her mouth to say, "Never mind, I'll get it later," but fortunately she was forestalled. Tucky's son had overheard their words and now he said to Ashcroft, "Pardon me, sir, but *Keeper* won't be back yet. When she returned from fueling, Dad sent her over to Jamestown to the Swedes. Remember that line they borrowed from us? Since we'll be packing up in the morning, he didn't want to forget to collect it."

There was a God, she thought, looking at Tucky's son in silent gratitude. He glanced at his wrist watch.

"*Keeper* should be back in an hour or so, Miss Westerly," he said, smiling at her.

Telling herself to remember she was walking through a mine field, she slid off the bar stool. With Billy on one side and Ashcroft pressed to the other, she made her way through the crowd, across the vestibule, and into the Clark Cooke house restaurant. The candles burning steadily under the large hurricane lamps lit the beams of floor and ceiling with a mellow glow. Ashcroft can't do anything at dinner, she told herself. Relax. Use the time to collect yourself. You almost goofed everything there.

Ashcroft's face after he seated her was inscrutable. She repressed the desire to shudder as he took the place next to her. Just as she was wondering where his wife might be, Mrs. Bachelor arrived with news of her.

"Leona is dining at Spouting Rock with the Potters," she said, dropping into a chair opposite her son. "She told me to say they didn't feel up to this scene. My, it is a madhouse here." Mrs. Bachelor went on to ask Billy about "that nice Australian boy, Rob," and for a while Mrs. Bachelor and Billy provided most of the conversation.

Under the table, Sebastian Ashcroft let his leg drift over toward hers, almost touching her, and she wished that she could hitch her chair closer to Billy's on her other side, but she forced herself to smile sweetly and sit still. They ordered from the elaborate menus, waited what seemed an interminable length of time for the courses to begin arriving, and finally got hors d'oeuvres. Her appetite was at zero but she made herself eat a few bites, for strength later. Pretty obviously, she was going to need it.

The hour *Keeper* would take to return had passed several times over before they finished dessert and coffee. At this point she had still not completely decided what to do. She could at any time have said she was going to the ladies' room, of course, but just running over to Newport Shipyard wouldn't get her past the guarded gate. She doubted that the people in charge there would go get the pocketbook for her; what proof would she have that it was hers? And what if anyone looked inside? She had to get Billy to accompany her.

When dinner was completed at last, Tucky invited them all over to the bar for brandy, or whatever they liked, and they moved in a body back to the porch. People at the bar now looked the worse for wear.

On their way in she felt Ashcroft's arm again encircling her waist.

"I'm afraid there's nowhere to sit," she said. She smiled at Billy. "Maybe we could go downstairs and dance for a while."

"Sure—" Billy began eagerly, but Ashcroft's arm tightened.

"No, you don't get away. You're my consolation prize."

Billy's protesting glance at her was cast under the protection of another crew member's crowding up to ask Ashcroft how long the syndicate house would stay open. There was a general discussion, joined by several other *Trophy* sailors; the room seemed packed with people connected to the *Trophy* effort.

"Where are the Australians tonight?" she asked, looking over the crowd. There was a sprinkling of T-shirts advertising the presence of almost every other twelve-meter.

"The Aussies have a team meeting on Thursdays; they'll come in later," Billy said. As he spoke, the small brunette of the night before appeared at his side.

"Your parents told me where to find you," she said, flicking her dark eyes over him.

Billy bent his head to catch her words, in the noisy room, and in a moment he was deep in conversation. Ashcroft, still holding her by the waist, was talking about the details of *Trophy*'s imminent departure from Newport. Amid the din, in the darkness of the smoky, talk-filled room, she suddenly found herself unable to keep standing there doing nothing. She had to make a move.

"Where is the ladies' room?" she asked the bartender when she could catch his eye.

"In the hall downstairs," he answered.

"Excuse me, I'll be right back," she said.

"Ladies' room?" Ashcroft said, catching her words. He interrupted his conversation with one of the other syndicate members. "It's on the way downstairs, my dear, so why don't we go on and dance? Big Ed, my little girl wants to disco."

Big Ed was far gone and did not seem to take any particular notice of this; the brunette had Billy trapped for the moment.

"I'll join you soon," Billy murmured under his breath as she was led off.

Going down the stairs, Ashcroft stumbled slightly, and she wondered if he were feeling the drinks he had consumed before dinner. Like her, he had turned down both wine with the meal and brandy afterward.

When he had to let go of her, at the door of the ladies' room, the relief she felt at being released was overwhelming. Don't be so jumpy, she said sternly to herself, closing the door behind her. She had no particular plan in mind with regard to the ladies' room, but if she had, it would have been doomed to failure. There was no window; the room was as small as a closet. In the mirror over the wash basin she checked her face. Her eyes stared back at her, opened wide and with enormous pupils. My God, she looked frightened! Trying to steady herself, she took deep breaths. A plan will come to you, she said to herself. Calm down.

Someone knocked on the door and a woman's voice called, "Is somebody inside?"

When she stepped out she had only the faintest of hopes that Ashcroft wouldn't be there. He was leaning against the wall in the hallway, talking to a young couple sitting on the stairs.

"See you later," he said to them. "This young lady and I are going dancing."

There was a line of persons waiting to get into the disco, but the man in charge recognized Ashcroft and immediately ushered them downstairs, despite a woman's voice lifted in complaint. "We were next—"

The reason for the line became clear as they descended. The small, dark room below was jammed with people. It looked as if someone would have to come out before anyone else could get more than a step inside. Music blasted from the speakers and dozens of dancers gyrated on the tiny dance floor. A long bar with dim Victorian glass lamps could be glimpsed at one end.

Ashcroft pushed into the throng, pulling her with him. A waitress squirmed her way around the dance floor and asked him for his order. He shouted something into her ear. Then suddenly space opened between some of the dancers as a slow piece came on, and Ashcroft cried, "Here we go, Dorinda." He grabbed her by the waist and pulled her to him, and they swayed back and forth together. There wasn't room to do more.

All right, she thought to herself. Here you are. It's obvious that he isn't going to let you go off alone. You have to face that. You have to forget the gun—

The panic that rose in her at this thought had to be swiftly controlled. She needed the gun! Well, then, put your mind on it, she said to herself. How can you get it? Is there anything in this situation you can take advantage of?

As Ashcroft pressed his body to hers, an idea began to form at the back of her mind. For a moment, she weighed the risks. Then she made up her mind.

"Do you know what I'm thinking?" she said into Ashcroft's ear, licking her mouth with her dry tongue and pulling her head back to gaze directly into his eyes, her lips almost touching his.

"What are you thinking, sweetie?"

She didn't answer at once, but let her lips brush his lips lightly, suppressing a shudder at their touch.

"Well, shall we go back to *Morgana*?" he said, squeezing her tightly to him. She could feel the bones in his legs, and the hard bulge where his penis pressed against her pelvis.

"What about your wife?" she murmured into his ear.

"Never mind about her."

"But you know what I thought yesterday, when I saw all those sail bags on *Trophy*?" She made her voice breathy, and tried to sound excited. "I thought, what a super place to make love. Did you ever do it?"

"Do what?" He stared intently into her eyes.

"Make love on board *Trophy*? That's what I want to do. Don't you?"

Ashcroft chuckled. "There's a night watchman, sweetie. Although tonight he's probably gone or drunk. Do you really mean it? Wouldn't you rather go back to *Morgana*?"

She shook her head.

"I want to be able to say I did it on a twelve-meter." She managed to put a young, guileless, almost petulant tone into her voice.

He rubbed his body against hers.

"All right," he said. "Fine."

The slow piece ended. He had turned her, while they danced, so that a light shone directly into her eyes, and she couldn't see the expression in his face. From the bar, the waitress was fighting her way toward them with a bottle of champagne and two glasses. Ashcroft pulled some money from his wallet, put it on the waitress's tray, and said, "Want to leave now?"

Gratefully, she nodded. The last thing she wanted was to have to pretend to drink champagne. There was nowhere to sit down, anyway. A fast piece started and they quickly maneuvered off the dance floor and, turning sideways, squeezed up the stairs. Jostled and shoved in their exit, they finally made it.

"Good night, sir," the doorman said in respectful tones as they passed him.

After the noise and bustle it was almost disorienting to step outside. The night was black and the salt air warm. Down the short cobblestone street tourists were still wandering, looking into the windows of the lighted shops. Long ago, this had been Blood Alley; the thought darted through her mind and was gone, a silent lightning-strike. Put your mind on this moment, she said to herself. Behind them, the porches of the Candy Store buzzed with conversation. Someone laughed wildly; glasses clinked. She glanced back at the bright windows. Suddenly it seemed as if all safety had been left behind. *She was alone with Mr. Bellevue.* Steady, she told herself.

They walked through the parking lot and, his arm again around her waist, he guided her past a factory building with dark windows.

"This is the way to the side gate," he said.

He couldn't just kill me here, she told herself, surprised at how coolly she could think those words. Her mind seemed to be working well, seemed almost to be picking up signals from his. If he tried to kill her here, he'd have to carry her too far. He definitely couldn't just leave her dead. They had been seen together all night. No, he was intending to get rid of her entirely. Then he could announce "Dorinda went back to New York early this morning—" In all of tomorrow's confusion, people going off in every direction, undoubtedly no one would question that she had left. He'd have to get rid of her car—

Her thoughts chilled her so much that she was afraid she might have shivered, and to cover up, she pressed against Ashcroft's side and, lifting her lips, softly kissed his cheek. His arm tightened around her as they traversed the uneven ground in the darkness. The water in the harbor on their right seemed a black sheet of nothing, faintly luminescent under the dark sky. Little ripples lapped softly at the edge of the weeds under their feet; the soil was boggy. Panic rose another degree in her, but she managed to walk calmly, as if nothing were the matter. At last they reached the gate in the chain link fence that surrounded the shipyard.

"Here we are," Ashcroft said. He seemed to be breathing a bit hard, although they had not walked quickly. A light was on in a nearby shipyard building and she could see that the gate was chained and locked.

"We can't get through," she said. Her voice sounded funny in her own ears, too high-pitched. She laced her right hand through the links of the fence, and put her left arm firmly around Ashcroft's waist. She didn't want him to see her hands shaking with fright.

He smiled, not quite meeting her eyes with his.

"I have a key." He fumbled in his pocket and pulled out a key ring. Her sensation of relief when he took his arm from around her was again so sharp that she clutched the fence to keep from falling. She hoped Ashcroft thought she was drunk. He held the key ring up to the light and searched for the small key that fit the padlock.

"I think it's this one," he said. In a moment, the key had clicked the padlock open, and he removed the chain. The gate squeaked loudly as it swung forward under his push. Smiling at him, she stepped through. He followed, rechaining the gate and fastening the padlock; as he did so, she took a few steps until she could see down the pier. The first two boats were an Australian twelve-meter and its tender, tied side by side. Past them she spotted *Trophy* and with a rush of relief she saw that *Keeper* was there, too, docked beyond *Trophy*! There was a light showing from *Keeper*'s cabin, but no sign of anyone on any of the boats. The pier itself was deserted and silent.

Ashcroft said something as he walked toward her, but she didn't hear what it was.

"I'll be back in a minute," she said quickly, moving before he could reach her. Her voice sounded shrill; she attempted to lower it, adding, "I left my pocketbook on the deck of *Keeper* this afternoon, remember? I'll just run down and get it—"

As she spoke, she broke into a run without waiting to see what Ashcroft would do. She had only one thought now: get the gun.

She sprinted over the uneven boards of the pier, past the long white shape that was the Australian twelve-meter. "I'll just be a minute," she called back over her shoulder, turning her head for only a second.

He didn't answer. He wasn't chasing her, unless he could run like an Indian. She heard no footsteps behind her as she ran. "Dear God," she prayed, "Please just let me—"

A bullet ripped through her body from back to front, catching her in mid-stride. She was close to the edge of the pier, and when her right foot came down it turned under her and she fell sideways onto *Trophy*.

She heard rather than felt the crash of her body on the deck of the twelve-meter. The impact of her fall tumbled her over once and then she fell further, into one of the open hatches on the deck.

Pain more intense than any she had experienced pierced through her. She wanted to scream in agony, but she felt shock follow the pain like a wave that engulfed her totally. Her back smashed against something. She felt that, then nothing more. Only her eyes worked. They saw her arms flung wide against the sides of the compartment, saw her legs in a split—one down and one stuck straight up out of the hatch. She was like a rag doll that has been violently thrown into a toy box.

The boat trembled. Someone stepped on board. In the dim square above her she saw the silhouette of Sebastian Ashcroft. He was holding a gun that had something attached to its muzzle. A silencer, she thought. There had been no sound when she was struck.

She wondered if he were going to squeeze the trigger again.

He stared at her.

She's dead, she thought to herself. She felt as if she were watching the scene from a little way above it. "She's dead, you bastard! You killed her!" she wanted to scream. "You won."

But she could make no sound. The expression on his face was unreadable. What little light there was came from behind his head and she could barely make out his features. She stared blankly at him. He withdrew his head, dropping the gun into his pocket.

"Oh, just having a look around," she heard him say. He laughed. Someone had come down the pier. She heard a woman's voice; then a man's. They were standing beside the boat, talking to him; she heard the woman laugh. He stepped off the boat and walked a way down the pier with them. She could hear their voices retreating. *Scream*, she begged herself. Tears came into her eyes with the effort she made, but no sound emerged. She was immobilized, feeling as though pinned through the middle by a red hot poker.

The boat trembled again. She saw his head outlined once more against the square of light above her. He stared down. After a minute, apparently satisfied that she hadn't moved, he withdrew his head. She heard him drop into the rear cockpit two feet away and go past her compartment into the bowels of the twelve-meter.

What was he doing?

Her mind worked as if it were out of her body, detached from the leaden, pain-filled physical parts of her. She heard a strange sound in the stillness. It was a soft sound, repeated over and over, a dragging sound as of heavy material being pulled out of something. She heard a grunt. He was working hard. But why?

She hadn't been breathing—suddenly, she realized it. She gasped. She wasn't dead. She took deep breaths.

The dragging sound was terrifying. But what was it? How could it be frightening, if she didn't know what it was? She struggled for air, filling her lungs deeply. The sound went on, a regular pulling, like—

Abruptly, she knew what it was. It was someone pulling

a huge sail out of a bag. It was Sebastian Ashcroft; he was going to pull a sail out of a bag and put her into it, instead. He could carry the sail bag on board *Keeper*, start the engine, run out into the bay, and drop her overboard. A piece of the twelve-meter's heavy equipment would carry her to the bottom for good. She would be gone without a trace.

She was forgetting to breathe again. She forced air into her lungs. Could she feel anything? Her right leg must be broken or wrenched, the leg that stuck up the hatch. The left leg was bent strangely, too. And her arms. Did she have any feeling in them? She took inventory. The back of her left hand felt cold, colder than the rest of her. Either it was already dead or it was resting on something cold. She concentrated. Her hand lay against something slippery and cool, something in the shape of a tooth.

A tooth. The marlinspike! The cold steel tooth. So slowly that it seemed to take millennia, she turned her head. In the faint light from above, she could make out the leather strap nailed to the side of the hatch, the strap that held the tailer's equipment, the knife, and the marlinspike.

The dragging sound went on without pause.

She begged herself for strength. She drew a deep breath, willed it, and amazingly her right arm slowly lifted, moved over, and touched her left hand. With both hands she managed to grasp the large, heavy spike and pull it up out of the holster.

She tried to straighten her body. The pain that shot through her was so excruciating that after the first shock she felt nothing more. She was numb. She pulled up her left foot and braced it against the hatch flooring. Then she stiffened her body and pulled her right foot away from the edge of the hatch. She bent her knee and drew the foot down.

With both feet beneath her, she stopped. The sound from the front of the boat continued. Ashcroft hadn't heard anything. Holding the spike in her right hand, she put both hands up onto the deck. Her feet, first one and then the other, found the rungs of the ladder on the side of the hatch. The hatch wasn't deep—only a little more than waist-high. It didn't take as much effort as she feared to drag herself up out of it.

Once she was up and crouched on the lip of the hatch, she rested. She was perched on the small strip of deck between the tailer's compartment and the large open-back cockpit. As she gasped for air, the dragging sound stopped. The boat moved slightly. He was coming aft.

She grasped the marlinspike in both hands. She couldn't straighten up from her crouch but she managed to raise the spike.

When Ashcroft ducked up into the cockpit, she threw her body down, diving off the deck, the heavy spike seeming to carry her with it. She aimed it for his chest and just before she lost consciousness, she felt it sink deep. He let out an amazed cry as she fell on him.

Six hours later, the sun came up.

Rusty Babcock walked through the front gate of the shipyard with the first of the shipyard workers. His parents were in the *Trophy* syndicate, and Rusty loved the boat. All summer, he had been allowed to help out with odd jobs around the dock and to run errands for the crew. He had taken a lot of photographs of *Trophy*, both docked and sailing. Now, he wanted to take the final pictures of her, with her silver mast gleaming in the early morning light, before her mast was taken out and she was towed out of Newport. Someone had told Rusty that the boat would be dismantled right away. Not knowing the condition *Trophy*'s crew had drunk itself into the night before, Rusty was afraid they might start early.

Passing the Australian twelve-meter, Rusty wondered if she were as fast as the Aussies claimed. He stopped beside her bow. A good breeze rippled the water of the bay and ahead, *Trophy* bobbed gently, riding her broken white reflection. Rusty backed up and took five shots of her at medium range. Then he approached her.

A minute later he rushed down the dock, yelling. Two Australians just arriving intercepted him. Everyone knew Rusty. His eyes were wide and his face red with excitement. He was babbling.

After taking a quick look at the cockpit of *Trophy*, the Australians joined Rusty in running for help. A crowd of workers and the policeman from the front gate came back with them. Their report turned out to be true. There were bodies in the cockpit of *Trophy*. A girl's body lay on top. Her blood had soaked into the clothing of the man beneath her, and his blood had soaked into the sail bags beneath him and collected in a pool beneath the floorboards.

The man was quickly identified as the head of the *Trophy* syndicate. He was dead.

When they lifted the girl off his body, she moaned. None of the men remembered seeing her before; Rusty was as ignorant as they. She was still alive when the ambulance reached Newport Hospital, and she was entered as patient Jane Doe. It was afternoon before she was identified as Dorinda Westerly.

PART III

Chapter Fifteen

"DORINDA?"

She heard her name. Paul had climbed down into the bed and was gently shaking her by the shoulder. It was warm under the covers and she had been asleep for only an hour. She resisted opening her eyes but he shook her more insistently and finally she came to.

"Oh, hi," she said, squinting at Paul in the light from the reading lamp he had turned on over the bed. The light was behind his head and, not seeing his expression, she assumed he had just come in from the theater and was waking her to make love. She lifted her arms to his shoulders, ready to be embraced.

"Dorinda, I've got some news," he said softly. He didn't move toward her as she expected and she blinked, changing her position so she could see him. Paul's face was very grave.

"What is it?" she asked, alarmed.

Paul was wearing a sweater and jeans, the way he always dressed to come home after a performance, and he had a newspaper clutched in one hand. For a moment, he seemed to ponder how to proceed, and her vague uneasiness escalated.

"Tell me right away," she said, sitting up.

"It's your mother, Dorinda."

"*Mother*? What is it? Have we heard from her? Where's—"

"Wait a minute, honey." She seized Paul by the arm and he put his hand on her hair, as if to soothe her. "It's not good news—not entirely good."

"What do you mean? Paul, tell me quick."

"She's in the States, in Newport. In a hospital. The operator's getting the hospital number for us now."

"How do you *know*?" she cried, staring at his face.

"I read it in tomorrow's *Times*." He indicated the newspaper he was holding. "I'll show you the story in a moment. But first—"

Before he could continue, the telephone beside the bed rang and Paul picked up the receiver.

"I see," he said, writing a number on a pad. He broke the connection with the operator and punched the numbers on the dial.

"Dorinda, be prepared," he said as the call went through. She was still kneeling beside him, unable to move. "The newspaper story said she was in critical condition from a gunshot wound."

"A gunshot wound! My God, why? Why is she in *Newport*?"

He shook his head. Faintly, she could hear the hospital answering on the other end.

"Can you tell me the condition of the patient Dorinda Westerly?" Paul said into the receiver.

Dorinda's mouth opened in amazement. Putting her hand on Paul's arm, she started to object, but he shook his head again as he listened intently.

"Good," he said. "Please transfer me." There was a

pause, and he repeated his request. Dorinda was unable to do anything but stare at Paul. He listened, then seemed to relax his stern expression slightly. "I see," he said. "I'm speaking for a relative of Miss Westerly's. We're in London; we'll get to Newport just as fast as possible. If there is any doctor you need to call, anything she needs, please do it for her. Could we speak to her doctor? I see. We should be there tomorrow, easily; that is—how far are you from New York? Oh, I see. Yes, we'll be there. Thank you."

He hung up the telephone and looked at Dorinda.

"She's alive. She's still critical." He lifted the receiver again and started punching buttons. "I've got a friend in a travel agency—remember Beatrice? I'm calling her; she'll help us."

Dorinda still stared at him blankly as he began to speak again.

"Beatrice, it's Paul Innowell; did I wake you? Oh, good. Look, we have an emergency. We've got to get to New York immediately. Can you find the first flight—will a Concorde be leaving tonight? Whatever's fastest. And could you arrange a charter plane to fly us to Newport— that's—where is it?" He said the last to Dorinda.

"Rhode Island," she heard herself say.

He repeated it into the phone.

What was happening suddenly began to register on her. Her *mother*—dear God, she prayed, don't let her die. Please.

"I see. And have a car standing by at that airport. Dorinda's mother is in critical condition in a Newport hospital and we must get there. Thank you, Beatrice."

He hung up. "We have to wait till morning. I'm sure Beatrice will get us on the first flight."

"Paul, what *is* in the paper?"

He looked down at his hand, and let her take the newspaper out of it. It was open to page four and she sat back against the pillows, quickly scanning the columns. There seemed nothing until she reached "Magnate Slain on Cup Yacht." Her eye caught her own name in the first paragraph and she exclaimed out loud.

"I tried to warn you," Paul said, sliding down to sit beside her. "They think—they think your mother is you."

"Me? But *why*?" Dorinda looked from the newspaper page to Paul.

"She wanted it that way. It was her plan before she left. Dorinda, she went to Miami Beach and had some plastic surgery done to make her look like you, or something like you."

"My God! You knew this? You mean, she hasn't been here at all?"

"I knew—I—she called me twice from over there. She was afraid to keep in close touch, but she called once from Miami Beach, and then just after she went to New York, to your apartment, as you. She went to New York to see if anyone was interested, if anyone would try to contact you."

For a few moments Dorinda was too flabbergasted to think of another question.

"She hasn't been in England!" she cried at last, repeating the strange news.

"No. When she left Ibiza she went straight to America."

"But, Paul. Why did she let me think she'd come here?"

"She didn't want you to know she was leaving you. She wanted you to feel that you would be safe."

"But then, why did she go to America? Why pretend to be me?"

Paul took both her hands in his, looking earnestly into her eyes.

"You know she was terrified that you were both in danger from someone," he said. "She thought if she went back to the States to investigate, and she were killed, that they would come looking for you. She was afraid that if he—they—whoever it was, existed, they might be able to find you no matter how hard you tried to hide. But she said that if she could make the person believe she *was* you, then if he did get to her and kill her, he'd think he'd killed you, and you'd be safe. She told me that if that happened, if 'Dorinda Westerly' were reported dead, that I should explain everything to you and say that it was what she wanted for you. That you would be safe."

Paul spoke these words in low tones, with a serious expression on his face.

"God!" Dorinda cried. For a moment she had no breath. "That's why she faked the drowning?"

"Yes. She said the person might not believe that Emma Westerly was dead, that they might hunt for *her* later, but of course they'd never find her, and they would never look for you if they believed they had killed you."

"Oh, my God, Paul." Tears began to run down Dorinda's face.

"But she's not dead, darling. She may be all right. We'll be there soon."

"Oh, please dear God. She has to be all right." Dorinda bent her head and said a prayer for her mother. The clawing feeling of helplessness inside her was eased a little, after a few moments. It would be all right, she told herself. She looked back at the newspaper story, this time reading it as Paul sat beside her, his arm around her shoulders.

"Paul, it says here that a man is dead. A man who lives in Newport. Do you think that he was the man who was after us?"

"Dorinda, I think—wouldn't it have to be? I mean, why else—"

She looked again at the story. It said that the police could supply no motive for a fight, but that it was assumed Sebastian Ashcroft had been killed by Miss Westerly in self-defense. A weapon was found, the marlinspike that had inflicted Ashcroft's injury, and her fingerprints were on it. The nearly fatal gunshot wound that had put her in Newport Hospital had been caused by a bullet from a gun owned by Ashcroft, who was the head of the *Trophy* twelve-meter syndicate that had built a candidate for the America's Cup this summer. Ashcroft's gun, along with some weights, had been found inside a sail bag that he was grasping. The police conjectured that he had shot Miss Westerly and was making preparations to put her into the sail bag when she managed to stab him. She was still unconscious and not able to be questioned.

The last paragraph detailed the fortune and widespread international holdings of Sebastian Ashcroft, who had recently entered politics and was a candidate for the governorship of Rhode Island in the election to be held that fall. "Dorinda Westerly" was identified only as a New Yorker who had been visiting the yacht owner.

The fact that the twelve-meter yacht *Trophy* had been

excused on Wednesday from further trials for the America's Cup defense was mentioned in the last sentence.

"I don't know what to think," Dorinda said when she finished reading the story.

"I'll tell you what I think," Paul said, giving her a squeeze. "I think your mother did exactly what she set out to do. She is one fantastic actress. When she first told me her plan I thought she was crazy, but she really convinced me. She told me why the man was after you—she told me everything. Of course I objected; I said it was too much risk—but she wouldn't listen. She said her life wasn't worth anything if she couldn't believe you would be free of fear. She's the most remarkable person I've ever known."

"But could they do that? Make her look like me?"

"I suppose they could make a version of you that would fool people who didn't know you."

Dorinda shook her head. "It's just amazing," she said. "I can't—she must have bleached her hair, and—"

"The whole thing took time, I know. She—"

The telephone interrupted him and Paul grabbed it.

"Beatrice?" he said. "I see." He glanced at his wrist watch, listening to what she was saying. "We'll be sure to do that. And at Kennedy we do what—Air Charter Inc. desk, all right. Yes, I've got an International Hertz card. You will? Wonderful. Beatrice, thank you—yes, *The Starling*'s turned into a big hit, I'll send you tickets."

He listened a moment longer and then hung up and turned back to Dorinda, who hadn't moved.

"Okay, an eight-thirty Concorde—we have to pick the tickets up an hour early so we must start out by six, not too long from now. There'll be a plane waiting to fly us to the airport in Newport, and a Hertz car from there. Beatrice says to tell you she hopes your mother is better."

Dorinda felt tears come into her eyes again.

"Thank you, Paul," she said. "What about you?"

He grinned. "Tomorrow's Sunday, you know, the theater is dark. If I don't get back, though, on Monday night Donald Snee will have the chance of his life. He's been dying to do my part. Reminds me, I must call Reggie."

While he made this call, Dorinda tried to sort out her thoughts. At least she knew where Emma was now. All the uncertainty was ended. But ended in such a way! She squeezed her eyes shut and prayed again, over and over, that her mother would not die.

When Paul hung up, she had a final question for him.

"Remember when you proposed to me? Was that why?"

"Was what why?"

"Remember, when I got so upset and said I was going home? I was packing, remember? And you begged me not to, and asked me to marry you. Was it all just to keep me from going back to New York and spoiling everything?"

Paul gave her a brief grin. "Darling, any time you will marry me, I will marry you," he said. "You know that. I love you."

"I think you must." She gave him a smile. "You're being wonderful, Paul. But you *did* keep me from going home; admit it."

"What I wanted was to keep you safe. If your mother could do so much, surely I could do a little, too. Oh—that reminds me, Trevor's going to want to know this news. He's been asking me constantly how Emma is coming along. He knew just a bit about what she was going to do, and he's been nervous. I should call him."

"Wait," she said. "Do you still have the hospital number? Let me call again, and give them this number, in case—well, in the next hours—" She felt tears come into her eyes again. "Oh, she *has* to be all right!" she cried.

"Hang on," Paul said. "We'll be there soon."

It did not seem soon, and yet the trip to the airport, the Concorde flight, the hour in the chartered plane, the drive to the hospital through heavy rain kept her occupied, moving, at least. It was only ten in the morning, Newport time, when they entered Newport Hospital. As they came out of the revolving door, Paul put his hand on Dorinda's arm.

"Look, let's say you are her sister. It will avoid a lot of confusion and explanation—don't you think?"

"That's a good idea."

In a minute, Dorinda was at the reception desk.

"I'm Miss Westerly's sister," she said. "How is she?"

The woman behind the desk checked the wheel of cards before her.

"She's in the intensive care unit," she said. "You'll have to speak to the nurse there about whether or not you can visit her."

At least she was still alive! Dorinda couldn't believe she was about to see her mother. The receptionist gave them directions, and they got into an elevator. It seemed to take forever to reach the floor with the intensive care unit; Dorinda's heart beat heavily and she was grateful for the support of Paul's hand.

They walked down a long corridor until they reached a nurse at a desk in front of a window lashed by rain. The nurse picked up a telephone and said something. After a few minutes a motherly looking, middle-aged woman came out of the intensive care unit beyond.

"Miss Westerly?" she said to Dorinda. "You're her sister? I can tell that. You look exactly like her. Yes. You can come in. Your friend—" she glanced up at Paul, "—had better wait out here. She hasn't yet regained consciousness."

"But how is she? Will she be all right?" Dorinda asked.

The nurse hesitated. The pause wasn't long, but it seemed to Dorinda that it lasted hours. Finally, the nurse spoke.

"The bullet did not hit any vital organs. Your sister's principally suffering from shock and the bleeding she did before she was found. She has been operated on; the bullet was removed. If there aren't any further complications, she has a chance."

"A chance." Dorinda repeated the words. They were puzzling; she couldn't seem to understand what the nurse was saying. "Please let me see her."

Giving Paul one glance, she followed the nurse through a heavy double door and down a short corridor. There, in a cubicle without a door, a form lay on the bed.

Dorinda walked in. Although she knew what to expect, a shock went through her as she looked at the person lying there. The pale face, with its eyes closed, was a ravaged version of her own. The scars from the plastic surgery, if there were any scars, were hidden up in her hairline or somewhere; they weren't visible. Still, for all the roundness of her cheeks, Emma lying there did not look young. She looked a sort of indeterminate age, and she was as white as a marble statue. A sheet covered her body but Dorinda could see the outline of bulky bandages around her abdomen. Tubes and sensors connected her to monitors and bottles. Her right hand lay on the outside of the sheet and as Dorinda stared at it, it seemed all that was left of her mother that she could recognize.

"Mother," she said, taking the hand, terribly afraid.

Emma did not know where she was, except in darkness. A smooth wall stretched around her in a circle and she could find no door anywhere that led out. Some part of her senses still worked, felt, moved along to find any crack in the dark sides of this world that encased her and trapped her. A man was trying to wake her, or had tried long ago.

"Hello! Wake up now! Hello!" he shouted as a tube was pulled straight up from her stomach, through her throat, and out her mouth. "Can you hear me?"

Or had anyone called her? She could feel pain but she didn't know where she hurt, in what part of her body. There was more quiet darkness and then Emma thought she found an opening at last, an opening in the slippery sides of the dark circle, but there was only more darkness beyond.

"We are going to take you back to your room," the man's voice shouted in her ear. "Will there be anybody waiting for you there?"

She couldn't whisper no. She didn't know where the pain was or where she was. A nurse spooned something into her mouth and she felt ill. She couldn't say no. She choked on some spoonfuls of ice cream and when the nurse threatened her with soup after that, she moaned. Another voice said, "Don't make her eat if she doesn't want to." That voice was clear, very bossy, and Irish-sounding, a woman's voice.

The nurse who fed her was Cuban, big and jolly. "You are my baby," she crooned. "Come on, now, baby, be good and eat."

But if she heard things it was strange because she couldn't feel her ears at all; they were in a new location perhaps, pinned beneath a heavy helmet on her head.

Floating, then. She sat in an office showing pictures of her daughter Dorinda to a plastic surgeon.

"I want to look like that."

He stared at her, horrified.

"I would *never* take on such an assignment," he said. "Why, in heaven's name? You are beautiful. You are years away from needing any operation. Why do you ask it?"

And the next doctor she consulted wanted to probe even deeper.

"Are you happy in your marriage?" he asked, looking closely at her face.

"I'm a widow."

"I *see*. A widow." The doctor pondered the photographs she gave him. "Now this particular shape of face, nose— yes, it is similar to yours, but you are beautiful the way you are. You look even better than this girl—certainly just as good, and more *suitable*. Now may I be frank? You don't need a face lift or a new nose. Many women come to me, for many reasons; they expect a miracle, and I've learned—"

He was full of himself and his wise insight into women and again she rose and left.

... The Irish nurse had called for the intern. "That's not much blood," Emma heard him say. "She'll be all right."

But the nurse was fussing still. Emma could not see because of something over her eyes but the nurse sounded peeved. ". . . bleed to death," she heard her grumble. She gave Emma some glycerine swabs to suck and put iced bandages over her eyes. It must be night outside, Emma thought, because she was so tired and the Irish nurse sounded tired, too. In the afternoon she had seen the jolly Cuban nurse who had pink cheeks. "Now you're my baby," she had said. But what afternoon was that? Was the nurse in her room after all? She had thought no, there won't be anybody there. Who would be there? Once she thought of Trevor York, and wished it might have been he . . .

"You're my baby, eat now." She couldn't tell the flavor of the ice cream and it made her sick and was all a part of the way she felt the morning they came for her and a different nurse gave her a shot. That needle didn't hurt at all and she began to feel wonderful and floating and it was nauseating to be so lighthearted and gay when really you were frightened and terrified and sad. The euphoria built even higher while she was in the elevator and then her bed was parked outside the operating theater. That room was round, all stainless steel and blue walls, no windows but many fluorescent lights and reflectors hanging from the ceiling. Many shiny cabinets were around the sides and many, many drawers of instruments and there were tables of instruments and cloths and sinks around the smooth walls. She wanted to scream, "Don't take me into that circle!"

The anesthetist stood beside her bed while she looked helplessly through the slid-back doors into the room. "They're not ready for us yet, for a few minutes," the anesthetist remarked conversationally to her. In the hall where her bed stood there was a window. The light she saw from outside was steely and cold, early morning light. If she could have spoken she would have begged them not to take her into the round room but her tongue and mouth were paralyzed and all she felt was a total happiness and well-being that was false and wrong. In the round room knives were waiting. But there was no one to hear her scream "No!" and the anesthetist picked at his fingernails and seemed bored. "Not quite ready for us yet," he repeated.

Then they were ready. They took the bed in and something cold was taped onto the front of her thigh. She stared up at the round lights above her and someone said to breathe, it wouldn't take long . . . not long. And then the undulating began, a series of throbs in her stomach, and then the tube came up through her throat and the shouting began. "Wake up." And she did not feel happy anymore; she felt in pain.

"When you go back to your room, will there be anybody there?"

Oh, who—who would be there?

It didn't matter because she was floating. The third doctor she consulted was so popular that she had to wait a month to get an appointment. A model in New York had once given her his name. Her hopes rose when she walked into his suite in one of the expensive high-rise hotels on the beach. Forty or more persons were waiting for him, sitting stiffly on elegant satin sofas and love seats. The waiting room was huge and overlooked the sea. Gulls wheeled past the plate-glass windows. A tiny poodle trotted over the white carpet to nuzzle her; his neck was circled by a diamond collar. From overhead came the twittering of birds swinging in wicker cages, and on a tea wagon were offerings of coffee and tea and cakes.

At this reception desk the girl who greeted her wore tight melon-colored pants and a loose orange mesh top that made no secret of the fact her pretty breasts were not confined in a brassiere. Her lovely facial bones and splendid body were an excellent advertisement, if the doctor had done it and not God. One of the telephones rang and, flinging back her long blonde hair, the girl answered it and whispered into the receiver.

Emma sat and waited; the poodle scampered from person to person. . . .

At last she was ushered into the doctor's empty office and asked to wait. On a large ornate desk was a small, gilt-edged mirror; behind the desk was a bookcase with popular best sellers in it, and on top a picture of a young man with ruffled hair and a gorgeous young woman. The ceiling of this room was a skylight, and beneath it from crisscrossed beams hung hundreds of plants, their foliage filtering the light from above.

When at last the young man in the photograph strode in person into the room, he picked up his telephone, sat down without glancing at her, and conducted a long conversation with a friend about taking a vacation in the Alps. He exuded breezy confidence. Finally he hung up, rose, came around the desk, and pulled up a chair next to hers, sitting so close that his knee pressed against hers. She was startled, and wondered if it were meant to be reassuring to nervous would-be patients, this human contact with the doctor.

Smiling very charmingly at her, he asked solicitously what she wanted of him.

She drew out the pictures of Dorinda and still he smiled, his knee firmly pressed to hers. She began to tell him what she wanted but the telephone rang and he went around the desk and talked, this time apparently to a patient. When he came back to Emma he was still smiling. He gazed at her, touched her chin gently to turn her head right and left, and let his knee find hers.

"Are you sure you need this?" he said softly.

She nodded.

"Then you will have just a little scar here," he said, and touched the skin in front of her ear. "And here," he added, touching the other side. "And a little scar under your chin."

"Why? Do I have to have scars?"

He smiled into her eyes without answering.

"How long will it be until the scars fade?" she asked when he was silent.

"Oh." He cocked his head. "That's difficult to say. Many people are perfectly presentable in ten days."

"Presentable? But I mean—"

"You can use makeup."

"And later?"

He fidgeted as if impatient to have the interview done. The telephone rang again, and as he rose to answer she said something about thinking it over and fled.

That left only one doctor. He was the one most difficult to see; she had made that appointment first and gone to the other doctors while she waited. Renata had been the one who'd told her about Dr. Ronald Hamilton, world-famous rejuvenator, the magician of Miami Beach. At last the day came when she could get in to see him. His office was shrinelike in its hush, furnished with eighteenth-century furniture, Oriental rugs, and Chinese vases. Only a few other people waited there. Either his nurses scheduled his appointments more carefully or fewer people wanted to pay his famous fees.

This interview went well all the way. Dr. Hamilton appeared promptly, with a handsome assistant at his side. The two men were all business and gave her wishes a respectful hearing.

"Yes, we can do this," Dr. Hamilton said, looking at the photographs with a seraphic smile. He was rotund and florid of complexion, and seemed extremely good-natured.

"What about scars, doctor?" she asked.

"We do the operation inside your ears and up in your hairline," he answered. "There are no scars."

"Not even—under my chin?"

"No. We go in from the ear. You will have small scars behind your ears but they will be hidden in the fold."

"And I can look like this? Like the pictures?"

He nodded. "Yes. We can do that."

Then he passed Emma on to his secretary, a sensible-looking young girl who told Emma it would cost ten thousand dollars for the surgery she wanted. The girl did not seem at all surprised when Emma agreed at once.

"This is so different—" Emma said hesitantly to the girl. "I mean, some of the other doctors I've consulted—they'd ask me all these questions. Why I wanted surgery—"

"That would make me so mad," the girl said. "That would make me furious. If anyone asked *me* that question I'd say it was none of their damn business."

For the first time in what had seemed an endless period, Emma laughed.

She'd felt good that day. Not the artificial delight of the hospital, the bliss that covered terror. Not the terrible floating above the floor...

She turned out to be allergic to the anesthetic. In her hotel room a week after the operation she lay alone and bit on a washcloth to keep from screaming in misery.

"The anesthetic breaks down in the body, you see, and some persons turn out to be allergic to some of the by-products that form," the young assistant explained to her. Her face was battered and bruised and where it had been "wire-brushed" the skin was broken out with blisters that itched unbearably. She could not sleep or eat and time moved leadenly. She wanted to die. She wept.

"Some people experience deep depressions as a result of

GREEN LADY

the anesthesia," the handsome young assistant told her. "It usually bottoms out in ten days; then, slowly—"

They were jerking up the tube. *Will there be anybody there?* the man shouted. But the pain was in her abdomen; Emma located it at last. Where was the Cuban nurse? Had that been in another time, some other place? She didn't know. Here, she was alone and in pain and darkness but it was different, too. Now she couldn't move at all. In the hotel room alone she had been tired, tired and weak, worn out . . . now she was tired, too, but she was somewhere in the dark and couldn't move at all and the tiredness was deeper. It went down levels and levels, seeping through her body, washing through her arteries, beating against her will . . .

After the hotel room, she had gotten better. Young girls —she looked at young girls . . . she could move just the way they did; she practiced. She took lessons in disco dancing, and bought jeans and satin sweatshirts. Young girls waved their arms as they talked, they walked from their hips, and jumped up stairs rather than climbing.

Her face cleared up finally, the blisters and bruises fading. She bleached her own hair because she was embarrassed to go to a hairdressing salon where they would feel her scars when they gave her a shampoo. The scars were hidden in her hairline, high over her temples, small ridges that the assistant told her would flatten.

The bleaching process took all morning and she was afraid of what the result might be but then, *there* in the mirror, when she finished, she saw her reward. Dorinda was in the mirror. It had worked! It was a miracle. She blessed Dr. Hamilton and forgot all the hours of pain, the sadness, the loneliness of the hotel room—she had to use heavy makeup over the remains of the bruises and rashes but she could see that she was going to make it, to look *young*. To look like Dorinda . . .

On the street a boy whistled at her and called "Hi, blondie." People in stores addressed her as "Miss." And she ran up stairs and practiced her dances and learned the lyrics of rock songs and read *Mademoiselle* magazine for teenagers' tips. She practiced giggling.

Another boy whistled at her, on the beach this time.

"My name's Dorinda," she told him.

And still she was afraid. It was like the euphoria before the operation, a happiness on top of fear. The operation had worked, and she could fool persons who had never known Dorinda—but who were the persons? Or person? *Was* there anyone to fear?

That's the question you're going to answer, she would tell herself. You *will* know.

And now she did know. And yet there was so much pain, pain from long ago that came back to her with the present pain, nailing her to the hard bed. She couldn't even moan. Where was the Cuban nurse?

"She'll bleed to death." She heard the Irish nurse talking.

"That's not much blood."

"*She'll bleed to death . . .*"

Someone took her hand.

"Mother," a voice said.

It was the voice of a young girl; almost her own voice. Had she spoken? But she would never call, "Mother." The idea of having a mother—she had been a mother, but she had never really *had* a mother, not since so long ago when she had been ordered to leave home.

Emma heard the voice repeat the word. The effort to open her eyes was too great. She wanted to drift, to see if she could drift away from the pain and separate herself from it. But someone was holding her hand.

Slowly Emma realized that she was alive. Parts of her seemed to collect out of the air and settle down inside her body. She could feel the bed under her back. Her midsection was bandaged tightly. It was today, she was living, and Dorinda was alive too, because she heard her say, "Mother?" It must be her child. She felt a rush of pure happiness, and she spoke.

"Sweetheart?"

"Don't talk, Mother. Please rest. You're all right. You're going to be all right."

If only I could make it all right for *you*, Emma thought. If only I could change the world, change history, make no one want to kill you, make your life safe. The thoughts were familiar, they had been her thoughts for so long, whenever she thought of Dorinda—

Then she remembered.

She *had* done something. The man who had frightened her for so long was gone. Wasn't he?

"Is he dead?" she whispered to Dorinda.

"He's dead, Mother," Dorinda said, squeezing her hand. "We're safe. You did what you wanted to do—you saved us both."

Emma couldn't speak; she just smiled and looked at Dorinda's face. *Dorinda was there in the room. There was somebody*.

"You must think I'm—" Emma tried to gesture toward her face with her free hand.

"Hush, lie still." Dorinda held Emma's hand up and pressed it for a moment against her cheek.

"I mean, my face—I'll—" Emma tried to speak clearly but the words came out in a mumble. "I'll have it put back."

Dorinda blinked and looked down, gazing at her mother through eyes that wanted to fill with tears. As she studied Emma, she realized that a little color had already come into her mother's cheeks. Emma was smiling at her.

After a moment the serious expression on Dorinda's features began to give way. A gleam of mischief came into her eyes. She let herself grin and finally, she spoke.

"Mother, Trevor might prefer it, but otherwise I'd say leave your face the way it is. I kind of like it."

Emma's dark eyes widened as she gazed into her daughter's. Together, they laughed.

**EVERY GENERATION HAS A WOMAN
FOR WHOM THE WORLD IS NOT BIG ENOUGH...**

Emma Harte was that kind of woman. Born to a poverty-stricken Yorkshire family, seduced and left pregnant at age 15, she fled to a grimy manufacturing town to pursue her twin dreams—riches and revenge.

From the moment you meet her, en route by private jet to the Manhattan headquarters of Harte Enterprises, the hub of her vast financial empire, you will be held inescapably in her spell: through two turbulent marriages... one great love... and the plot by her children that threatens all she has built—and challenges her unshakable faith in herself.

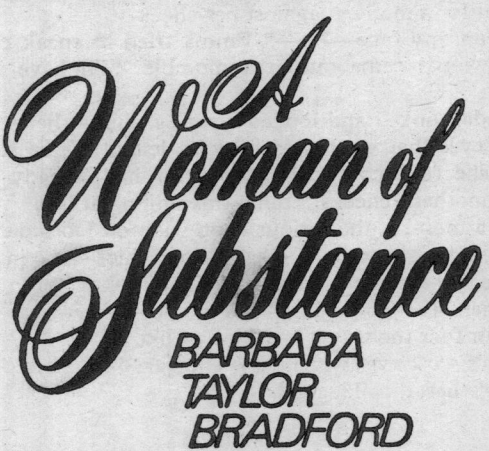

A Woman of Substance
BARBARA TAYLOR BRADFORD

THE IRRESISTIBLE NATIONWIDE BESTSELLER

"A wonderfully entertaining novel"
The Denver Post

 AVON   49163 $2.95